A COUNTRY DILEMMA

Also by Sasha Morgan

A Country Scandal
A Country Rivalry

A COUNTRY DILEMMA

Sasha Morgan

An Aria Book

This edition first published in the United Kingdom in 2020 by Aria,
an imprint of Head of Zeus Ltd

Copyright © Sasha Morgan, 2020

The moral right of Sasha Morgan to be identified as the author
of this work has been asserted in accordance with the Copyright,
Designs and Patents Act of 1988.

All rights reserved. No part of this publication may be reproduced,
stored in a retrieval system, or transmitted, in any form or by any
means, electronic, mechanical, photocopying, recording, or otherwise,
without the prior permission of both the copyright owner and the above
publisher of this book.

This is a work of fiction. All characters, organizations, and events
portrayed in this novel are either products of the author's imagination
or are used fictitiously.

A CIP catalogue record for this book is available from
the British Library.

ISBN 9781035907250

Typeset by Siliconchips Services Ltd UK

Cover design © Heike Schüssler

Aria
c/o Head of Zeus
First Floor East
5–8 Hardwick Street
London EC1R 4RG

www.ariafiction.com

Printed and bound by CPI Group (UK) Ltd, Croydon, CR0 4YY

For Zac, a much loved, loyal friend and sorely missed.

1

Megan read the gold, italic writing on the cream card:

> *'Mr Dermot O'Grady, has the pleasure in inviting you to the marriage of his daughter, Miss Finula Dolores O'Grady, to Mr Marcus Devlin on the 23rd July, 1pm, at All Saints Church, Treweham.'*

Seeing it in writing gave her an excited thrill. Finula, her best friend since moving to the village of Treweham over a year ago, was marrying the sexy, TV producer Marcus Devlin, who was also her brother-in-law, so it had recently transpired. Megan was adapting well to being a new mum and also Lady of Treweham Hall, her husband's ancestral home, an impressive sandstone building with four corner turrets and sturdy buttresses, giving it a castle-like appearance.

It was a far cry from the modest, cosy cottage Megan had first moved into, after having inherited her gran's home in Treweham. It hadn't taken long for her to strike up a friendship with Finula whilst working behind the bar at The Templar, and even less for Tobias to spot the brunette with brown almond-shaped eyes and a shy smile. He had been captivated by Megan and within six months had married her. Having Edward had been the icing on the cake, not to mention being the much-awaited son and heir to the Treweham Hall estate.

Baby Edward was three months old now and had finally slipped into a routine of sleeping mostly through the night, giving Megan and Tobias a fairly decent rest. Megan had refused point blank to employ a nanny, although had almost succumbed after constantly dragging herself out of the warmth of their four-poster bed to the relentless cries of her son. Bobbing him up and down on her lap now and watching his cheeky face chuckle in delight made it all worthwhile. He was just adorable, with his twinkling green eyes and dark curls, just like his father. Megan kissed his cheek and received a playful slap in the face from his chubby, little hands.

'Aah, you munchkin!' Megan laughed, tickling him under his dribbling chin. She was interrupted by Henry, the butler.

'Madam, Sir is asking you to join us all in his study.'

'OK, thanks, Henry.' On seeing Henry, Edward gurgled with joy, making the butler's stiff upper lip curve into a smile. Even Henry, who was renowned for his rather pompous manner, couldn't help but melt when it came to Master Edward. Hardly surprising, given that he had practically assisted in his arrival on finding Megan lying on the drawing room floor in agony. A bond had been made and Henry's allegiance knew no bounds. 'Come on, Edward, let's see what Daddy wants.' She scooped Edward up and followed Henry to Tobias' study. On entering, she was greeted by a smiling team of estate workers sat round her husband's desk. Tobias immediately rose to take his son who was reaching out for him.

'Come here, you.' He laughed as Edward snuggled into him. Megan took a seat next to him. 'We're discussing the opening times of the Hall,' Tobias informed her, whilst clutching a wriggling Edward.

'Right.' Megan nodded. As a tour guide her opinion would matter.

'Would you like a later start, bearing in mind you've this one to attend to?' asked Tobias grinning.

'Hmm, maybe, just on the two days I cover.'

'Ten-thirty OK with you?'

'Yes, that's fine. It should give me enough time to hand him over to your mum.'

Lady Beatrice was more than happy to babysit her only grandchild, and would take over a lot more, given half the chance. Megan was pleased to act as a tour guide. It gave her a break and an opportunity to socialise with the rest of the staff. She still missed her best friend Finula terribly though, which made her all the more excited for her pending wedding. It would be great to have Finula back in Treweham for a short while.

'Right. That's settled then. Opening times ten o'clock Monday to Wednesday, ten-thirty Thursday and Fridays.' He turned to a middle-aged lady sitting at the end of his desk. 'All set to open next week, Mrs P?'

'Yes, Lord Cavendish-Blake, all the catering's been ordered and the tea shop rota's been drawn up.'

'Good.' Tobias then looked towards the two men sat opposite him. 'Security and car park at the ready?'

'Yes, Sir, all the CCTV equipment has been serviced and the security and car park staff fully trained and updated.' Tobias nodded his head in approval. 'Henry, you will as always be extra diligent during opening hours, particularly to the South Wing.' He was referring to the set of private rooms allocated to himself and Megan. Now his son and heir would be there too, which meant upping safety measures.

Megan took in the efficient, business-like way Tobias conducted himself. He was well respected, yet still approachable, making him popular amongst all the staff at Treweham Hall. Not to mention easy on the eye, with his long, dark hair, piercing green eyes and muscular build. Any wonder he'd been the subject of many a tabloid with his rakish good looks and devil-may-care past.

'Right then, let's do it,' he said, cheerfully glancing round the room. Edward started to gurgle again, making everyone laugh.

2

Dermot O'Grady rubbed his hands together and surveyed The Templar. He'd arranged to have the pub thoroughly cleaned before proudly handing it over to the new owners. His eyes took in the freshly scrubbed stone floor, the large inglenook fire twinkling warmly, the rustic wooden tables with mismatched chairs and the clean, whitewashed lime walls. The lighting was subtle, creating a snug, intimate atmosphere. The Templar was a sixteenth-century former coach inn, oozing with character, and had been home to Dermot and his daughter, Finula, for over twenty years. Now it was to be someone else's home.

On meeting the young couple, Dermot had recognised the same enthusiasm he had once felt whilst being shown round the pub. They, like him all those years ago, had instantly fallen in love with its history and charm. It was hard not to be enticed by its squeaky, uneven floorboards, old stone walls, beamed ceilings and open fires. A huge vase of fresh lilies stood on the bar next to a bucket of ice chilling a bottle of champagne, ready to be opened in celebration.

Stephen and Christie Newbury, the soon-to-be new owners, would be arriving any moment. Dermot couldn't help but feel a touch emotional about handing over the keys to his pub, but was at the same time glad it was in safe hands, and not about to be taken over by a large brewery, which would no doubt rip out the heart and soul of the place. He'd witnessed first-hand how excited the Newburys appeared as they explored each room, discussing every nook and cranny of the place with eagerness. It felt right to be passing on The Templar to such young, vibrant people, ready to make a go of it.

Dermot had agreed to sell The Templar on the condition it would still host his daughter's wedding and he would oversee all the arrangements. The Newburys were more than happy to agree to this, glad of the opportunity to learn the ropes from his valued experience. And he too had a new chapter in his life to look forward to. His comfy little cottage stood invitingly, waiting for him to enjoy the autumn of his life. His retirement was well earned and past due. Being landlord of a pub was heavy, relentless work and Dermot fully intended to embrace every minute of his retiring years. Besides, The Templar wasn't the same without Finula; he was ready to move on.

His thoughts were interrupted by a loud knock at the door. It was mid-morning and the pub wouldn't be opening until afternoon lunches were due to be served. Rubbing his hands together again, Dermot gave the room one last check before striding to answer. He unbolted the large, oak door and pushed it open with a bright, welcoming smile – only to be greeted by a woman standing there, alone and on the verge of tears. Dermot halted.

'Mrs Newbury?' He hardly recognised her. Gone was the fresh-faced young lady who was brimming with enthusiasm to get into The Templar. Instead a pale face, with bloodshot eyes stared back at him soberly.

'Yes.' She bit her lip nervously.

'Err... please... come in.' Dermot looked over her shoulder for any signs of the husband. There were none. Sensing Dermot's puzzlement, she supplied an explanation.

'I'm, afraid it's just me...'

'Ah, I see,' replied Dermot, not understanding at all. An awkward moment passed briefly, before he continued. 'Right then, let's start with a cup of tea, shall we?' Judging from this poor woman's state, he suspected a good chat was in order before any champagne was popped. 'Take a seat, Mrs Newbury, I won't be long.'

Her eyes darted round the beautiful country inn she'd loved at first sight. Ever since clapping eyes on its Cotswold honey stone and small leaded windows that peeped out from lush, green ivy, she'd known it was for her. Dermot left the room and soon returned to the bar holding a tray of tea. He sat down next to her and poured, waiting for her to speak.

'I don't know where to start, Mr O'Grady,' she attempted in a quiet voice.

'Well, you can start by calling me Dermot.' He smiled encouragingly.

'I'm Christie.' She shakily smiled back.

'Where I come from Christie's a boy's name.'

'It's short for Christina.'

Dermot nodded. 'OK, Christie, what's to do?' he asked gently. Although clearly something was wrong, Dermot knew the sale transaction had completed. All the monies had cleared. It was only because they'd agreed Dermot would still be hands on for a while that he was actually still there to officially hand over the keys. Christie's shoulders started to shake with emotion.

'He's left me…' Tears started to pour down her face. Dermot swallowed. It was hard watching someone of a similar age to his daughter so upset. As a father his heart went out to her.

'Oh, Christie,' he sighed, 'want to tell me about it?'

3

The moment Christie's eyes met Stephen Newbury's, the attraction was instant. Across a hectic, rowdy pub packed to the rafters with rugby players and hen parties, they homed in on each other like radars. When their gazes locked, time stood still. Stephen's pint glass hovered mid-drink, whilst Christie halted, her conversation abruptly stopped. An urge between the two pulled like a magnetic force, bringing them together in the thick of the crowds.

'I'm Stephen,' this huge chap with broad shoulders and an infectious smile said. He held out his hand. Christie shook it and noticed the firm, confident shake.

'I'm Christie.' She grinned back. They could hardly hear for the noise amongst the drinkers.

'Christie, let's go someplace else.' It was more of a direction than a request. He seemed desperate to get to know the girl with dark, corkscrew curls and pale blue eyes he hadn't seen before. Christie was only too happy to follow him, admiring the way his tight black T-shirt emphasised his muscular arms and his legs bulged out of faded jeans. He had blond hair cut in a short, snappy style. She suspected he was one of the rugby players, judging by his physique, so he must be a local. Whereas she was partying with her girlfriends on a hen do. Chester seemed the ideal place to celebrate, given its culture and nightlife. The fact it was brimming with hunky rugby players was a big plus too. The girls had giggled about that whilst making arrangements.

Stephen chose a small bistro tucked away down a tiny alleyway named Benedict's after the owner. It was cosy, intimate and proved the ideal spot for Christie and Stephen to fall in love. Which is precisely what they did. They talked about just everything, from their childhood and teenage years, where they came from, families, friends, careers, to lifetime ambitions. Christie's had always been the same: to own her own hotel. Being in the accommodation business, she had grown from being a chambermaid to the assistant manager of a very prestigious country inn in the heart of the Lake District. It was hard work, but it paid off when seeing visitor after visitor return with smiles and compliments, not to mention generous tips.

One day, thought Christie, one day I'll own my own place. Often she would dream of exactly how it would be: rustic charm meets country sophistication that the more discerning traveller would flock to. That had been her ultimate wish, and it had almost come true, almost. Stephen had soon latched on to Christie's aspiration and he too could see the fascination of owning his own fabulous hotel and rather liked the idea of being his own boss, instead of working for the tyrant at the estate agents. He too was assistant manager, not that it stood for much under Burns' regime. Bill Burns was a ruthless, sexist pig who made the small team of Abbott and Reedley's miserable. From touching up the young girls in the tea room, to refusing annual leave whilst he took himself off golfing made him the most unpopular manager ever. Stephen couldn't wait to leave, but he appreciated, as did Christie, timing was crucial.

From the first evening they had met, Stephen and Christie had been inseparable. Weekends were spent with either Stephen travelling to the Lake District, or Christie to Chester. They had lots in common, both middle children to two sisters, with a close-knit family and circle of friends. A whole new group had been formed, as both sets of friends genuinely gelled well. Once they had announced their engagement after exactly one year, they all went wild and a mother of all parties had been thrown. Happy days.

Then, after a year of blissful marriage, the cracks began to show. Christie badly wanted to save and save, to achieve her goal of buying a hotel. She was by then the manager of a small, boutique hotel in Chester city. And whilst Stephen still liked the idea of owning his own business, his lifestyle somehow didn't involve making the necessary sacrifices to accomplish this. He still played rugby, every weekend now, as well as attending practice nights during the week. These inevitably would end in a drinking session, often followed by slipping into town and finishing up in a club. Basically, he'd reverted back to his single days. Christie had begun to feel helpless. It was hard watching her husband who had once shared her ambitions gradually morph into a drunken slob who only lived for his boozy nights with his mates.

After three months of growing tired waiting for Stephen to come home sober in an evening, or even come home at all, Christie had had enough. She packed her bags one Friday night after returning home late from work to a note saying, *"Gone out. Probably stay at Ash's tonight."* Well, good for him, thought Christie. Ash was welcome to him. With grit and sheer determination, she hauled two suitcases and a rucksack to Chester railway station and never looked back.

Within a week Stephen followed, full of remorse. He'd promised her the earth, anything, *anything*, if only she'd come back home with him. Even a baby. This was his trump card, knowing full well Christie had secretly started to yearn for one. Up until now he'd always brushed away the notion of parenthood, claiming they were both too young and ambitious. When Christie had pointed out he actually didn't seem as motivated as her anymore, he vehemently swore he'd change. So compelling were his claims, that Christie – convinced of her husband's promises – found herself back in Chester and trying to conceive.

Then more cracks appeared. It just wasn't happening. Month after month saw Christie on the verge of tears as the blue line on the pregnancy testing kits refused to play ball. Why? What was happening, or not happening? It further saddened her when Stephen feared it could be his fault, as though his manhood was in question. Well, a rugby player being labelled a "jaffa" was hardly what one envisaged, was it? So much so, that he made Christie promise not to tell a soul. The party line was they weren't trying. They didn't want children just yet – that was the patter she'd have to rattle out if anyone asked. Even though, deep down, having a baby became the only thing Christie did want. So badly it graduated into an obsession.

After another year of relentlessly hoping to start a family, Christie noticed another change in Stephen. He wasn't going out on drunken nights anymore, but was putting in prolonged working days, which was a first considering how much he'd hated his job. Then the odd weekend involving a conference, or training course would crop up, which he simply couldn't miss.

Once, she found an earring under the car seat, which most definitely wasn't hers. When she challenged Stephen, he declared no knowledge of it. But he never was a good liar, blushing pink and scraping his hand through his hair. Christie knew. Then it suddenly stopped. It was as if the old Stephen – the one she'd first met – had reappeared. The man she'd fallen in love with a few years ago had come back. He seemed more relaxed, happy to be with her, and together they built bridges again. Deciding they'd saved enough money now for a decent deposit for their hotel, the search was on.

It hadn't taken long to spot The Templar in the glorious Cotswolds. After making the trip to see it for themselves and being shown around the quaint country inn, they didn't hesitate to put in an offer. When it was accepted, they were overjoyed. Anxious to make the move and get started with their new, exciting life, Christie and Stephen pushed for a speedy sale. Luckily the landlord was very accommodating and the transaction was soon completed.

Then Stephen dropped a bombshell. It was their last night in Chester. Christie had booked a table at Benedict's to celebrate. Stephen was joining her there straight from work. As it was his last day at Abbott and Reedley's, she was expecting him to be in extra high spirits. Instead she took in his grim expression, the dark bags under his eyes, his pale skin, slow walk, and a sense of foreboding filled her. He hardly looked at the menu before ordering a large whiskey. Christie frowned. This was unlike him, who usually enjoyed a glass of wine with his meal.

She looked him in the eye. 'What's the matter?'

Stephen knocked back his whiskey, gulped, then spoke. 'I can't do it, Christie.' There was a pregnant pause before he continued, 'I'm going to be a dad.' The statement rang in her ears. As though being punched in the stomach, Christie doubled over in pain. 'I'm sorry, Christie… I'm so sorry.'

'Who is it?' she demanded. Anger started to replace shock. She glared at him. He dipped his gaze, unable to make eye contact.

'Sophie from the office.'

'Sophie? The one you introduced me to at the Christmas party?' She pictured a young girl with long, blonde hair and an enormous chest. Typical. How cliché, thought Christie with venom. Stephen dully nodded his head. 'So it was her earring then?' she spat. 'Obviously been going on for months.'

'I ended it, honestly. But now… she told me she's pregnant…'

'And obviously it's yours?' Christie threw out sarcastically. 'But of course, that's what you want to believe, isn't it?' Her voice rose hysterically, causing the other diners to glance over. 'So, not seedless after all?'

'Christie, please,' Stephen hissed.

Christie knew when she was beaten. Sophie was clearly able to give him the very thing she couldn't: a child. The injustice of it all made her want to vomit.

'Listen, Christie, this doesn't change things for you,' Stephen urged.

Her eyes widened in disbelief. 'How can you say that?' she whispered faintly.

'Go for it. I mean it. The Templar, your hotel, take it. I don't care about the money.' He spoke firmly.

Christie looked at him and realised he intended to give her everything to alleviate his guilt. Well, let him. She looked him firmly in the eye. 'I'd like that in writing.'

'Of course, yes I'll… get a contract drawn up.' He seemed desperate to appease her. Yes, she would go and follow her dream and if he was prepared to say goodbye to her and his share, then so be it.

4

Flora glided through the air with ease, then gently landed the horse. Phoenix's balance was almost perfect, she reflected with glee. All the long, strenuous days they'd worked tirelessly together had certainly paid off. Flora had known right from the start that he had real potential. The trouble was that he'd been trained in the wrong direction, as a flat racehorse, rather than a jump horse. Having convinced her boyfriend, Dylan Delany, the ex-champion jockey, to keep him at his training yard, Flora had more than proved her point.

Dylan had been dubious initially about taking on the horse, mainly due to its history. Poor Phoenix had been flogged over many a finishing post, trailing in last. His then owner, a ruthless, heartless man called Graham Roper, had lost all patience with him and demanded Dylan do something with his horse to improve his form. In the end, after witnessing how Flora had bonded so well with Phoenix, he had arranged for himself and a neighbouring friend, Gary Belcher, to buy the horse.

Dylan had boxed clever though, never revealing Phoenix's potential as a first-class jump horse. He just told Roper that his horse would never win a flat race. Which he wouldn't. The fact that Phoenix jumped like a dream and he and Gary had formed a partnership with the intention to hurdle race him remained silent. It wasn't just a good business deal for Dylan; he adored Flora and would do anything to keep her happy. Actually, he'd do anything to keep her, which at times had proved difficult, for Dylan had had quite a chequered past. His dark, gypsy looks and deep, blue eyes, not to mention his very toned body, made him appealing to most women. Up until meeting Flora, who he'd encountered in the Treweham Hall stables, Dylan had taken full advantage of all the attention that came his way. He had been the Romeo of the racing circuit, weaving his way in and out of relationships, but never fully committing.

Then he met Flora, who had been employed by his close friend, Tobias Cavendish-Blake, as a groom in his stables. Dylan had been smitten by this young, fresh-faced girl with wavy blonde hair and a kind, caring temperament. Most of all he'd sensed a real connection, their love of horses. He'd never felt this with another human being, let alone a girlfriend.

When Dylan had decided to retire as a jockey and set up his own racehorse training yard, he had had no hesitation in asking Flora to be his assistant trainer. It was a no-brainer. Who else could he trust to do the job better? No one, and the fact she made his pulse race with her curvaceous body in jodhpurs was purely coincidental. Dylan and Flora genuinely enjoyed one another's company. Not only being girlfriend and boyfriend, but best friends too, meant that both living and working together wasn't a problem. Although Dylan was ten years older, Flora having recently celebrated her twenty-first birthday, the age gap hadn't mattered. If anything, Flora had often given wise counselling regarding the running of the yard and Dylan had valued her input; and, she'd been absolutely right about Phoenix. All the staff in the yard agreed, he was going to be a star.

Flora led Phoenix back to his stable.

'Come on, old boy, let's get you fed and watered.' She patted his side and pushed the door open. After tending to Phoenix, she made her way into the office where Dylan was busy behind his desk talking on the phone. He raised his hand to acknowledge her, openly admiring her pert bottom in those tight britches.

'Will do – OK, Tobias, bye.' Dylan ended his call. Tobias was not only his close friend, but his landlord too, as he rented acres of his land from the Treweham Hall estate where his yard had been set up. Originally being the old stable block to Treweham Hall, Tobias had renovated it into the first-class training yard it now was, housing up to twenty stables, complete with paddocks, an all-weather gallop and mile after mile of white running rails, which the horses thundered along.

Dylan grinned. 'How's your boy?' The touch of playful sarcasm wasn't lost on Flora. He was of course referring to the amount of time she spent on Phoenix.

'Jumping like a gazelle. I think he's ready, Dylan.' Dylan nodded his head. He'd clearly thought as much after watching her in the paddock with him. 'I've been thinking, let's enter him in a point-to-point to start with.' Flora searched Dylan's face for a reaction. After a few moments' consideration he nodded his head again.

'Yes, something low-key. We need to go gently on him,' he

warned. The last thing Phoenix needed was any reminders of how he'd been treated in a racing environment previously.

'Absolutely,' agreed Flora. She moved to sit on the edge of his desk. 'You know and understand Phoenix as well as I do,' she said smiling.

'I know and understand you more,' he replied, pulling her onto his lap. Flora giggled.

'Dylan, we're at work!' She attempted to fend off his wandering hands, which had made their way into her check shirt.

'I don't care, you're totally irresistible,' he murmured into her ear, whilst he cupped her breasts. His thumbs began to slowly circle her nipples, making her gasp. He always knew what buttons to press – Flora was putty in his hands. He kissed her neck, then quickly unbuttoned her shirt and tugged it from her shoulders. He sighed in pleasure at the black, lace bra, which Flora was bursting out from. Instinctively Flora stood up for him to gently pull her jodhpurs down, revealing a matching black, lace thong. Dylan groaned with lust as his fingers crept inside and edged them down too. He dipped his head and ran kisses across her hip bone and down to the centre of her. Flora gripped Dylan's shoulders as his tongue probed inside her.

'Dylan,' she whimpered. All cares of getting caught were forgotten as he continued to lick and explore her. Just as she thought she'd burst with desire, he stood to unzip his huge erection and slid inside her hot slickness. She cried out loud now, all inhibitions vanished as he pushed harder and further into her whilst clutching her buttocks against the desk.

He could feel her tighten against his cock and with a final guttural moan he released himself, while Flora clung on to him. Both panting for a moment, they looked into each other's eyes. 'One of these days, somebody will walk in on us,' whispered Flora.

'It's worth the risk,' replied Dylan with a wink.

5

Finula was busy blending the fruit cake mixture. Taking great care to add the exact amount of sherry, she squinted at the jug measurements. Well, it wasn't every day you baked your own wedding cake was it? Marcus grinned to himself, watching his soon-to-be wife concentrate, her tongue slightly protruding from her mouth. She caught him watching her out of the corner of her eye.

'What are you smirking at?' she asked.

'You.' He laughed.

'Well, it's got to be right!' she exclaimed in frustration. 'It's all right for you, sitting there, tapping away on your laptop.'

Marcus was in fact emailing the BBC, informing them his documentary was on schedule as originally planned. The documentary, entitled *Green and Pleasant Land?* was based on the village of Treweham and explored the quintessential customs and traditions of the old English way of life. It also provided the ideal contrast to the harsh realities of the rising figures of homelessness and poverty, which is why Marcus rather cleverly decided to add a question mark to the title. Treweham had been hand-picked because of its charm and character, not to mention Marcus' ancestral family who resided in Treweham Hall. The documentary was set to be a showstopper, culminating in the revelation that he, Marcus Devlin, the award-winning producer, was in fact the firstborn son of the late Lord Richard Cavendish-Blake.

None of this was coincidental of course. Marcus had originally intended to dishonour the Cavendish-Blakes, believing, incorrectly, that his father had hushed up the whole affair by banishing his mam to Ireland. When the truth had finally come to light, via the late Lord's diaries, Marcus learnt that his father had never even known of his existence. In short, his mam had bolted, without any trace, shedding a whole new light on the matter. Only now was Marcus able to put the past behind him and fondly acknowledge his half-brothers, Tobias and Sebastian.

Meeting Finula whilst he and his crew stayed at The Templar when filming had been the ultimate icing on the cake – and now here was the love of his life, baking their wedding cake. He smiled at the flour on her freckled face. It had even ended up in her long blaze of red hair. Not for the first time he had likened her to the colleens of Roscommon in Ireland, where he had been brought up. Choosing to move to Shropshire a few years ago meant he was handier for London, where he often worked. He had filmed on location there and instantly felt at home with its open, green countryside, golden cornfields and space. He'd bought a black and white framed Tudor cottage, nestled in the rolling hills, and found the solace he needed to let his creative juices flow.

And flow they did. Some of his most dynamic, hard-hitting documentaries had been produced since his move to Shropshire. Marcus Devlin was fast becoming a big name in the TV world and the latest of his work involving the village of Treweham was set to top him. His only regret was that his beloved mam wasn't there to witness it all. Marcus had been fiercely close to her and had nursed her to the end of her torturous days suffering with cancer. It was in the early hours of her last dawn that she managed to tell him, between gasps, who his father actually was, sending Marcus into shock.

After the shock came anger, an anger that had bubbled and festered into revenge. Marcus, believing his mam had been abandoned, sought to discredit his father. However, he never got the chance, as Richard Cavendish-Blake died a month after his mother. When the truth had exploded into light, it had been Finula who was there to comfort him. She had arranged with Megan and Tobias for Marcus to access his father's diaries. After the dust had settled and Marcus had been rightfully acknowledged, relationships gradually formed and now he considered both Tobias and Sebastian as true brothers, and they him as their older brother.

The interview the three of them gave on the documentary would prove heart-warming as well as sensational. A part of Marcus wanted the truth out, while the inner, private side of him lay in trepidation for the inevitable onslaught. He'd seen how the media had taunted Tobias throughout his adult life and didn't relish the same. The fact he was so closely linked to them could prove even more tantalising, he shrewdly thought, knowing no loyalty would be shown. A story was a story – end of. He wisely chose to get married before the documentary was aired, having seen first-hand the pandemonium Tobias and Megan's wedding had created. He had stayed at The Templar whilst Treweham village had endured the complete and utter invasion of the press. He grimaced at the thought of the intrusion. Luckily, he and Finula would enjoy their wedding day amongst family and friends without any fuss or reporters present.

'All done,' cried Finula with relief, sliding the cake tins into the oven.

'Me too,' replied Marcus, closing his laptop. He moved away from the kitchen table to stand before her. He wrapped his arms around her body, not bothering about the flour covering her apron. 'Love you, Mrs Devlin-to-be.'

Finula felt the stubble of his jaw against her cheek and breathed in that familiar citrus smell of him. 'You better,' she replied.

6

Christie woke to the sound of birdsong. Opening her eyes, she saw sunlight flicker through the floral curtains. Filled with an optimism that spring always brought, she threw back the covers and got out of bed. Drawing the curtains, she surveyed the view before her; acres of fresh, green and golden fields rolled before her, separated by stone walls and surrounded by woodland. A brook gently bubbled through, creating a calm, tranquil atmosphere. Christie opened the window wide and breathed it all in.

Despite her circumstances and being thrown in at the deep end, she was remarkably positive. It had been a hectic fortnight at The Templar, but she'd enjoyed every minute of being constantly on call, whilst familiarising herself with the staff, plus the customers had taken all of her time and concentration. Christie felt blessed to have Dermot on hand, always there to guide and advise her when called upon. It had gone down well with the locals too, still having their old landlord about, showing Christie the way. The two worked seamlessly together. She saw Dermot as a father figure, a tower of strength, not just at work, but also on those rare occasions when the gravity of Stephen's actions had finally hit home. On those moments, Dermot would offer wise counsel and huge support. He was a brick.

All in all, Christie was coping extremely well. She took the responsibility of owning and running her own country inn seriously. She had to – it was all down to her now, no one else. Once or twice amongst the mayhem of her new life, she would allow herself to think about Stephen. Her thoughts travelled to Chester, wondering what he and Sophie would be doing there. Would he be excited, preparing himself for parenthood? She pictured a pregnant Sophie, smiling smugly, patting her swollen abdomen. Amazingly, Christie didn't feel jealous. It had almost taken her by surprise at just how calm she really was, especially when considering her desperate need for a baby.

Maybe this was telling, she reflected in her most quiet moments. Had she been desperate for a baby, or a fix to her marriage? Was the idea of starting a family some sort of remedy for a relationship not working? And if being completely honest with herself, Christie had to concede she hadn't been happy. Yes, in the beginning when Stephen had been the same man she had fallen in love with, but not towards the end when her husband had turned into a lying cheat she couldn't trust.

She tried to imagine him here, in the Cotswolds, drinking in the scenery, and found she couldn't. He would have been a fish out of water, preferring the bright lights and buzz of a city, somewhere he could party with his rugby mates, not cosy up with her beside a roaring fire. Christie, in a very short space of time, had concluded that being in charge of her own destiny was definitely the way forward. Fulfilling the lifelong dream she had had of owning her own business was all-consuming. It took every ounce of her strength and sapped all her energy. At the end of each day, after an early start and busy evening, she would sink into a heavenly hot bubble bath with a glass of wine and stare out of the bathroom skylight at the stars. I'm here. I've made it, she would tell herself and raise her glass.

The Templar was starting to get more bookings now with it being spring. Dermot, in his wisdom, had suggested employing a few more members of staff to help with the housekeeping. Christie had also approved the new chef who had taken over from Dermot's daughter, Finula. She knew Dermot missed his daughter dearly, but her impending wedding kept him occupied and focused.

Christie chose to skip breakfast and just made herself a filtered coffee. Sipping it by the reception desk, she glanced down at the paperwork before her. Two new visitors were expected today.

'I've just cleaned rooms three and five, Christie,' said one of the recently employed girls, keen to make a good impression.

'Thanks, Emma.' She smiled. It was important to her that she knew each member of staff's name and used it. It paid off – in turn all the workers liked and respected their new employer. Christie also made a point of paying over the minimum wage and sharing all the tips out fairly. This too had gained The Templar a good name and it was rated a reputable place to work, with a friendly, welcoming atmosphere.

Dermot was more than happy with the way Christie was running the place. Initially it had been a wrench to give up his pub, but to hand over to someone like Christie was a pleasure. The Templar was in safe hands, he had no doubt. He did worry about her though, despite his jovial outward appearance. Often he would catch her with a pained expression, as though the past was jabbing and taunting her. It was gutting, reminding him of the heartache Finula had once suffered. He was determined to make things work for Christie. She so deserved it and he'd do all in his power to ensure a smooth transition.

'Christie, we need to talk flowers,' he said whilst passing the reception area, carrying a crate of wine. Christie looked up. 'For the wedding,' he explained.

There was enough chintz in this place without any more flowers, she thought wryly.

'Hmm, maybe let's think about a little refurbishment first?' she replied.

Dermot's eyebrows shot up. 'What's wrong with the decoration?'

'Perhaps a little dated in places?' she attempted gently.

'Where?' he asked, somewhat defensively. This was the first time Christie had ever challenged his taste. He looked bemused at her laughter.

'Where, Dermot? Well, let's start with the wood-chipped wallpaper in the hall and landing, the red carpet on the stairs and the bloody awful floral curtains in my bedroom.'

'That was Finula's bedroom,' he retorted, offended, making Christie giggle even more.

'Oh, Dermot, how long have they been there?'

'Since she was... a little girl...' he replied lamely.

'Exactly. Years.'

'Oh.'

Seeing how deflated he looked, Christie continued

soothingly. 'I'm not saying we need a whole new makeover, just in one or two areas, mainly the hallway and the bedrooms.'

'I see.' He clearly didn't, judging by his look of confusion.

'A new pair of eyes can see how we could... freshen the place up. Let's go for country chic, something a touch more sophisticated; think... rustic charm, warm colours, tweeds.'

'Right.'

'Not wood-chip and floral,' she added dryly.

Emma, who had witnessed the conversation, couldn't help but laugh too.

'Christie's right, the bedrooms are a bit old-fashioned.'

Dermot turned to face her. 'Oh, are they really? Well, I know when I'm outnumbered,' he replied with light sarcasm, making Christie smile with real affection.

'We want the place perfect for Finula's wedding, don't we?' she appeased.

'Yes, Christie, we certainly do,' Dermot called over his shoulder as he made his way to the bar. Emma and Christie exchanged grins, which were quickly interrupted by the opening of the front door. In came a tall, blond-haired man carrying a huge rucksack over his broad shoulders. For a moment Christie jolted. He instantly reminded her of Stephen. Then, as he approached, she realised he had a kinder face, with soft, blue eyes.

'Hello, I'm Daniel James. I'm booked in for a few days. I know I'm a little early.'

Yes, he did look like a Daniel, thought Christie, probably because closer up he resembled Daniel Craig with his charming smile and strong jawline.

'Ah, yes.' Christie glanced down towards the paperwork on the desk. 'That's fine, you're in room three, Mr James – it's ready.' She smiled and reached down under the desk for the room key. She passed it to him. 'I'll show you to your room.'

'I'll do that,' butted in Emma with enthusiasm.

'Thanks, Emma.' Couldn't blame her, Christie thought grinning to herself, as she watched Emma's eyes shine at the latest visitor.

7

Once alone, Daniel dropped his rucksack and fell on the bed. He was exhausted, physically, mentally and emotionally. Travelling round the Cotswolds trying to find a bolthole was draining him. He desperately needed to get away, not too far from home, but far enough from his everyday surroundings, concerned friends and family – and most of all Jenna. Just the thought of her made him tense.

But with Jenna, came Emily, and his body began to relax. His little Emily was the one thing worth living for. His heart melted, picturing her face the last time he saw her the previous week. She was the image of him with her pale blue eyes and blonde hair. Thank God, he thought, knowing full well what Jenna was capable of – any possibility of his fatherhood being questioned and she'd use it. The fact that Emily so clearly resembled him put paid to any schemes Jenna may have concocted.

Daniel took a deep breath and tried to calm down. He closed his eyes and just lay still for a moment. He followed the advice of his counsellor and tried to concentrate on his breathing, steady in and slowly out. He listened to the peace and quiet, with only the soft lullaby of the birds at the window. He veered his thoughts from the impending court hearing and all that encompassed. He had one month before his world could potentially be shattered. One month to try and find the perfect home for him and Emily and prove to the powers that be that he most definitely could and *would* provide and care for his daughter, as a single, competent, loving father. Emily was due to start school that summer; the idea of a close-knit community appealed to Daniel, which is why his search for a wholesome, country life took him to the Cotswolds.

Despite his efforts, the dark thoughts in his head wouldn't escape. What if it all went spectacularly wrong? His chest tightened. Surely, they wouldn't let Jenna take his little girl away from the daddy she adored? Daniel wanted closure on his relationship with Jenna, *real* closure, not the half-hearted attempts at separation that ultimately led to them drifting together again for convenience – for him access to Emily, for her money. Well, someone needed to fund the lifestyle Jenna had carved out for herself, and as she point-blank refused to work, on the convenient excuse of not wanting to leave Emily, it was apparently down to Daniel to bring home the bacon.

Jenna didn't mind continually dropping off their daughter at the nursery, with childminders, or his parents while she set off on shopping sprees. Then came the weekend breaks with the girls, which often resulted in a tearful Emily waving her mummy off, as Jenna giggled excitedly with her friends. It broke Daniel's heart the way Jenna could be so dismissive of their daughter. He'd relish having the time she could have with Emily. Didn't she realise what she was missing out on?

Then it all came to a climax one Sunday morning when

Jenna announced she'd met someone. Immediately Daniel had panicked. Where was this going to leave them all? He'd prayed Jenna would just choose to clear off with her new boyfriend and leave him and Emily in peace; but no, it was never going to be that simple with Jenna. Daniel knew full well that she'd use Emily as a lever, and boy did she. As long as Daniel was prepared to carry on supplementing her lifestyle through the extortionate maintenance he provided, things could pretty much stay the same regarding Emily. Jenna agreed not to move in with her boyfriend, thereby safeguarding Emily from being taken out of her family home, as long as Daniel moved out. He did so, and moved in temporarily with his parents nearby – anything to keep his daughter safely close to him.

But after a few months Jenna decided this wasn't enough. She now wanted to live with the new love of her life – a Scouser called John Jones, which he shortened to "JonJo". What a wanker, thought Daniel. JonJo rated himself as a singer-songwriter and toured the local circuits, which is precisely where he had met Jenna. She'd been so easily flattered by his boyish good looks and cheeky charm. He had practically serenaded his last song to her and she in turn had fallen under his spell. Now JonJo fancied returning to his beloved Liverpool and taking Jenna with him. Which meant bringing Emily also.

Daniel went ballistic when she'd told him of her plans. No-way, never, *ever* would she take Emily away from him. He'd fight with every bone in his body to keep her, which is exactly how he'd been left feeling now; like every bone in his body was breaking under the heartache and stress of it all.

8

Tobias gazed out of his drawing room window and considered how much things had changed in such a short space of time. It was just over twelve months now since he had first met Megan and whilst it had been one of the happiest periods of his life, it had also been tainted with worry. Treweham Hall had been left with crippling debts, due to his late father's financial inadequacy. It beggared belief that Richard Cavendish-Blake had produced an heir with such business acumen. Tobias had managed to turn the place around, from running headlong into the red, to the thriving operation it now was.

The estate contained acres of orchards and vegetable plots that supplied local businesses; it also housed the training yard, allowing his close friend Dylan the space he needed to train his racehorses, which in itself brought in a huge income. Then Tobias had persuaded his family to open Treweham Hall to the public. By securing private quarters and carefully restricting access, he had cleverly made certain rooms free for visitors to share, always accompanied by a tour guide. Unbeknown to his wife Megan, he had also installed extra security on the open days. Tobias was ever mindful of how the media, plus any other undesirable opportunist, could operate and had learnt to be protective over his family, especially Megan who hadn't been used to such invasion in her life. Now that they had Edward, his vigilance had reached fever pitch and security was of paramount importance.

His gaze moved to the woodland where the folly was nestled. There lay the latest venture. He smiled to himself. The Folly Players was his brother Sebastian's newly set up theatre company. Sebastian was an actor who had made a huge success playing Richard III at The Royal Shakespeare Theatre. The part had catapulted him into stardom, making him a household name. He had met his partner, Jamie, who'd been a runner in the documentary TV crew whilst filming in Treweham. Together they had created The Folly Players, using the beautiful, tall, stone building, with small slits of windows and a castellated top, tucked away in the Treweham Hall woods as their headquarters. Their debut play was *A Midsummer Night's Dream* and seemed the ideal choice as an open-air production with its leafy surroundings.

Tobias was pleased for his brother, who had had his fair share of heartache. Now it appeared Sebastian had finally found happiness with Jamie.

So, all in all, things were on the up, Tobias thought with satisfaction as he surveyed his estate. Gone was the deep feeling of uncertainty. He wished his father could see it all now, and was saddened to realise that his last days must have been riddled with money worries. Not for the first time he cursed himself for not spotting it, not seeing for himself the pressure his father must have been under; but Tobias had been too preoccupied running his own business, renovating and selling property, to notice.

He shook his head and vowed never to let his relationship with his son suffer like that. Tobias had learnt a valuable lesson the hard way – family came first. On that note, he decided to call in to the folly to see his brother. Whilst he appreciated how happy Sebastian obviously was, he couldn't help but notice how tired he was looking too. Clearly setting up his new theatre company and preparing for the production was taking it out of him.

As he strolled through the woods, he could hear voices in the distance. Sebastian, in true form, was playing the court jester. Squinting through the trees, Tobias could see his brother place a donkey's head over himself and call out, 'Ee-oo, ee-oo!' to a small crowd of actors who cheered him on with laughter. He chuckled to himself, then stopped suddenly when seeing Sebastian lose his footing and fall over. The crowd carried on laughing, thinking it was Sebastian fooling, but Tobias knew different.

As Sebastian lay on the ground, Tobias saw Jamie quickly pull off his donkey head and help him up. Sebastian quickly recovered and took a bow to a still-cheering group. As Tobias approached through the woods, they dispersed quickly, leaving him alone with Jamie and Sebastian. He overheard the tail end of their quiet whispers.

'You need to be more careful, Seb,' urged Jamie.

'Stop fussing,' came the curt reply. Tobias frowned. Sebastian quickly changed the subject. 'Ah, very kind of you to pay us a visit.' He bowed again theatrically.

'I take it that's Bottom?' He nodded towards the donkey's head on the grass.

'It sure is,' laughed Jamie.

'All set?' asked Tobias.

'We're getting there,' Sebastian replied looking more serious now. 'It should all come together for the opening night.'

'You sure?' Tobias looked at the props and wooden scenery scattered on the ground. He knew the costumes were carefully labelled and hung on racks inside the folly. The play was due to open in a fortnight.

'It's all under control,' reassured Sebastian. He picked up the donkey's head from off the grass and threw it on a pile of outdoor rugs. Lanterns, blankets and rugs were to be supplied to the audience, creating a cosy, comfortable atmosphere in the early evening dusk. Tobias noticed Sebastian's hand tremor slightly.

'If you need any help, just ask.'

'Will do, thanks,' replied Sebastian, then he turned to Jamie. 'Right, let's crack on. We need to work on the programs.' Tobias turned to go.

'I'll leave you to it!' he called and made his way back to the Hall, feeling a touch of concern.

9

Christie was sat near the bar. On the table in front of her lay samples of wallpaper, swatches of fabric, colour charts and brochures. She was on a mission, wanting to get the alterations just right. It baffled Dermot the way she seemed to be agonising over shades, patterns and textures. Surely it wasn't that hard, was it?

The breakfasts had just been served and the guests were passing her. Daniel smiled to himself and stopped.

'Thinking of a refurb?'

Christie, deep in concentration, suddenly looked up.

'Just the bedrooms and hallway.' She smiled too. To her surprise he took a seat next to her. His beautiful pale blue eyes glanced over the samples. Christie wondered what he did for a living. It would be a stroke of luck if he was an interior designer – he looked the arty type. He definitely had style. His clothes, although casual being khaki green combat pants and a long-sleeved olive T-shirt, fitted him perfectly and were obviously of good quality. He had a sharp haircut and just the right amount of stubble to look ruggedly handsome, rather than unkempt. He smelt fresh too. Christie caught a whiff of sage as he sat close to her. His broad shoulders brushed up against her.

He noticed her sizing him up and grinned back at her. 'Hope you don't think I'm being nosy.'

'Not at all!' she exclaimed, blushing slightly.

'I enjoy this kind of thing. I'm actually an architect, but love seeing how a building I've designed comes to life inside.'

Christie's face lit up. She really could do with a second opinion, especially from someone who knew what he was talking about.

'Ah, I see. In that case, Mr—'

'Daniel,' he cut in. Those eyes bored into her, making her stutter a little.

'I... I'm Christie,' she replied faintly.

'Well, Christie, what did you have in mind?' He nodded towards the table and laughed. 'You've quite a bit to choose from.'

She laughed too. 'I know, Dermot thinks I'm bonkers.' She gestured towards him behind the bar, where he was busy replacing bottles. Daniel smiled again. Christie noticed his cheeks dimpling, then realising she was staring once more, forced herself back to the issue at hand. 'I thought of a warm, rich colour for the hall, something welcoming, like this Hawthorne Yellow.' She pointed to it on a colour chart.

Daniel nodded his head in agreement. 'Yep, like the sun's shining through it permanently, keeping it airy and light.'

'Precisely!'

'What about curtains?'

'I thought this tweed, with pale creams, browns and the same yellow running through it?' She looked eagerly for his approval. Again he nodded. Christie was on a roll now, keen to show him her ideas for the bedrooms. 'Let me show you my bedroom,' she gushed.

Daniel's eyebrows rose in mock seduction. 'If you insist,' he replied playfully, making Christie blush again.

'Sorry.' She giggled, then opened a book of wallpaper samples.

Her hands stopped on a page that was pretty enough, but slightly too girly in his opinion, with its pale pink background and swirly silver pattern. Was there no husband sharing this bedroom with her? Instinctively he looked down to her left hand and noticed a pale ring mark where clearly a wedding ring had recently been removed. Plus, wouldn't she have said "our bedroom" not "my bedroom"?

Christie took his pause to be a negative. 'Maybe not – it was only going to be a feature wall.'

'No, it's nice,' he quickly interrupted. 'What about the rest of the guests' rooms?'

'That's where I'm undecided. Should I keep them all similar, country-chic style, or individual?'

'Definitely individual, give them a theme.'

Christie's face lit up again. He *really did* get it, she thought. 'That's an excellent idea!' she gasped with enthusiasm, making Dermot glance over.

'Just one thing though.' Daniel appeared a touch more serious, making Christie frown.

'Yes?'

'You've no family room. Maybe take the biggest bedroom and put a sofa-bed in there, to cater for a couple of children, if need be.'

Christie blinked. Of course – how could she have missed that? All her rooms were either double or twin. None provided for a family.

'You're absolutely right,' she conceded.

'Just a thought.' Daniel shrugged, then rose from the table. 'I'll let you get on.' He gave another charming smile and left her with lots to ponder, and not just the décor. Had he suggested a family room because he had one? She watched him stroll out of the bar with a quiet air of reassurance about him, like he was happy in his own skin. He wasn't showy, or overconfident, unlike someone she could mention, but friendly in a down-to-earth manner.

Dermot noticed her perusal of him and chuckled to himself. Christie might kid herself she could take on the world single-handed, but deep down he sensed she wasn't meant to be alone. He'd also clocked the guest scanning her hand for a wedding ring, and gave him credit for it. Most young men nowadays wouldn't have bothered. Hmm, watch this space, he told himself with hope.

Daniel made his way back to his room. He too was wondering a few things. Like what was the set-up here? He'd learnt from chatting to the locals that Dermot had been the landlord of The Templar and Christie had recently bought it. Obviously, Dermot was still working here, but what had happened to Christie's husband? The ring mark on her hand told him she must only have just separated from him. Why? Then he reprimanded himself; after all, it was none of his business was it? Even so, it left him a touch perplexed that someone as sweet as Christie clearly was, and a beauty to match with her fresh complexion and dark corkscrew curls, could possibly end up on her own.

10

Dylan read with interest all the details of the Cotswold Races and Country Fair on the computer screen in front of him. It told him all he needed to know – that Phoenix would be eligible to enter. He also needed a rider for the horse. Having been a professional jockey, he was ruled out, as the meeting was run entirely for veteran and novice riders. Despite the objections he knew full well would come from Flora, Dylan had approached Josh, their best groom, who was more than happy to ride Phoenix. Josh was used to riding him and knew the horse, albeit not like Flora did, but Dylan just couldn't put her in what he knew to be a dangerous position.

His thoughts turned to his last race, the only one he had fallen in. Although he had suffered concussion, bruising and broken ribs, it was minor compared to what he could have sustained. He knew jockeys who had been paralysed through racing and his blood turned cold at the very thought of Flora being injured in any way at all. Josh, who had showed interest and potential in jump racing, had had the necessary training, plus he would be stronger than Flora. All Dylan needed to do was submit his entry and fee to the Point-to-Point Racing Company Ltd, which he was about to do online, when Flora entered the yard office. She sidled up behind him and kissed his cheek. She then narrowed her eyes to see what was on his screen.

'I'm registering Phoenix in the Cotswold Races,' he explained.

'So I see. Dylan, I've been thinking—'

'No way,' he replied flatly.

'You don't know what I was about to say!' she replied in exasperation.

'Yes I do. And the answer is no, you are not riding Phoenix in the point-to-point.'

'But, Dylan—'

'Flora, no. It's not going to happen. I'm entering Josh as the rider.'

Flora had suspected this would be the case. Just then Dylan's mobile rang. Sighing he fished it out of his jeans pocket. The caller display apparently told him this call may be a lengthy one, so he eased off his chair, took his cup of coffee and sat on the nearby settee for comfort. Flora was still standing by his computer. The keyboard was calling her. All she had to do was delete Josh's details, retype her own in and press send. Job done. She quickly glanced over to Dylan, who was deep in conversation now. On impulse she did it. Dylan was too engrossed to notice what she had done, all in a few split seconds.

A sly smile spread across her face. She, Flora Tudor, would race her beloved Phoenix at the Cotswold Races. A message pinged back confirming the submission was received. She quickly marked it as read; meanwhile Dylan was still talking on his phone. When eventually he hung up, he returned to his computer. Flora was sat at her desk in the corner of the office. She knew Dylan would assume he'd sent his submission on seeing the email from the racing company.

'It's all gone through,' Flora called casually, hoping he wouldn't read the confirmation message with her details on.

'Good,' replied Dylan as he took another phone call. Phew, thought Flora in relief.

11

Finula sighed and continued to look at the glossy bridal magazines. Nothing was catching her eye. Everything was so over the top. Being a big believer in "less-is-more" she obviously wasn't included in the target audience that was supposed to swoon with delight. Finula winced at the huge, meringue creations, which to her wouldn't look out of place in Disneyland. She frowned at the ten-foot silk and lace trains, dragging behind the brides and wondered how they were supposed to move with ease. All the wedding dresses looked far too complicated with detail, having thousands of pearls, diamonds or sequins stitched into them.

What was wrong with a classy, simple gown that oozed elegance and style? It was almost as if the bride *needed* a statement dress, thought Finula. Tossing the magazine to one side, she picked up another one and turned the page to "Bride of the Season". This time she laughed out loud. Bride of the Season? Finula read the narrative underneath the photograph, *"Congratulations to Petula Pinkerton-Jones, the proud winner of our beautiful Bride of the Season."* Finula took in Petula's bucked teeth and crossed eyes and couldn't help spluttering.

'What's so funny?' asked Marcus as he entered the bedroom. Finula was unable to stop giggling at poor Petula. Curiosity getting the better of him, Marcus made his way over to the bed where Finula was sat up, surrounded by magazines. She pointed to the photograph. Marcus squinted to read the caption. 'Jeysus,' he muttered shaking his head, sending Finula into hysterics. He then started to undress and got into bed. Finula calmed down and put all the reading material on the bedroom floor.

'Blimey,' she sighed, 'I don't think I'm ever going to find the dress I want.'

'I'm sure you will,' replied Marcus dryly, judging by the amount of time she was spending trying to find one. If she didn't have her head buried in some wedding brochure, she was scouring the internet or trailing round bridal shops. It made him wonder what on earth she did before he had proposed.

'What I need, is a second opinion.'

'I'll tell you—'

'And not yours, silly, you're the groom,' she interrupted impatiently. 'No, I need a female's view.'

'Hmm,' Marcus replied, knowing it was hard for Finula being in Shropshire with just him, instead of her home village in Treweham. 'Why don't we go to visit your dad for the weekend? You could go dress shopping with Megan – she'd be happy to help.'

'Oh let's!' Finula's face lit up, making him smile. 'Dad'll be pleased to see us and I've not seen baby Edward for a while.' She then turned to face him. 'You sure you can spare the time?' Marcus pulled her onto his bare chest and wrapped his arms round her.

'For you, anything.' He kissed her cream shoulder, sprinkled with freckles. Finula ran her hands across his dark, broad chest and reached her lips to his, kissing him gently. He tugged her flimsy nightdress up over her head and flung it across the bed. 'Come here,' he whispered thickly and pulled her fully on top of him. Finula snuggled into his warm, lean body, enjoying the feel of his touch as he stroked her back and bottom. She loved the smell of him, drinking in that familiar citrus scent. Leaning up, her eyes met his and she smiled. Her breasts were grazing his chest and she felt the stirring of his erection against her thighs.

'Just think, in two months' time, we'll be husband and wife,' she said gently in between kisses.

'We sure will, darlin',' he replied, slowly easing himself into her.

12

Daniel sighed as he waited for his breakfast in the dining room. Only one more day left at The Templar and he was due to go home. If that's what his parents' house was, he thought sadly. How had it come to this? He reflected over the happy times with Jenna, when she held him in high esteem and he enjoyed her carefree company. They'd always been opposites, but then wasn't that the attraction in the first place? He had been a solid influence, with a promising career, whilst Jenna's sense of fun had been a breath of fresh air. Together they had made a home, albeit at his expense, but it hadn't mattered at the time; he was just happy to be with her. Then along came Emily, their beautiful daughter – it was all he'd ever wished for, a contented family life.

But as the years passed by, a growing unease had rooted. Jenna clearly hadn't taken to motherhood, preferring the company of her friends to that of a small child she had to occupy. It bored her being at home all day with Emily. Jenna hadn't been one for the mum and toddler groups. The thought of a bunch of cackling mothers, cooing over their children made her eyes roll. Basically, Daniel concluded, she was selfish. He'd seen the way Jenna always put herself first and he'd started to voice his concerns. Jenna wouldn't listen, refusing to admit she was a bad mother.

Daniel recalled one Christmas morning when Emily had been three years old. Instead of making the most of the precious time with their excited daughter, she'd stayed in bed with a hangover from the night before, only rising to pick at the Christmas dinner he'd made for them. His parents had been there, quietly accepting Jenna's inappropriate behaviour. Although they'd never said a word to Daniel, he knew they didn't approve of her. Well, who could blame them? Forever taking them for granted with her constant requests to babysit at every opportunity and never actually thanking them. They saw first-hand how miserable she had gradually made their son and resented her for it, not to mention the blatant neglect of their granddaughter.

Daniel sighed again. Once more his mood was beginning to sink to a low. He honestly thought that finding a prospective home in an area such as the Cotswolds would be the fresh start he desperately needed – somewhere he could settle down nicely with Emily. The horror of his little girl moving to Liverpool gripped his stomach, just as his full English was placed down before him.

'Thank you.' He attempted a smile at the young girl waiting on the tables.

'No problem.' She flashed her most dazzling beam at him. He didn't react. Instead he cast his eyes on the printed house details he'd brought down with him. He had just two more cottages to view. The four he'd looked at in the surrounding area hadn't met his expectations, not that they were too high. Surely wanting at least two bedrooms with two reception rooms, a decent-sized kitchen and a biggish garden wasn't asking too much? Apparently so, on his budget anyway.

His intention was to work from home more, enabling him more time with Emily, therefore he had to have a room to designate as an office, or some kind of outbuilding he could renovate to a studio. But it just wasn't happening. They were either too small, not quite in the right location or were listed, thereby restricting any renovations he might want. His parents had even offered to sell and relocate with him, joining funds to get somewhere together, but Daniel had gratefully declined. He wanted it to be just his and Emily's home.

Looking at the two houses left, his hopes weren't particularly high. They looked to be of similar ilk to the other properties he'd viewed, essentially charming on the outside with honey-coloured stone, covered in wisteria and roses blooming round the door, but poky and dark on the inside. He felt his future dream slipping through his fingers and gulped back his steaming tea. It burnt his lips, making him wince. Deciding he couldn't face eating after all, he collected his paperwork and made his way through to the reception area. Christie was displaying leaflets on the shelves by the desk and smiled at him as he passed.

'Morning!' she called cheerily.

Daniel stopped. 'Hi, Christie.' Then looked at what she was holding.

'They're local walks – fancy one?' He hesitated, badly wanting to get out there, deep into the countryside to clear his head, yet debating whether he'd have enough time.

He was due to meet the estate agents that morning, but hopefully he'd be free in the afternoon.

'Yeah, why not?' He smiled and took a leaflet from her.

She, in turn, looked at what he had in his hand.

'House specs,' he informed her, 'I'm looking to buy a property in the area.'

'Really?' This surprised Christie.

'Hmm, if I can find the right one.' He showed her the brochures for two cottages.

'They look pretty.' But fairly small, she thought. Was this to be just for him, or a family home?

'They do, but not sure how practical they're going to be for me and my little girl.'

'Oh, right. How old is your little girl?' She smiled, genuinely interested. Daniel's face immediately softened.

'Emily's four. She's due to start school this September, which is why I want to get somewhere quite quickly.'

'I see.' Christie nodded her head and sensed his dilemma. He was due to check out tomorrow.

'Anyway, thanks for this.' He waved the leaflet in the air and went up the stairs to his room, leaving Christie deep in thought, and with an idea hovering on the surface.

The morning proved to be just as he suspected. Whilst both properties did have good points, they sadly didn't tick all of Daniel's boxes. The local schools also hadn't rated as highly as he'd liked. He drove back to The Templar in low spirits, so decided to take that walk after all to lift his mood a little.

After surveying the map, he made his way over the small, humped-back bridge, past the church and the village green and took the public footpath to the side of Treweham Hall, which led partly through the woods. Breathing in the spring, country air he could feel himself unwind. Just listening to the stream gently trickle through the woodland and smelling the earthy, wild garlic made his shoulders relax and his heart beat rhythmically, instead of pounding through his chest. He had a real affinity with this place.

He heard voices in the distance and peered through the leafy branches. Narrowing his eyes, he saw a group of people outside some kind of tall building. They appeared to be in costume. Then he realised, they must be the actors, "The Folly Players" as advertised on the posters dotted about the village and in the reception area at The Templar. He smiled, thinking how quaint it was to have something like that on your doorstep. Following further along the footpath, he found it veered right onto a slight opening, where trees had evidently been felled to make a clearing for the stone house that was standing rather neglected by the side of the woods.

Daniel frowned, assuming he'd lost track. He glanced down again at the map; no, he definitely was still on the footpath and wasn't trespassing. Curiosity getting the better of him, he walked towards the building. Judging by the state of its crumbling walls and dilapidated slate roof, it had been derelict for some time. The wooden door was slightly ajar, tempting Daniel to explore further. He did so, with caution, not wanting any debris falling on him. He coughed from the dry, stale air inside and waved away the dust. His eyes took in the huge inglenook fireplace and the stone mullion window frames. The room was large with two doorways either end, leading onto a hallway.

Daniel slowly and carefully went from room to room. The layout was exactly what he had been looking for; two reception rooms and a large kitchen, although obviously a hell of a lot of restoration would be involved, but even so, what a place it could potentially be and in such a fantastic location. Sensing he had stumbled across something special, Daniel took photos of all the rooms on the ground floor. He didn't want to risk climbing the rickety, wooden staircase. As an architect, his imagination was running riot and his hopes began to soar. But who did it belong to, and why had it been left to ruin?

13

Edward gurgled and kicked in his cot, as Tobias wound up the musical mobile again. He watched his son's eyes sparkle with delight at the small, suspended teddy bears slowly spinning round above his head and his heart melted. He turned on hearing Megan enter the nursery.

'That was Finula on the phone,' she said joining them. Her gaze fixed on the bundle of joy that was their baby. 'She and Marcus are coming to Treweham at the weekend.'

'Do you hear that, Edward?' Tobias picked him up out of his cot, 'Uncle Marcus and Aunty Finula are coming to see us.' Edward burped and grabbed Tobias' nose.

'Charming, young man.' Megan laughed, then wrinkled her nose. 'He needs his nappy changing.' She reached out to take him.

'I'll do it,' said Tobias, relishing spending time with his son. It wasn't often enough that he could get away from running the Treweham Hall estate and all that encompassed. Moments like this, with just the three of them together, were precious to him.

'I'm looking forward to seeing Finula.' Megan missed her best friend dreadfully. 'She wants us to look at wedding dresses.'

'I see,' replied Tobias, gingerly taking off Edward's dirty nappy. 'I could do to talk to Marcus.'

Megan turned sharply. 'What about?' She waited while he wiped Edward clean and put a fresh nappy on him, which was proving difficult to manoeuvre as he kicked and wriggled. Finally Tobias managed to change him. He looked at Megan.

'I'm worried about Sebastian.'

'Why?'

'I can't put my finger on it, but somehow he's not his usual self.'

Megan had noticed that her brother-in-law did seem a little tired, but had put it down to all the organising he'd had to do setting up The Folly Players.

'Do you think it's stress?' she asked.

'Possibly, but before he set up his business I think he looked drained.' Megan paused and pondered for a moment. Thinking of it, she too had been a touch concerned about Sebastian. She remembered asking him if there was anything wrong, towards the end of her pregnancy. For a split second he'd looked as if he was about to open up, but then the shutters had come down and he'd closed up on her.

'Mm, do you think Marcus could help?'

'Yes, they gel well – he might confide in him. Also, with Jamie knowing Marcus too, it could encourage him to talk.' Jamie, as the runner in the TV documentary crew, which Marcus had headed, had always looked up to him. In turn, Marcus had seen Jamie's potential and had arranged for him to interview the three brothers as part of the documentary. It made sense that Sebastian would feel comfortable enough to share something with Marcus.

'Have you tried speaking to him?' asked Megan.

'Yes, but I sense resistance. I suspect it's because he thinks I may involve Mother. At least with Marcus, there wouldn't be that risk.'

'True,' she agreed. With Marcus being the eldest brother with a different mother to his younger half-siblings, Sebastian may subconsciously talk more freely, without the worry of any impact on his family.

'So, when you and Finula are out busy shopping for a wedding dress—' Tobias handed over a sweet-smelling Edward '—I'll be having a word with Marcus.' Megan took hold of him. 'Right.' He kissed her on the lips and rubbed his son's head. 'The estate manager wanted to see me at some point today; hopefully I won't be too long.'

'OK.' She smiled, waving Edward's podgy, little hand. 'Say bye-bye to Daddy.'

14

Later that evening, Daniel decided to have dinner early. He had returned from his afternoon walk full of optimism, had a long, hot bath and was famished, especially having not eaten his breakfast and skipping lunch. He was due to check out the following morning, but was reluctant to do so just yet, especially on finding the derelict cottage. He badly wanted to know who it belonged to. The more he thought about it, the more determined he was to make it his home. It wasn't just pie-in-the-sky dreaming, he'd convinced himself. If he could buy and restore it back to life, surely that would sound appealing to whoever had left it to languish in the woods; after all, what use was it at the moment? He'd be doing the owner a favour, taking it off them for a reasonable price, wouldn't he?

He was ordering a pint at the bar and thought he'd ask Dermot if he knew anything about the cottage.

Dermot nodded his head. 'Oh, that'd be Keeper's Cottage on the Treweham Hall estate,' he'd replied, passing him his drink. Daniel immediately warmed to the name. 'It belonged to the old gamekeeper, years ago. When he died, the then Lord Cavendish-Blake didn't replace him, so it's been left abandoned ever since.'

'I see,' said Daniel, taking a gulp of his pint. 'So it's owned by the Cavendish-Blake family then?'

'Yes, Tobias is the current Lord Cavendish-Blake.' Daniel had heard of the name. 'He got married last year to Megan. It was all over the press. She used to work here,' Dermot informed him.

'Did she?' Daniel was surprised, assuming that Tobias Cavendish-Blake as an aristocrat wouldn't have mixed with barmaids. Dermot chuckled, following his line of thought. 'He's a grand chap, the whole family is. In fact—' he leant forward over the bar '—my Finula is marrying his older brother, Marcus.'

'Really?' Daniel's eyebrows rose.

'Well, half-brother to be exact. They only share the same father.'

'I see.' Daniel's mind started ticking into overdrive. 'Dermot, do you think Tobias would talk to me? I'm really keen to buy and renovate that cottage.'

Dermot shrugged. 'Don't see why not. You could try ringing the estate manager and ask to see him,' he suggested.

'Hmm, I might just do that.' His stomach grumbled loudly, telling him to go and eat. 'Thanks, Dermot, you've certainly given me food for thought.' He moved to a small table at the side of the bar. Once his order had been taken, he took out his phone from his pocket and flicked through the photographs he'd taken of the cottage.

'Hi, Daniel.' He turned immediately and smiled at seeing Christie.

'Hi there.'

'Could I have a word with you? There's something I'd like to ask.'

Daniel's interest flickered.

'Yeah sure, take a seat.' He nodded towards the chair opposite him at the table.

'I've been thinking about your suggestion of a family room.'

'Right.' He waited for her to continue.

'The largest bedroom is free at the moment. I plan to make a few alterations, putting in a sofa bed for one, as you recommended, plus one or two other tweaks. The thing is, I could really do with some help, someone with a natural flair for interior design, which I believe you have. I like your idea of giving each bedroom a theme.'

He smiled back at her.

'Well, in short,' she quickly said, feeling slightly embarrassed, 'I'd like you to stay in the family room, obviously with your little girl, free of charge and... help me renovate the rooms. Does that sound a fair exchange?' She looked anxiously at him, hoping he wouldn't laugh at her proposal.

Instead he looked thoughtfully at her and gave a grin. Christie's heart leapt in her chest. Hell, he was handsome. He took a swig of his beer. Was he stalling for time? Her eyes never left his face, patiently waiting with bated breath for a response from him.

'Yes, I think that's a fair exchange.' He stared straight at her. Her cheeks were slightly flushed, he noticed, finding it utterly endearing. She had an open, honest way about her. He suspected that what you saw, was what you got – no hidden agenda. That in itself made a refreshing change, he thought bitterly.

'Good. Good.' She looked away, as if self-conscious.

'To be honest, I was thinking of staying a little

longer anyway and I've got Emily for a short while, so it would suit me fine.' Christie's face lit up. Once again Daniel warmed to her reaction. Then, taking his phone he showed her the pictures of Keeper's Cottage. Christie seemed genuinely interested.

'It looks like it's got bags of potential,' she remarked.

'It has, plus it's in a fabulous spot.'

'On the Treweham Hall estate? Wouldn't that cause complications?'

'Possibly – depends on what Lord Cavendish-Blake's view is,' he replied soberly. Christie noticed the frown burrowing on Daniel's forehead and hoped she hadn't burst his bubble of excitement.

'Do you think Emily will enjoy staying here?' She smiled. Immediately the frown disappeared.

He beamed. 'She'll love it.'

15

'You what?'

'Shush,' hissed Flora and pulled Josh away from the view of the office window and into a stable. Once alone, Flora took a deep breath and tried to appease him. 'Listen, Josh, this is my doing – you won't take the rap.'

'You kidding?' he rasped. 'Dylan will kill me!'

'Keep your voice down,' Flora whispered urgently and quickly looked out of the stable door. Good, no one was about. Turning back, she continued in a low voice, 'Dylan won't find out, not until the race starts and he realises it's me riding Phoenix, not you.'

'Your name will appear on the programme,' cut in Josh dryly.

'We'll have to make sure he doesn't bloody well see the programme then, won't we?'

'*We?*' Josh's eyes widened.

Flora tried again to win him over. 'Josh, there's no way Dylan would agree to me riding in that point-to-point, or any other race for that matter. He thinks it's too dangerous—'

'Which is exactly why I'm not agreeing to this either,' he interrupted, folding his arms defiantly.

'Yes you will.' Flora glared at him. 'I'm the assistant trainer of this yard.'

'And Dylan's the owner of this yard,' he retaliated. 'He'll fucking sack me!'

'No he won't,' replied Flora in a stern voice. 'I will tell him the truth: that I made you promise not to say a word. Look, we all know I'm the best rider for Phoenix.'

With that Josh couldn't argue; he remained silent.

Flora quickly continued, 'Just let me show Dylan that I *can* do it, and safely. Once he realises I'm fine racing, it won't be a problem.'

Josh pulled a face in disbelief. Even she had to concede this may be pushing it a bit.

'Please, Josh, don't tell him.' Her eyes searched his face.

He gave a deep sigh and looked away.

'Please?' She touched his arm until he faced her.

'OK,' he agreed reluctantly, already regretting his actions.

'Oh thanks, Josh!' She hugged him with gratitude.

Dylan walked past the stable and saw through the gap of the door. Blinking, he glanced again to see Flora's arms around Josh. Gulping, he quickly strode into the office, his heart hammering in his chest. *What the fuck?* Surely not? Flora... and Josh? But that's what he'd seen, with his very own eyes. He slumped down at his desk and rubbed a shaking hand through his hair.

His first instinct was to tear into that stable and rip the bastard apart, but the voice of reason quickly intervened. Josh was actually a very good groom and he wouldn't be able to replace him that easily. Also, he was riding for him in the point-to-point next week. A nauseating sensation settled in his gut, threatening to spill out of him. He took in a long, steady breath. Flora, his precious Flora – how could she? Tears began to well in his eyes. He quickly blinked them away on hearing her enter the office.

'Hi!' she breezed. His mouth was dry, unable to answer. He took in the back of her, as she poured herself a drink. Her blonde hair was plaited and coming lose, her petite frame nicely showcased in a fitted, quilted jacket and tight jodhpurs. He swallowed away the bile that edged up his throat. She turned to face him. Her cheeks held a rosy glow. Was that from sexual excitement? thought Dylan miserably. 'You OK?' Flora asked, looking concerned. 'You look pale.' Still unable to speak, he dragged his chair back and got up. 'Dylan?'

'I need to go home,' he said gruffly and strode out of the office, leaving a rather puzzled Flora staring after him.

16

Finula's spirits lifted once they drove past the sign of Treweham village. It felt good to be home, not that she didn't enjoy living in Shropshire, but her roots were here, deep in the Cotswolds. As always, her dad was there at the front door of The Templar, ready to meet them, making her heart tug a little. Marcus pulled into the car park and opened the boot of the Range Rover to carry in the luggage. Finula ran to hug Dermot.

'Oh, Dad, I miss you,' she half wailed.

'Now, come on, Fin.' He laughed, blinking rapidly. He turned to Marcus. 'How are you, Marcus?'

'Fine, Dermot, and yourself?'

'Good. Come and meet the new owner of The Templar.' He ushered them both inside. Christie was on reception and gave them all a wide smile.

'Hello, you must be Finula and Marcus?' Finula instantly warmed to the pretty girl with dark, curly hair and a kind, welcoming face.

'And you must be Christie.' She held her hand out to shake Christie's.

'Hello, Christie.' Marcus nodded his head. 'Which room are we in?'

'Room one – it's all ready for you.' She handed Finula the key.

'It seems strange taking a key from you, instead of just going up to my room.'

'Ah, I'm, in there now,' replied Christie with a grin.

'And wants to redecorate it,' butted in Dermot.

'I should think so, Dad!' reprimanded Finula making Christie chuckle to herself. A hunch told her she was going to get along just fine with Finula.

Once upstairs and in their room, Finula wrapped her arms round Marcus.

'Do you remember the first time we were in this room?' she whispered sexily. Marcus raised his eyebrow.

'Do I ever, you little minx.' He lowered his head and kissed her slowly. Finula hugged him harder. Just then there was a knock at the door, prompting them to stop suddenly. Dermot poked his head round the door.

'Come on, there's drinks at the bar for you, then we'll eat.'

'OK, we're on our way, Dad,' called Finula. When he'd left she giggled at Marcus' face.

'No change there then,' he said with a wry grin.

Finula loved being back in The Templar, but as a guest, and not having to work behind the bar, which was getting busy.

'Business still good then, Dad, even though all the locals know you're leaving?' They'd all enjoyed a lovely evening meal and were relaxing with coffee in the far corner of the dining area.

'Yes, they've all taken to Christie. I'm not surprised – she's a good girl and loves this place.' He turned towards her as she chatted and served drinks to various people.

'She seems to fit in well,' observed Marcus. His eyes narrowed to the blond-haired man propped up by the bar who appeared very comfortable talking to Christie. 'Is he a local?' He nodded in his direction.

'No, well not yet anyway. That's Daniel. He's staying here at the moment, but wants to find a house here in Treweham. He's going to help Christie renovate the bedrooms. He has "an eye" for that sort of thing apparently.' It clearly perplexed Dermot that Christie felt the need to change anything, but then he was no longer the owner.

'Good for Christie,' said Finula, pleased that The Templar was in safe hands.

'Daniel fancies buying the old Keeper's Cottage,' Dermot told her.

'Didn't know Tobias was selling it,' she replied surprised.

'He isn't. Daniel stumbled across it and wants to persuade him to sell it.'

'Can't blame him for wanting to settle here.' Finula looked at the man at the bar. He didn't look the swanky city type who just wanted a holiday home somehow. She noticed his easy, relaxed manner and the way he mixed with the locals. Judging by the appreciative looks a few of the women were giving him, Finula guessed he'd blend in perfectly. Christie noticed her looking and waved her over.

'Finula, meet Daniel. Daniel, this is Dermot's daughter.'

'Pleased to meet you.' Daniel smiled and warmly shook hands with her. Marcus and Dermot followed behind. Turning to them, Finula introduced Marcus.

'Hello there.' Marcus gave him a firm handshake.

Daniel asked casually but deliberately in Marcus' direction, 'So, all ready for the wedding?'

'No idea – Finula's the person to ask,' he replied dryly, making them all laugh.

'We're getting there,' Finula cut in with a smile, 'and with the help of Christie, I'm sure it'll all go to plan.'

'Don't worry, it will,' Christie assured her. 'Come on, let's drink to it.' She reached up for a bottle of champagne.

Dermot smiled to himself – the very bottle he'd had on ice for her first arrival at The Templar. How much brighter things looked for her now. She expertly removed the cork and poured the fizz into flutes. 'To the wedding!' she cheered.

'And to the new Templar,' added Dermot with a wink.

17

Daniel woke the next day with a headache. Not surprising, given the amount he'd had to drink the night before. But he considered it all to be in a good cause. He'd made the most of the opportunity in talking to Finula and Marcus, whom he genuinely liked. Dermot's words rang in his ears about how the Cavendish-Blake family were good, grounded people. Certainly chatting to Marcus proved this, although it was Tobias who he was desperate to win round over Keeper's Cottage.

Deciding to strike while the iron was hot, he rang the number of the Treweham estate office, which he'd looked up. Within a few minutes he had been given definite instructions by a well-spoken, extremely efficient-sounding manager. He'd been told to email, giving detail to who he was and why he wanted to speak with Lord Cavendish-Blake, which he had done, after great deliberation. Daniel had tried to pitch the message just right, eager not to appear cheeky or intrusive.

Shutting down his laptop, he sighed. Everything he did and thought seemed to revolve round his future. Once again, the court case that was looming invaded his mind, causing his chest to tighten. Then he tried hard to take deep, steady breaths as he'd been advised. Stress was a killer, he'd come to realise. Yet how could he switch off and not contemplate losing Emily? Because for all Jenna's shallow reassurances, her taking their little girl to Liverpool would mean hardly ever seeing his daughter. He knew better than to believe or trust anything Jenna promised. He was well aware of how she operated.

He cast his mind back to a few months ago when Jenna had refused point blank to attend any mediation that the court had tried to arrange. Daniel had been more than willing to go, hoping it would encourage some sort of compromise, or at least make Jenna see his point of view, but no she didn't want to know. He had appointed a solicitor, an expensive one at that, but was prepared to pay whatever the costs to ensure Emily was safe with him, in the only place she'd known. Alana Frost was very cold and hard and didn't take any prisoners. She specialised in family law and had a sharp, legal mind. Alana had been direct and honest from the start. He pictured himself sat opposite her deadpan face in the tiny attic office of his local solicitors'. After outlining why he was there, a barrage of questions had followed.

'Is your name on the birth certificate?'

'Yes, of course,' he'd replied shocked. 'Who else's name would be on it?'

'Nobody's. It could be left blank,' she'd stated flatly. And on it went, question after question regarding his income, lifestyle and parenting. Then she'd focused her questions on the child's mother. Even her face flickered with emotion when Daniel had summarised, honestly, how Jenna was with Emily. This seemed to open up a can of worms and Alana had leapt into full vigour. 'Does she take drugs?'

'No.' Did she? Would he know? 'Not that I know of.' He swallowed. His stomach felt like he'd been punched.

'Drink?'

'Yes.'

Alana's face shot up. 'How much?'

'Err… well, quite a lot when she's on a night out with her friends, but—'

'How often does she go out?' she fired, making Daniel swallow again. His mouth had become very dry.

'Quite often. That's how she met… John Jones.'

'What does he do?'

'He's a…' dickhead, thought Daniel, '… a musician apparently, he tours the… pubs.'

Alana rolled her eyes. 'A two-bit singer without a professional job then?'

He was beginning to warm to her now. 'Yes,' he replied with force.

Alana nodded her head. 'Well, I'll be straight with you,' she stated, staring into him. Daniel flinched. 'You've got a good case. It won't be easy – these things never are – but…' she nodded her head again '…I think you've got substantial grounds for a Residence Order.'

'You mean custody, right?' His heart soared.

'Yes. But I must counsel patience and, remember, I can't promise anything.'

'OK.' Daniel had been given the first ray of hope since this whole sorry mess had started. He'd been interviewed, as had his parents; there had been visits, child reports and he felt like his whole life had been put under a microscope. Now here he was, frantically trying to build a home and future for himself and Emily.

18

Tobias made his way towards the woods to the Folly. An early evening dusk had settled over the Treweham Hall grounds and the sounds of the night forest echoed through the trees. In the distance he could see the Folly, illuminated now with beams of light strategically placed that Sebastian had had installed. It gave the building a dramatic, theatrical presence, completely striking the right tone. Outside people scurried about with urgent voices, putting together the last-minute arrangements for the opening show the following night.

Tobias stood back and watched the mayhem, smiling to himself with affection. He was pleased that his brother had finally found happiness, not only with his partner, but with his new business as well. The Folly Players too. There was no doubt that Sebastian was totally in his comfort zone as he gave instructions to the other actors, whilst still managing to make them laugh. He had a way with them, Tobias had noticed. People liked Sebastian. It was easy to see why, with his easy-going nature and humorous outlook on life.

His little brother had always stolen the show with his entertaining drama, often sending family and friends into hysterics, even Aunt Celia. He was a wicked mimic too, with a wide range of voices. Look how he had shone in his performance of *Richard III*. Tobias had been beyond proud of him. But there was something, deep down, that concerned him and he just couldn't put his finger on it. He observed him as he walked holding a bundle of costumes in his arms. Tobias narrowed his eyes and scrutinised the way Sebastian's left shoulder slightly rose and fell. He turned his gaze downwards to his left leg and saw how Sebastian's stride didn't flow naturally. He was limping.

Thinking back now, Tobias realised that he had noticed this before, but hadn't thought too much about it – putting it down to fatigue, which Sebastian had complained of at the time. He'd known his brother had been to a physio too, but that was due to his forced posture whilst playing *Richard III* and having to hobble across a stage for weeks on end in character. But it looked like the limp hadn't disappeared. Tobias cast his mind back to the other week when he'd seen Sebastian fall over and a disturbing feeling began to settle. The sooner he spoke to Marcus, the better. They were all coming to the opening night tomorrow, so hopefully he'd be able to confide in him then.

Sebastian turned and saw Tobias making his way through the small crowd.

'Evening, my Lord.' He bowed. 'Good of you to call.'

Tobias grinned – typical Sebastian, always the player.

'Yes, well I thought I'd see if you're all set to go for the opening night.'

'Think so.' Sebastian suddenly looked anxious as he glanced round at the hub of activity. Nerves were clearly starting to kick in; it was all becoming very real now.

'I'm sure it'll all go to plan,' Tobias reassured him. 'Where's Jamie?'

'Inside, discussing lighting with the techies.'

'They've done a good job lighting up the Folly.' Tobias looked up at the tall, stone building in admiration.

'They have,' agreed Sebastian. He began hanging the costumes onto a rail. 'There'll be spotlights in the woods too, for a couple of the scenes.'

'It sounds fantastic.' Sebastian carried on with the costumes. For all his bravado, he actually found it hard to accept compliments. 'Seriously, Sebastian, well done.' Tobias patted his back.

'Thanks, bro.' He looked straight at him, giving him his full attention. Tobias decided to broach the subject that was on his mind.

'Is everything—' But he was suddenly interrupted by a flustered Jamie.

'Seb, we need you in here a minute!'

'No rest for the wicked.' Sebastian rolled his eyes in good humour. 'Got to go, Tobias, but see you tomorrow?'

Tobias smiled. 'Absolutely, we'll all be here, cheering you on.'

19

Flora snuggled up to Dylan and felt his whole body turn rigid. She frowned, finding the response unusual. Normally he would turn and envelop her into a warm hug, loving the feel of her skin on his. But not tonight. In fact, on reflection, not for a few nights now. She recalled how instead of stretching out his arms in welcome, he had slept with his back to her. As broad and muscular as it was, Flora was beginning to sense a form of rejection and missed being held by the man she adored. What was wrong?

'Dylan?' she whispered, kissing his neck. Still no response. She paused for a moment, then turned on her back when hearing his gentle snores. Flora gazed up at the ceiling. She knew he couldn't be asleep so soon, especially when he was obviously so tense and stiff. What on earth was the matter? Had he guessed she had defied him by signing up to race Phoenix? But how? And surely the first thing he'd do would be to confront her, not give her the silent treatment; that just wasn't his style. Then another dark thought crept into her head, one that had often strayed and trespassed through her mind before. Was there someone else? Had Dylan been unfaithful? Gulping back tears, she turned on her side and fought hard to sleep.

Dylan lay still. It was torture resisting Flora's kisses, when all he badly wanted to do was ravish her. He missed that soft, sweet body under his as he sunk into her, loving the taste and smell of the girl who had stolen his heart. And now his heart was breaking. Literally, he could physically feel a sharp pain in his chest, which utter sorrow brought. Flora, his beautiful, stubborn soul mate, who was more in tune with him than any other human being.

A tear plopped out of the corner of his eye and dribbled onto his pillow. How could she? Sheer anger replaced the heartbreak when the memory of her and Josh's embrace in the stables stung him. He'd rip the bastard apart, once the point-to-point was over and he'd done his last job by riding for him. Once that was over, he'd give Josh his marching orders, plus a good hiding to boot.

20

'Daddy!' Daniel opened the front gate to his parents' house and watched Emily run down the pathway to greet him. He crouched down, arms open wide as she bolted into him.

'Emily.' He hugged her hard and breathed her in, then kissed the top of her blonde head.

'Daddy, Grandma says we're going on holiday?' She beamed up at him excitedly.

'We certainly are, Sweet Pea.' He lifted her up and walked down the path. His mum was standing by the open door smiling and waving. His dad was behind her. Once inside he asked, 'Everything all right?' That was code for *"Did Jenna drop her off without any hassle?"*

'Yes, love, everything's fine,' his mum reassured him. Daniel looked to his dad for confirmation, knowing how his mum had a tendency to smooth over situations, without letting on the whole truth sometimes. The firm nod of his head told Daniel that all was well.

'Good. Right then, Emily, do you know where we're going on holiday?'

'The Codswallops,' she replied, making everyone laugh.

'The Cotswolds,' corrected Daniel with a grin. How he

loved this child of his, with her big, blue eyes, cute button nose and blonde waves. His mum had tied them into a ponytail with a lemon satin ribbon. Jenna would never have done that; she'd think it too twee. 'And tonight, we are going to a see a play in the woods.'

'What's a play?'

'It's when people act out a story, like the pantomime we went to at Christmas, remember?'

Emily's face lit up. 'Yes!' She started to jump on the spot. 'Will there be a horse?' She was referring to the panto horse, which she'd howled with laughter at.

'Hmm, kind of. A man grows donkey's ears, which is like a horse.'

'Oh.' She gave a puzzled look. 'What's he called?'

'Bottom,' Daniel replied, knowing full well what was coming next.

Emily started to giggle. 'Don't be silly, Daddy!'

'He is,' insisted Daniel with a grin. His mum and dad looked on, obviously loving the interaction.

'Emily, why don't you show Daddy your new dress? It's upstairs on your bed, sweetheart.' His mum obviously had something to tell him and his stomach contracted slightly. As soon as Emily had disappeared, he looked at his parents.

'You've a letter, son.' His dad handed him the white envelope. Judging by their serious expressions, they'd guessed it was an official correspondence. Daniel placed it in his back pocket. Not wanting to spoil the day, he chose to read it another time when he was alone.

There was a moment's silence. Then he told them about Keeper's Cottage and how he'd contacted the Treweham estate.

'It sounds ideal, love. Do you think Lord Cavendish-Blake will let you have it?' asked his mum.

'Possibly, at the right price,' he replied.

'Everything has a price,' his dad added, whilst Emily came into the room proudly wearing her new dress.

'Look, Daddy!'

'Emily, you look beautiful,' he gushed, picking her up to sit on his knee. After spending time with his parents, he and Emily set off back to Treweham. He loved having her in the car, chatting away and looking out of the window. He didn't want moments like this to end. His heart was breaking at the possibility.

Back in The Templar, Christie was at pains to make sure everything was just right in the new family room. Instead of putting in a sofa bed, she had opted for a day bed. The room was plenty big enough and the white, iron, open bed with pretty patchwork bedding looked more suitable for a little girl than a sofa bed that would have to be set up every night. Who wanted that fuss on holiday? Christie had thought about bunk beds for the future, but was undecided. Looking round the room, she gave it one last inspection. Had she more time to prepare, Christie had thought about buying a trunk to put toys in, but she was clueless as to what toys to buy. A nasty voice entered her head, *"Stephen will soon know,"* it whispered with malevolence. A dull pain throbbed in her chest.

Stop it, she told herself, *concentrate on what's going on in your life.* Then, as a welcome distraction, she looked out through the window and saw Daniel pull onto the car park.

She smiled and watched him open the door for his daughter. What a cutie! Out popped a blonde tiny tot in a pink dress and matching pink, glittered pumps, carrying a teddy bear. She was skipping, obviously excited to be here with her dad. Christie's heart melted. Again her mind cast back to Stephen. Would he have a son or daughter? Gulping back the tears, she made her way down to reception to greet them.

Dermot had beat her to it. By the time she had got down the stairs, he was chatting away to them. He glanced over at her as she approached them.

'Ah, here she is. Emily, meet Christie. This lady has been getting your room ready.' Christie bent down to the little girl's level.

'Hello there, Emily.' She smiled.

'Hello, can I see my room please?'

'Of course, come on, I'll show you.' Expecting Daniel to follow them, Christie was surprised when Emily automatically took her hand.

Daniel grinned. 'You go on ahead, I'll bring in the cases.'

Entering the room, Christie looked anxiously at Emily for her reaction and was filled with relief when her face lit up.

'Is this my bed?' She ran and sat on it.

'Yes, do you like it?'

'Yes! And so does Snuggles.' The teddy bear she'd been carrying had been plonked on the pillow.

'Good. I'm glad.' Christie laughed.

Daniel entered the room. 'Everything to madam's liking?'

'Look, Daddy, this is my bed.'

'So I see,' he replied, then turned to Christie. 'Thanks.

That's a lovely touch, better than a sofa bed on second thoughts, isn't it?'

'Yes, saves on messing about—'

'We're going to a play in the woods tonight,' interrupted Emily.

'Are you?' Christie smiled.

'Will you come with us?' asked Emily, staring up expectantly.

'Oh, I…'

'If you're not too busy, we'd love you to join us,' said Daniel softly, looking into her eyes.

Christie swallowed. How handsome he was with those mesmerising eyes. 'Err… well yes then, thank you, that would be lovely.'

'Yes, but there's a bottom in it, with donkey ears,' warned Emily, folding her arms, making Christie laugh out loud once more.

21

A tense, nervous thrill hung in the air, as was always the case for an opening night. But for Sebastian, this wasn't just any opening night, it was *his* first production. Tonight's performance would make or break The Folly Players. A lot was hinging on the next few hours. He knew full well the critics would be out there, ready to analyse and appraise, not just the acting, but the performance as a whole – its venue, scenery, costumes and direction – all of which Sebastian was responsible for.

A fine layer of perspiration covered him. He dropped the programme he'd been clutching. It fell to the floor, open with the central pages showing the cast and the team who had made this happen. His eyes homed in on Jamie's photograph and for a moment all the anxiety evaporated. There he was, his closest ally and confidant. Where would he be without him? His eyes then cast over his own portrait, making him chuckle. With pointy ears and horns, and a mischievous grin, Sebastian made the perfect Puck. Originally he'd wanted a minor role, but couldn't resist playing the clever, impish jester of a fairy. Well, who better? the rest of the cast had joked.

Sebastian picked up the programme and called the cast together for that last-minute pep talk. He knew what to say; he'd listened to enough words of wisdom from experienced directors before. He wanted to eliminate all the actors' nerves and encourage them to enjoy the performance. Doing this convincingly meant he had to compose himself. He peeped outside the Folly's slit windows and took a deep breath. The grounds were filling up. *That's a good thing,* he told himself and with an air of confidence, pulled his shoulders back, inhaled fully and spoke with utter conviction to the team surrounding him.

Tobias and Megan sat on the front row, eager for the show to begin. Baby Edward was sound asleep in his pram, oblivious to the commotion around him. The two seats empty next to them were to be occupied by Finula and Marcus. Megan bobbed her head into the pram.

She turned to Tobias. 'If he wakes up and cries, I'll have to take him back.'

'No you won't. I've got Henry to do that.' He thumbed the row behind them, where Henry dutifully sat. Megan smiled to herself. Given the choice, she suspected Henry would much rather wheel Edward back to the Hall than sit through the play.

She caught sight of Finula out of the corner of her eye and waved to get her attention. Waving back, Finula ushered Marcus to the front row to join them. Tobias stood up to kiss Finula and shake Marcus' hand. He discreetly whispered something to him, which Marcus nodded his head at. After admiring Edward, Finula sat next to Megan and chatted excitedly about the shopping trip she'd arranged for a wedding dress. As the two girls exchanged chit-chat, Tobias and Marcus spoke quietly.

'I'm worried about him, there's something he's not telling me,' Tobias said in a low tone.

'Do you think he'll talk to me though?' replied Marcus with a frown.

'He may do. If not, I want you to approach Jamie – obviously you know him better than me.'

'I'll see what I can do.' Marcus looked into his brother's eyes and saw how troubled he was. 'Don't worry, Tobias, we'll get to the bottom of it.'

For Tobias, it was good to have his brother's reassurance. Up until now it had only ever been him shouldering the burden.

'Thanks, Marcus.'

Emily ran to the front, frantic to have the best view. Daniel called her back, but she insisted on the last three seats. She sat Snuggles on the middle one.

'Hurry up!' she called, making Megan and Finula laugh. Daniel quickly sat down, shortly followed by Christie.

'Now sit down and be quiet, Emily,' coaxed Daniel, feeling slightly self-conscious. He faced Marcus and Finula. 'Hello again.' He smiled.

'Hi,' replied Finula, then turned to Tobias and Megan. 'Meet Daniel and Emily – they're staying at The Templar.'

'Hello.' Megan grinned.

Tobias nodded his head. The name Daniel resonated with him for a moment. Then he recalled an email he had received the other day from someone staying at The Templar. Daniel politely included Christie.

'We've roped Christie into coming with us.' He laughed.

'Good for you. I'm sure she deserves a night off,' replied Finula.

Christie chuckled and thought how much Finula was like her dad.

'Ladies, gentlemen and children, please take your seats and be dazzled by *A Midsummer Night's Dream*!' An actress with long, flowing auburn hair, wearing a dark green, shimmering dress and fairy wings called across the crowds. Hushes and whispers followed in anticipation – The Folly Players were about to perform.

And perform they did with seamless grace and skill. As predicted, Sebastian stole the show with his hilarious interpretation of Puck. Little Emily howled with laughter, as Daniel had predicted, at Bottom and his donkey's head, whilst Christie soberly reflected on a line of his; *"And yet, to say the truth, reason and love keep little company together now-a-days."* The words dug deeply, sending her into another world.

Daniel caught her pained expression and had a sudden urge to kiss her troubles away. His own instincts took him by surprise for a moment, then when spending time discreetly observing those full, red lips she anxiously chewed, it seemed the most natural thing in the world to join his to them. A dark curl of hair had covered one of her eyes and he resisted the urge to sweep it back in place. She was naturally pretty, without the use of cosmetics. He remembered how Jenna used to plaster herself in make-up.

Christie didn't need it with her fresh complexion and rosy cheeks.

She caught him clocking her and looked into his eyes. For a moment they just stared at each other, until he whispered, 'You OK?'

She nodded her head and smiled faintly. He so wanted to reach out to her, but this was hardly the time and place. He glanced down. Emily was half asleep now, leaning against him. Hardly surprising, he thought; it had been quite a full, eventful day for her.

"Lord what fools these mortals be!" cried Puck. Daniel considered this for a moment. Was he being foolish? Hoping to start afresh in the village of Treweham? Was it a pipe dream? His glance moved to Tobias, sitting a few seats away. There was a lot hinging on his decision. Would he sell him Keeper's Cottage?

Marcus was observing Sebastian closely. Although by first appearances his brother seemed confident, Marcus' eyes narrowed at the slightly uneven steps he made. He also noticed his hand quiver slightly when pouring the "magic potion" onto his characters. He suspected Tobias' concerns were well founded.

After almost two hours of constant entertainment, Puck spoke the closing words of the play, *"If we shadows have offended, think but this, and all is mended. That you have but slumbered here, while these visions did appear."*

This was met with a thundering applause and a standing ovation from the crowd. The cast all lined up, joined hands and took their final bow.

Megan's eyes watered at seeing the utter pride and joy

in Sebastian's face. Then, on seeing Edward stir from the loud clapping and cheers, she picked him up from his pram. Luckily, he was happy to be tucked inside his mother's arms without wailing.

Tobias gently stroked the top of his head. Then he turned sharply towards the security staff, who were positioned round the audience. Their job was to swiftly guide every member of the public out of the grounds with minimum fuss. He was perhaps a little paranoid where his family was concerned, but always hid this from Megan. The last thing he wanted was to make her fearful.

Daniel carried a now sleeping Emily back to The Templar with Christie.

'She looks so angelic,' whispered Christie.

'I know,' agreed Daniel, his heart melting. 'I'll put her straight to bed. Then do you fancy a nightcap?' he asked, knowing Emily would be safe and not wake up.

'That would be nice.' She really didn't want to go to bed in this mood. Although she'd enjoyed the play, the feeling of melancholy it brought was proving hard to shake off. Would this empty emotion always haunt her? She prayed not.

After safely tucking Emily into her comfy bed, Daniel came back downstairs to join Christie in the bar. It was fairly quiet and Dermot had a bottle of wine chilling for them.

'You two go and relax with this.' He pointed to a secluded alcove near the inglenook fire. Christie smiled to herself. If she didn't know him better, she'd swear he was trying his best to match-make.

'Good idea, Dermot,' replied Daniel and carried the wine

and glasses to the table. Christie followed. 'There you go, get this down you,' he said softly, pouring generous measures. Hell, this pretty lady needed cheering up.

'Thanks. Cheers.' They clinked glasses. There was a moment's pause, then Daniel was horrified to see a tear slip down Christie's face. She quickly wiped it away with the back of her hand. 'Sorry.' She glanced at him, then looked away as if embarrassed. Daniel swallowed, then decided to take a leap of faith.

'Christie, what's troubling you?' Daniel spoke gently, his beautiful blue eyes full of concern. Christie gulped back her wine. Why not offload? It might do her good to talk, *really* talk and open up. She had to a degree with Dermot, but had always restricted herself, taking care not to divulge too much. Well, she was sick of playing it careful; she was growing tired of having to put on a front, for staff, customers, and even herself. Who was she kidding? Admitting to herself how exhausted, both physically and emotionally, she actually was, Christie made the decision to spill – everything.

As Daniel sat and listened in silence, it proved cathartic for Christie to finally get everything off her chest. To let go. It was a release, and a long-awaited one that had been building momentum for weeks. After several more glasses of wine, she finished her story, leaving Daniel dumbfounded.

'Sorry, was that information overload, Daniel?'

'Of course not. I... I'm just speechless. Who in their right mind would treat a girl like you in that way?' he asked incredulously. He truly was staggered at the man's actions.

'My husband apparently, especially if I can't have children,' she replied with a sad smile.

'Then he's a bloody fool, Christie,' he said with force, 'and so not worth your tears.' He stared into her face and that same impulse to kiss her gripped him again. He sensed her reading his thoughts. She held his gaze. Was she inviting him? In a split second he took another leap of faith and leant forward to softly kiss her.

Christie's chest was pounding. She felt her lips responded to his instinctively. That earthy smell of sage and the touch of his slight stubble intoxicated her. The kiss deepened, until they were both oblivious of their surroundings.

Luckily, being hidden in the discreet alcove meant that they were quite out of view of everyone except Dermot, who had seen them from across the bar and grinned. Good on 'em, he thought. They both deserved a break.

22

It was the day of the point-to-point and for Dylan it couldn't come quick enough. Feeling so isolated from Flora was killing him. He longed to be able to get Phoenix's race over, then he could give Josh his marching orders. Although, strangely enough, when he'd witnessed him and Flora together in the stable yard at work, he had only sensed a coolness between the two, which had him doubting what he had seen that day in the stables. No, he told himself, he'd definitely seen them in a clinch. Plus, Flora had been acting oddly too, kind of secretive; something had to be going on.

As for Flora, she was at breaking point. Her nerves were only just holding out regarding the race she had ahead of her. She yearned for Dylan's reassurance to calm her, but that obviously had been ruled out, him being unaware of her deception. Guilt had started to set in too, not helping her unease. Had it all been worth it? And had Dylan sussed out something was afoot? Judging by his coldness she strongly suspected so, and was dreading the aftermath once he'd learnt of her dishonesty.

The Cotswold Races and Country Fair were set in the parkland on the banks of the River Severn and showcased the best of British amateur horseracing over the jumps, combined with rural crafts and an action-packed country fair. Along with eight competitive races, visitors also enjoyed a gun dog display, falconry display, hound parade, ferret racing, wood turning, face painting and a bouncy castle. A tented shopping pavilion housed various stalls, from local and artisan food and drink, to homemade crafts and clothing.

With exception to the first two races, this meeting was run entirely for veteran and novice riders. Phoenix had been entered for the third race, which was due to start at 3pm.

The Delany Racing Yard team had arrived early with Phoenix. Flora had made Josh take her riding kit in preparation and she planned to get to the weighing in room with the rest of the jockeys as soon as possible once she had arrived with Dylan. It was all going to be a little tricky, but she was determined to keep a cool head and do this. She *had* to ride Phoenix; nobody knew him like she did.

Accompanying Dylan and Flora, were Gary and Tracy Belcher. The Belchers had invested in Phoenix and together they had formed a partnership, calling themselves "The Last Laugh". There was meaning behind the name, as the previous owner of Phoenix had callously written him off, after he had flogged the poor horse almost to death as a flat racer. In desperation he had ordered Dylan to train him into winning. Not having the gumption, or tolerance, to realise that the horse was a natural jumper meant that Graham Roper – a cruel ogre of a man – had lost patience and sold him on to Gary Belcher, not knowing that he formed half of the partnership with Dylan. Dylan had told Flora that Roper would rue the day he wrote Phoenix off and hence the name "The Last Laugh".

Gary and Tracy were fairly new to Treweham village.

They came from Lancashire and were true down-to-earth Northerners. A lottery win meant that Gary was able to pack in his job stacking fridges in Iceland and Tracy hers as a care assistant in a nursing home. Whilst Gary had adapted to the good country life, it had taken Tracy a little longer to become accustomed to the new privileged lifestyle she had been thrown into. Gary had excelled in the shooting club he had joined, the other members finding his Northern humour a breath of fresh air. As a result, the Belchers had never been short of dinner and party invitations.

They had been racing before with Dylan and Flora, which was when Dylan had approached Gary to join the partnership and buy Phoenix. Gary had welcomed the opportunity of owning a racehorse and he'd been looking forward immensely to seeing Phoenix race for the first time.

Once they all arrived, Dylan guided them to the marquee overlooking the course, which included the viewing area for the paddock where Phoenix would be. Dylan passed his binoculars to Gary and pointed the horse out.

'Blimey, he looks in good shape,' remarked Gary in awe. He still found it hard to believe he was the owner of a racehorse.

'Yes, we've worked very hard on him, haven't we?' Dylan turned to Flora who was looking more agitated by the minute.

'Err... yes. Dylan, I just need to check on something. I'll be right back,' and off she went.

'But—' Dylan was left in confusion and a sharp pain of dismissal stung him.

Flora pelted to the changing rooms where an even more

anxious Josh stood waiting for her. He was clutching her kit and passed it her as soon as she approached him.

'Quick,' he hissed, 'you've only just made it.' Flora hurried as fast as she could to the changing room and scrambled into her silks. She then quickly joined the back of the queue where all the jockeys stood waiting to be weighed. Flora knew she would have to have weights inserted into her saddle, as she was well under the twelve-stone limit. She forced herself to take steady breaths and calm her nerves. Finally, the procedures had been followed and the jockeys were led to join their horses.

Dylan stared at his watch. It was five to three and Phoenix's race was about to start. Where the hell was Flora? He clenched his jaw in anger, then was distracted by an urgent pull on his arm. It was Josh, looking anxious.

'What are you doing here?' rasped Dylan. 'The race is about to start.'

'She made me do it,' babbled Josh, looking genuinely petrified.

Dylan frowned. 'What are you talking about?'

'Flora, she's riding Phoenix – she made me promise not to say anything.'

Dylan's eyes widened, then the race was announced over the speaker. Looking through his binoculars he saw her immediately. He'd recognise that pert bottom anywhere. He gulped his rage. Realisation struck him: so that's what the secrecy was all about.

'The other day in the stables, Flora collared me, said she was riding Phoenix and I had to keep schtum.'

Dylan stared angrily at him. 'I saw you two embracing,' he said in a low, controlled voice, making Josh even more restless.

'No! No, it was *her* hugging me, in gratitude! Honestly—'

Then all heads turned as the race was about to start. Dylan lifted his binoculars again. My God, there she was, his precious Flora, about to jump those fences and race this course. His heart pounded. How had he not guessed? How could he think her capable of cheating on him? A cocktail of emotions flooded through him: relief, fury, but most of all fear. His beautiful, delicate girl was about to race. He knew more than any jockey the dangers of racing, having sustained bad injuries in a fall himself.

They were off. Phoenix shot out like a cork from a champagne bottle.

'Come on, Phoenix!' Flora shouted into her horse's ear, but he'd already found rhythm and was making good stride. She gripped her reins tight as they approached the first fence, willing the horse to take off and glide through the air with ease, as he had in the training yard. Flora dug her heels in and away he went, sailing over the fence like a gazelle with a smooth, flawless landing. Perfect. Phoenix needed little direction. It was as if the horse knew he was born to jump race; it was in his blood.

Gaining stride, Flora found herself sandwiched between the two leading horses and about to face the next jump, which also had a ditch. Desperate for more room she gave Phoenix a tap with the whip and in an instant he was off, shifting up a gear and passing the other horses. He took another mighty leap, leaving Flora breathless, but he landed again effortlessly, easily clearing the open ditch. She knew Phoenix was a quality animal, but she didn't know he could do *that* so naturally: switch into overdrive like some bionic wonder horse.

*

Dylan gripped his binoculars and held his breath. He was astounded at his horse's performance and Flora's, truth be told. It was hard to be cross when he was so infinitely proud of her. His chest thumped uncontrollably as they reached yet another fence. It was huge and he winced, barely able to look, as once again they leapt high, clearing it with ease. He swallowed, tears forming in his eyes, as he watched Flora jump again and again until she looked behind her to see the rest of the field so distant they could have been in another race.

Once safely over the line she raised her arms in triumph. Gary and Tracy cheered with elation, the crowd roared with applause, but Dylan was transfixed by the image of Flora standing up in the saddle as if she'd won the Grand National. Memories of his first win came back to him, along with that sensation of utter elation. He so didn't want to take that from Flora, but then he so didn't want her to race again. The very notion terrified him. He was torn.

'Come on, let's meet them!' called Gary, barely able to contain himself. Together they weaved through the crowds and finally made it into the winners' enclosure. There they were, the worthy winners. Dylan couldn't help but smile to himself. He didn't know who looked more pleased, Flora or Phoenix, as the pair basked in all the glory. It was as if the horse was saying, *"See, look what I can do,"* whilst Flora couldn't stop beaming and hugging him.

Dylan joined them, which brought all the cameras out. Well, it wasn't every day the former champion jockey was here at the point-to-point races. Flora looked sheepishly into his eyes, waiting for him to speak.

Dylan closed in to kiss her long and hard. The crowd went wild. Then he whispered in her ear, 'Don't *ever* do that to me again.' He patted Phoenix before he was doused with buckets of water and calmly led out to claps and cheers.

A local brewery presented a case of real ale to the winning yard in each race. Dylan made a point of letting Gary accept theirs, much to his delight. All in all, the day had been a triumph, but Dylan was still feeling unsettled. How was he going to convince Flora not to race again? *Could* he?

23

Finula and Megan slumped down at the first empty table they found in the coffee shop. It had been a harassing morning to say the least. Megan thought how lucky she was to have found her wedding dress pretty quickly. Not so Finula. Everything they'd looked at just hadn't been right. All attempts to cajole Finula by the persistent shop assistants were met with a shake of the head, a frown, a polite "I don't think so" or an outright laugh. Megan was beginning to lose heart. Would her friend ever find anything to suit her?

'Why don't you just get one made?' asked Megan after they'd both ordered cappuccinos and a sandwich.

'Because I don't know what to ask for.'

'You must have *some* idea, Fin,' replied Megan with a touch of frustration. She was beginning to feel sorry for Marcus and understood why he was taking the typical man back-seat approach.

'I'll know it, when I see it,' Finula replied with conviction. 'It's just a matter of time.'

'The wedding's in July, Finula; you haven't got much time,' added Megan dryly as their lunch arrived. The sight of a nice, warm cup of coffee and a bite to eat were welcome, after trailing round all the wedding gown shops the Cotswolds had to offer. They'd clocked up quite a few miles and both girls were exhausted. And still no dress. Still, they had bought Finula's wedding shoes and decided on the ladies' favours for the tables – organic, handmade mini soaps. But the main item, the dress, was proving more difficult to find by the hour.

'So what's little Edward up to today?' Finula smiled and then tucked into her sandwich. The mention of her son always made Megan beam.

'His daddy is taking him for a stroll round the estate apparently.'

'Showing him the ropes a little early, isn't he?' Finula laughed and Megan joined in.

'He's got a meeting with the estate manager this afternoon. No doubt he'll have Edward in on that too,' she joked.

After finishing their lunch, the predicament of the unobtainable wedding dress was discussed.

'So, you're sure you don't like *any* of the dresses we've seen so far?' reiterated Megan.

'Absolutely, they're all so... fussy. What happened to old-fashioned simplicity? Without all this need for layers of lace and frills?'

'Hmm.' Megan's mind pictured the sepia photograph of her gran's wedding day, where she stood outside the registry office in an elegant turquoise satin tea dress. Then an idea came to her. 'Finula, have you thought about second-hand dresses?'

'You mean from a charity shop?' Finula frowned.

'Not necessarily – there could be a website that deals with vintage clothing. It's worth a try, especially if you want that timeless, graceful look.'

'Now why didn't I think of that?' Finula took out her phone and started searching. Within seconds her face lit up. 'Look! *The Oxfam online shop is the home of beautiful second-hand bridal wear, offering a wide choice of gorgeous dresses, shoes and accessories. From strapless to lace, vintage bridal wear to ex-catwalk, you can find your dream wedding dress with Oxfam.*' She spoke with excitement, showing Megan her phone. Together they scrolled through the many dresses, dating back to decades ago. 'This is more like it.' Finula eyed the pictures with glee, then suddenly stopped. 'This is it. That's the one.'

Megan read out the description. 'A vintage, unbranded, sleeveless wedding gown in ivory silk. Size 10.' Turning to her friend she clasped her arm. 'Finula, it's perfect!' They both hugged each other with relief.

24

Tobias had thoroughly enjoyed himself strolling through the leafy grounds with Edward. Now and again he'd stop and chat to a member of staff either tending the perfectly manicured gardens or working in the vegetable patches and orchards that covered the estate. After lunch he pushed Edward in his pram to the estate office, where his manager patiently sat waiting for him. He stood up immediately on seeing Lord Cavendish-Blake enter the room. 'Good afternoon, Sir.'

'Hello there, Percy. Now what have you got for me?' He nodded for him to take a seat opposite him at the desk. He checked to see that Edward was sleeping soundly then looked at his computer screen.

'Everything seems to be running smoothly, Sir.' The estate manager seemed keen to reassure him. 'The play at The Folly has been a tremendous success.'

'Yes, it has,' agreed Tobias, then squinted to read his emails. Mentioning the play reminded him of that email from Daniel, who was staying at The Templar. He clicked on it again and reread it. 'Have you heard any more from…' Tobias moved closer to read the name '…Daniel James? The chap who wants to buy Keeper's Cottage?'

'No, Sir.'

Tobias nodded. Good. He didn't like pushy tactics. He seemed a nice enough guy, he thought, recalling how good he was with his little girl. Surely, it had to be the same person?

'Contact him. Tell him I'll talk to him.'

'Yes, Sir. When would be convenient?'

'Tomorrow,' replied Tobias firmly.

The email Daniel received had come at a good time. Having just reread the letter from the court, telling him of his pending hearing date, a response from Lord Cavendish-Blake was a most welcome distraction. His instincts to sit back and patiently wait had paid off. Now all he had to do was play his cards right when meeting the man. Hopefully, he'd remember him from the play, so the ice had already been broken.

Daniel's mood suddenly lifted – not that he hadn't had a great day, he had, with Emily – but reading the official letter indicating the date in bold writing of the hearing that would determine his future had frightened him. *Keep calm*, he kept telling himself. Now reading this email from Treweham Hall, Daniel took it as a good omen. He allowed happier thoughts to enter his head, like today when he had taken Emily on a local nature trail. He'd loved watching her face light up with enthusiasm as they'd wandered through the lush, green woods and paddled in the clear streams.

Despite all this quality time with Emily, the court case was forever in the background, dulling his senses. Now perhaps things were on the up, he hoped optimistically.

Emily had been shattered again and after supper and a bath, she was once more tucked up with Snuggles and she lay in a restful sleep. Daniel went downstairs to the bar, where Christie was busy serving. He smiled easily at her and she smiled back, perhaps a little self-consciously, he suspected. Had she regretted kissing him the other night? He hoped not. He certainly hadn't. If anything, it left him yearning for more. They'd only spoken a few times since "the kiss" and that was polite chit-chat with Emily on what they had been doing during the day.

Soon they would need to start firming up arrangements on renovating the bedrooms – that's why he was still at The Templar, after all. He appreciated that Christie had given him some time to be with Emily, but he was soon due to drop her back off at his parents', where Jenna had arranged to collect her. Once he'd done that, he'd get cracking with ideas and suggestions. He already had a few simmering in his mind. He'd also noticed furniture and textile shops whilst visiting local areas with Emily. They had inspired him, plus there were artisan craft shops supplying unique goods, holding relevance and history to the Cotswolds. All this had ignited his imagination and he was keen to get to work.

Shortly after he had separated from Jenna, Daniel had made the decision to work for himself, setting his own business up. Fortunately, he had made quite a name for himself as a talented architect and many of his former clients from the firm he had been with had followed him. He was slowly but steadily building up a decent workload, whilst managing his time for a better work-life balance with his daughter. Daniel saw it as a huge positive that he was able to work from home, giving him more flexibility as a parent.

So did his solicitor, when he explained the situation to her. Surely all this must help his cause? He dearly hoped so.

He was even more keen to get to work with Christie. He watched her serving the customers with ease and efficiency, not a trace of the vulnerable girl from the other night. He admired her delicate laugh, the way her dark, corkscrew curls rested on her elegant neck and shoulders, the faint dusting of freckles between her cleavage – he felt himself stir and harden.

She suddenly looked at him again as if reading his lustful thoughts. Daniel met her gaze unflinching – he was past caring. His mind was made up. He wanted her.

25

Marcus and Finula were due to go back home to Shropshire, but Marcus, conscious that he needed to speak to Sebastian, or Jamie, had made plans to visit the folly before setting off. 'We'll leave early evening and miss the traffic,' he'd told Finula.

'Good idea. I'll call in on Megan and Tobias and say goodbye,' she'd replied.

Having given it considerable thought, Marcus was still unsure of how to open the conversation with Sebastian. He'd have to be tactful, yet direct, judging by the way he'd been avoiding Tobias' raised concerns.

The folly, as usual, was a hive of activity, preparing for the performance that evening. Sebastian saw Marcus enter through the woods and waved him over. 'Hello there.' He smiled, looking genuinely pleased to see him. It warmed Marcus' heart, especially as he was so new to the family. It was incredible to think that this time last year, he hadn't even known of his two half-brothers, or indeed who his father had actually been.

'Hi, Sebastian. Do you have a minute? I'd like a word.'

'Sounds ominous.' He gave a laugh.

Marcus nodded towards the folly. 'Can we go inside, somewhere private?'

'Yeah, sure.' Sebastian frowned, clearly wondering what this was about. Marcus watched carefully as his brother led him into the old, stone building. He had a definite limp. He also noticed his hand tremor slightly as he pulled a dark green, velvet chair forward for him to sit on. They were in what used to be their father's bolthole, a room with two comfy armchairs beside a wood burner, complete with a drinks cabinet. 'Would you like a drink, Marcus?' Sebastian opened it up and began pouring himself a brandy.

'Yes, I'll join you.' Marcus would welcome a stiff drink. Once seated opposite each other, Sebastian stared into Marcus' face, waiting for him to talk. Marcus gave a cough. 'I'll get to the point, Sebastian. Tobias is worried about you. And when I see how tired you're looking, I can see why—'

'I'm running this show,' Sebastian interrupted, gesturing around the room with one hand.

'It's more than that, isn't it?' came Marcus' soft reply. There was a short silence. 'There's something wrong. Your walk, it's laboured. Your hand shakes.' Sebastian knocked back his drink and turned his head away from Marcus' intense stare. 'I'm not leaving until you tell me.' He spoke quietly, yet firmly.

Sebastian took a deep breath. 'OK. I'll tell you. I've got multiple sclerosis.'

Marcus nodded. 'When were you diagnosed?'

'A few months ago. Nobody knows, except Jamie, and now you of course.'

'Why haven't you told Tobias?'

'Because he'd only worry.'

'He's worried anyway,' Marcus immediately answered, his gaze never leaving Sebastian's. 'He knows something's wrong. You need to talk to him.'

Sebastian slowly nodded his head in agreement. 'I know. I will, but in my time.'

'Don't leave it too long,' Marcus gently advised. 'Give the guy some credit: he wants to help, not make things difficult.'

'I know. I just…'

'Listen.' Marcus leant forward. 'The three of us share the same blood. We all look out for each other, got it?'

Sebastian gulped and tears appeared in his eyes.

'Is your condition likely to worsen?'

'It's too early to say, hopefully not. I attend the MS clinic every six months. It's being monitored.'

'Good,' said Marcus firmly, 'it's early days I know, but you're not on your own. I mean it. When you're ready to talk properly, we'll be here.'

'Thanks.' Sebastian gave a wobbly smile.

26

'Come on, Emily, eat up,' encouraged Daniel, watching Emily dawdle over her breakfast.

'Daddy, do I have to go back today?' His heart broke as he looked into his daughter's sad blue eyes.

'It's only for a short while, Sweet Pea, then I'll be picking you up again.' Emily looked down. 'Mummy will be missing you,' he said with a forced brightness.

'Will JonJo be there?' He froze for a moment. Did he detect a touch of wariness in her tone?

'I expect so, why?' He tried to appear as casual as possible, which was excruciatingly hard.

Emily shrugged.

'Don't you like JonJo?' Should he be asking her this? He'd always got the impression she did, which was a relief in one respect, but mildly annoying too.

'Yes, but I want you, Daddy.'

Daniel's eyes instantly filled. He gulped back the emotion. For a moment he was speechless, then on cue, Christie appeared, making Emily perk up.

'Look what Daddy's bought me!' she said excitedly, pointing to her rag doll sat on the spare chair at the table.

'Oh, she's lovely!' What's her name?' Christie bent down

to Emily's level, making Daniel smile to himself. She had a real way with children. Another huge box ticked, his inner voice told him. His attraction to Christie was increasing by the day. He was desperate to touch and kiss her again.

'I haven't thought of one yet,' replied Emily, then turned to Daniel. 'Daddy, what shall I call her?'

'Any name you want.' He laughed, then looked to Christie. 'Any suggestions, Christie?'

'Well, I used to have a doll called Polly once.' Christie smiled at them.

'I like that,' Emily declared. 'I'm calling my dolly Polly too.' Then, noticing Dermot walk into the dining room, she grabbed the doll to show him, leaving Daniel and Christie alone.

Seizing the moment Daniel spoke first. 'Christie, I'm taking Emily back today. Are you free to start working on the bedrooms tomorrow?'

'Yes, I've got some suggestions to run past you. I've put together a few mood boards.' Daniel seemed impressed, she noticed, judging by the expression on his face.

'Great. I've been collecting ideas too, mainly from visiting the area.'

'Excellent!'

'Tobias Cavendish-Blake's agreed to see me later this afternoon, about Keeper's Cottage.'

'That's good.' Christie's face lit up. 'I hope he agrees to sell it to you.' The thought of having Daniel permanently around as her neighbour was a warm one that made her feel good inside. She took in his physique. He was wearing a black T-shirt that hugged his muscular arms and shoulders. Christie experienced a rousing that she hadn't felt in a long time.

Swallowing, she suddenly realised how blatantly obvious her assessment of his body had been. Looking into his pale blue eyes though, what she saw was a similar look from him. There was a definite connection. Kissing him proved that, the way their lips urgently sought and explored each other's was sheer magnetism that neither could ignore. She so longed to share another breathtaking kiss like that again.

'So do I.'

Christie blinked. Had he read her thought? 'Sorry?'

'I hope he agrees to sell Keeper's Cottage too.' Daniel laughed.

'Oh, yes...' They were interrupted by Emily running back to the table.

'Come on then, Sweet Pea, let's get a move on.' Daniel picked her up with gusto. Emily wrapped her small arms round his neck and cuddled into him, dropping her doll as she did so.

Christie bent to pick it up. 'Don't forget Polly.'

Emily turned to face Christie and suddenly reached an arm out to her. Christie allowed herself to be pulled in. 'Bye-bye, Christie,' she whispered.

'See you soon, Emily,' Christie replied and on impulse kissed the little girl's cheek. She couldn't help it – Emily was adorable.

By late morning Daniel had safely dropped Emily off at his parents' house as arranged. He swore it got harder having to say goodbye to her, however temporary it was. He refused point blank to let his mind wander into that bleak, depressive space, being determined to stay positive and upbeat for his meeting with Tobias Cavendish-Blake. He needed to come across as assertive. He did allow his thoughts to travel to a future at Keeper's Cottage and prayed it all worked out. Also, the prospect of living so close to Christie was a most welcome one. He could feel himself stir again at the thought of her and gripped the steering wheel tightly to concentrate on the drive back to Treweham.

Later that afternoon he made his way to the Treweham Hall estate office, as directed. Moments before reaching the office door, he mentally prepared himself and coughed before knocking. The estate manager opened it and showed him in. Tobias was sat at the desk waiting.

'Hello, Mr James.' He nodded.

'Daniel, please,' he answered reaching out his hand. A firm handshake followed.

'Please, sit down, Daniel.' Tobias looked at him expectantly, obviously waiting for him to take the initiative, which he did, as confidently as his nerves would allow.

'Thank you, Lord Cavendish-Blake, for your time.' He noticed another curt nod and took it as a sign to get down to business. 'In a nutshell, I'd like to buy Keeper's Cottage. I'm an architect and would love to renovate it back to its former glory.' *Former glory* – was that a tad melodramatic? Daniel coughed and continued, 'I would restore it to a very high standard and it would make an ideal home for me and my little girl.'

'Providing you have the funds to do so,' replied Tobias, 'which takes us to the point of the cost.'

'Yes, it does.' Daniel stared back. Inside he was shaking, but refused to let it show.

Tobias had thought long and hard about Daniel's

proposition. He'd learnt the hard way regarding selling property on his estate, having seen how the Belchers had desecrated the Gate House. This had left Tobias thinking twice before doing so again. But then, Daniel James did seem a different kettle of fish compared to the lottery winners that he'd made a handsome profit from.

However, Tobias was a businessman, and an astute one at that. To leave Keeper's Cottage as a crumbling ruin, when it could be restored to life and make him money would be a travesty, but under no circumstances did he want any undesirables living on his estate.

'A cottage with such potential, located on this estate, would fetch at least £400,000.'

Daniel gulped. There was no way he could afford that, plus the cost of the renovation. His heart sank.

'However, I don't want to sell all of it.'

Daniel frowned and waited for Tobias to continue.

'I do want to see it restored, and I want a say in who's going to inhabit it, which means I'd want joint ownership.'

Daniel listened carefully to what was being said and sat forward.

'Here's what I propose: you renovate the cottage to my standards, at your expense and we have joint names on the deeds. That way, if you ever decide to move on, I either buy you out, or we both agree on the purchasers. The last thing I want is no say as to who will be living on my estate.'

Daniel sat and digested the proposition.

'This way, you don't have to stump up the asking price, but the money for the restoration only, and still have part ownership.'

The more Daniel considered it, the more attractive it sounded, especially as he couldn't ever see himself moving from Keeper's Cottage.

'I own a building company. Renovating old properties is nothing new to me; along with your skills as an architect we could pool our resources. This could be a worthy project.'

This clinched it. 'Yes, I agree,' said Daniel firmly. 'I'd like to accept your offer.' He liked the idea of using Tobias' workmen. They were hardly likely to take advantage, with their employer having a vested interest.

'Good, then I'll have my solicitor draw up a contract and we'll get together to discuss a timetable.'

Daniel nodded his head with enthusiasm. 'Yes, yes of course and... thank you.'

Tobias smiled; his instincts told him they'd both made a good decision. 'Did you see the outbuilding?' he asked.

'No?'

'Hardly surprising – it's covered in ivy, but yes, there's a small stone outbuilding towards the back of the cottage, further into the woods.'

Daniel's imagination leapt. This could be converted into a work studio. It would be ideal, so close to his home, yet still providing a separate space. 'Excellent, I'll take a look at it.'

Tobias smiled again, warming to this man who looked like he'd been given the world.

27

Flora slid her hand down Dylan's bare back and rested it on his hip bone.

'Dylan,' she whispered seductively in his ear, 'are you awake?'

Was he ever. He'd slept like a log last night after their energetic lovemaking, leaving him fully refreshed, and it looked like Flora was raring to go again. A far cry from the past few weeks where both of them had virtually slept back to back in silence. Since the race Flora had returned to her old self, full of life and love for Dylan; and he was only too happy to reap the rewards having missed her lithe, curvaceous body beneath his. The sex between them was electric, taking him back to the early days when they'd first met and couldn't keep their hands off one another.

And whilst Dylan was making the most of it and relishing every minute of Flora's attention, it was tinged with a sense of foreboding. Flora winning the race with Phoenix so spectacularly would only leave her hungry for more. She'd proved a point, hadn't she? This left Dylan in a quandary. He was resolute in not wanting to endanger his precious girlfriend in any way whatsoever, and flying through the air on horseback in a steeplechase was most definitely dangerous.

The possibilities of what could happen didn't bear thinking about. He'd only just had a lucky escape himself, having taken a fall on his last race before retiring from the racing circuit. He counted his blessings that he'd only suffered a couple of broken ribs, bruising and concussion. Dylan knew jockeys who had never walked again from injuries sustained – paralysis was every jockey's nightmare. He understood, all too well, that wonderful feeling of euphoria from winning a race – of course he did, he'd been champion jockey – but looking at Flora's petite frame and knowing what risks lay ahead if she raced again turned his stomach. There was *no way* he could ever allow that to happen again. Non-negotiable. But for now, he'd bask in the welcome change of mood.

'Dylan?' Flora's hand moved from his hip bone and crept to cover his rock-hard erection. Gently she slid her fingers up and down the shaft. 'Hmm, something tells me you are awake.' She giggled and ran kisses over his shoulder and up his neck.

'Come here, you little minx.' Dylan turned on his back and pulled her onto his broad, dark chest. His mouth sought hers, running his tongue across her lips.

Flora's arms wrapped round his neck, pulling herself further into his warm, muscular body. He smelt delicious, and virile, making her want more. Dylan's head dipped to her full, firm breasts and caught a rosy nipple, flicking his tongue. It instantly stiffened, making her moan with pleasure. His tongue continued sucking and licking, whilst his hand moved down to softly stroke the insides of her thighs, before finding its way to her hot, slick core. He rubbed smoothly, gliding his finger in and out. Flora cried out again in ecstasy. She was ready for him and ground her hips urgently against his pulsing body. Dylan continued, slowly teasing her with his probing.

'Dylan,' she begged, turning him on further until he couldn't resist any longer. He turned to flip her on her back and he quickly nestled in between her legs. His cock edged into her and they both gasped. Flora clenched his buttocks as he moved further into her.

'Flora,' he groaned, thrusting deeper again and again until finally exploding with complete and utter satisfaction. They both lay still with exhaustion. Was now the time to tell her how he felt about her racing again, whilst she was so relaxed and peaceful? He looked into her face and she smiled and closed her eyes. Probably not. Then his thoughts were interrupted by the harsh ring of the phone.

Climbing out of bed, he grabbed his bathrobe and then made his way down the stairs into the hall.

'Hello—'

'Delany, you robbing bastard!' thundered a voice that he instantly recognised. It was Graham Roper, the previous owner of Phoenix. Roper had asked Dylan to train his horse, in a last-ditch attempt to make it a flat race winner. Once Phoenix arrived at his racing yard, it was blatantly obvious how he had been mistreated, judging by his wounds. Instantly Flora had taken a shine to the horse and together they had bonded so well, it was impossible to think of him returning to an owner who wasn't a horse lover, but purely a businessman, wanting to make money from him.

Flora had also soon realised that Phoenix was more suited to soft ground, having a high knee action; because he raised his legs far up and forcefully down, he needed to land on softer turf, which was why the hard, flat race courses were not for him. Phoenix needed the jump courses, which had a gentler landing for him. Dylan, in his wisdom, had simply told Roper that his horse would never make a flat race winner, which was true. He'd been economical with the truth in order to convince Roper to sell him, which he did, but to Gary Belcher. Dylan, for obvious reasons, kept his name out of the sale. Once the deal was completed, he and Gary formed their partnership aptly named "The Last Laugh". If Roper had seen Phoenix win so superbly at the point-to-pint, it wouldn't have helped seeing the names of the new owners in the programme. Dylan took a deep breath.

'You were paid for that horse, Roper,' he answered flatly.

'I was underpaid and you know it, you thieving swine!'

'I said Phoenix wouldn't make a flat race winner, which is true.'

'Yeah, no mention of him jumping like a stag, though, was there?' roared Roper down the phone.

'And why's that?' cut in Dylan icily. 'Perhaps it's because the poor horse was covered in whip lashes and clearly suffering from stress. You don't care for your horses, you bastard, they're just money-making machines to you. Well, tough shit, you won't be making any money from Phoenix,' and down went the phone. Dylan's hand was shaking slightly.

Flora, overhearing the conversation was behind him now. 'Could he take Phoenix from us, Dylan?' she asked wide eyed. Her bottom lip trembled.

'No, no of course not, sweetheart.' He reached out and hugged her to him. Although he sounded reassuring and confident, Dylan couldn't help but think he hadn't heard the last of Roper.

28

'Finula wants lilies on the tables, white linen tablecloths and soft lighting. I'm thinking candles.' Dermot was running through a few arrangements for Finula's wedding.

'I'm thinking fire risk,' replied Christie dryly, 'especially if the champagne's flowing, which by the amount you've ordered, it will.'

'I'm not scrimping on me own daughter's wedding,' said Dermot defiantly.

'You're certainly not.' Christie's eyes had watered when she'd seen the cost of the marquee alone, not to mention all the food and drink. Dermot's family were staying at The Templar, which he'd agreed to pay for too. 'Let's have tea lights, for that subtle look,' persuaded Christie. The picture of the marquee in flames, burning merrily on The Templar lawn, was not one she relished.

'OK,' agreed Dermot. 'Here's the full itinerary. Finula's just emailed me.' He passed her a sheet of A4 paper, with neatly written instruction on.

'Only just? The wedding's in a few weeks.' Christie felt a tad anxious. Although most things had been booked regarding venue, staff and catering, it was the finer details that needed finalising.

'Well… Finula's always been a bit… particular. She likes to take her time and get things just right,' explained Dermot unconvincingly.

Christie rolled her eyes. *Last minute, that's what,* she thought with exasperation.

'I see, let's have a look then.' Christie scanned the list. It read like a military operation with precision timing. Finula might be last minute, but she had indeed covered everything, leaving no room for error.

'OK. That's us told then.' She grinned up at Dermot.

'Like I said, my Finula's quite particular.'

'Have you written your speech yet?'

A wicked smirk covered his face. Christie laughed.

'Oh yes, I know exactly what's expected of me.'

'Don't tell me she's given instructions on that as well,' said Christie still laughing.

'No, but she's in for a surprise.' Dermot winked.

Christie had grown to love working with this man who she regarded now as a father figure. He was fun to be around, with his light-hearted banter and kind ways. She knew he was watching out for her and wanted her to succeed in running The Templar. She also suspected he'd been craftily playing cupid between herself and Daniel, by encouraging them to sit down with a bottle of wine he'd had chilled on the bar. She knew he'd approved of Daniel helping her renovate the bedrooms; and last night when Daniel had announced he was going to live in Keeper's Cottage, he'd practically rubbed his hands together.

As if on cue, Daniel walked into the bar. They were going to Gloucester. Daniel had sourced a company that made bespoke furniture and Christie was eager to collect sample swatches of material from a fabric shop. To say she was looking forward to it was a slight understatement, especially as her heart started to flutter at the sight of him. Looking very sexy in faded jeans that hugged his hard thighs and a dark, fitted jacket, he gave her a smile that displayed his dimples. Irresistible.

'Hi,' she breezed, trying to sound as casual as possible.

'Hi, ready to go?' he said smoothly, knowing from her expression his appearance was hitting the mark. Daniel had made a real effort, wanting to take things up a notch with Christie, especially now he knew he was staying in Treweham. Today was the perfect opportunity and he fully intended to use it. And, by the look of things so did Christie, he guessed, while assessing her skinny jeans showcasing that pert bottom and the close-fitting, white hoody that her black curls rested on. He longed to unzip it and see what lay beneath.

'Now you two have a good day,' called Dermot, 'and don't hurry back. I'll hold the fort, no worries.'

Christie smiled to herself. 'Thanks, Dermot.'

Soon they were entering the cathedral city of the Cotswolds. Christie's mind wandered back to when it hosted the Rugby World Cup and she and Stephen had visited. Quickly dispelling such thoughts, she glanced towards Daniel who was concentrating on parking his car. He smelt gorgeous, with that fresh sage scent she was beginning to associate with him.

'Right,' he said looking at her, 'I thought we could take a look at the bespoke furniture shop first.'

'Sounds good. We'll pick up the fabric swatches last, save carrying them about.'

Once inside the showroom, it was easy to pick out what they wanted, both being on the same wavelength. Deciding on old, rustic charm, rather than modern pine, Christie soon chose the double beds in a dark, weathered wood, which would match the beams beautifully. She chose individual wardrobes in the same wood, but a slightly different design.

'So, that's the basics,' said Daniel. 'Have you thought about themes for the rooms?'

'Do you think it's a bit twee to call them after flowers?'

'Yes,' replied Daniel, making her laugh. He grinned, longing to close his lips over hers. 'You need something that links with the area. What's the Cotswolds most renowned for?'

'Its honey-coloured stone?'

'Yes, and its textile – the wool merchants built churches and manor houses with their fortunes, encouraging the Arts and Crafts Movement. I think we should home in on that. Also, it's got strong literary connections.'

'Ah yes, Laurie Lee,' Christie reminisced about reading *Cider With Rosie* at school.

'Exactly! Talking of which it's also well known for its cider houses and old-world real-ale pubs, just like yours.' This made Christie tingle with pride. Daniel's enthusiasm was infectious. Then an idea suddenly hit her.

'Let's go to the antique centre! There could be pieces in there that would really add finishing touches.'

'Excellent, you're getting the idea.' Daniel patted her back, then let his arm slide round her side, pulling her into him. Christie felt happy and relaxed and snuggled into him as they made their way into the heart of the ancient city.

As predicted, the antique centre proved a worthwhile visit. Their eyes darted round the various shops, picking out period items that would blend in perfectly with the themed rooms; from a charming Georgian writing bureau, to rustic cider pots and lambs-wool rugs. Christie bought various prints of the Cotswolds, depicting its historic villages, landscape and ancient honey-stoned architecture. Daniel collected a few old vintage signs taken from alehouses, shops and cafés, which would look quirky on the room walls. All in all, it had been a very productive day.

After three hours of solid shopping and having heaved all their goods back into the car, they were more than ready for a sit-down.

'Come on, I'll buy you lunch.' Daniel directed them into a quaint-looking tea shop. Inside the cosy tea room, they sat in a corner and talked animatedly about their purchases. It had been a long time since either of them had felt so buoyant, well apart from yesterday when Daniel had been promised Keeper's Cottage. Happiness exuded from his face. His pale blue eyes were gleaming, Christie noticed. She so didn't want the day to end.

'Let's go and visit the cathedral after lunch,' she suggested. Anything to prolong her time in his company; she felt so chilled just being with him. Today's shopping trip proved they were very alike, always thinking along the same lines. He certainly had a creative mind, and style, not to mention being easy on the eye.

'The cathedral is one of the finest medieval buildings in the country,' boasted the guide, 'and traces a thousand years of architectural styles from Norman to the present day, where our team of stonemasons are still carving and casting.' Daniel and Christie absorbed all the impressive history of the cathedral, wandering through the decorative arched cloisters and into the Lady Chapel, which housed some of the finest Arts and Crafts glass in the country, as the tour guide told them. They climbed to the top of the tower to see the bells and the stunning rooftop views. Daniel looked sideways to see Christie in awe of the panoramic vista. He leant forward and kissed her cheek. She turned to face him and smiled.

'Thank you,' she said.

'What for?'

'Helping me.' Those two words were simple, but loaded.

'It's a two-way thing,' he replied.

29

Marcus was deep in concentration, staring at the screens in front of him. He'd had his cellar renovated into a studio to enable him to work from home. Here he could do almost everything that hiring a studio in London would provide, only on a smaller scale. It suited him perfectly, having all the equipment to hand, but in a tranquil environment that made his creative juices flow. Being an award-winning TV producer meant Marcus had a reputation to uphold, and his latest documentary, *A Green and Pleasant Land?*, in his opinion, would be every bit as cutting and dynamic as the others he was renowned for.

Marcus had a real talent for hitting home a message, invoking real emotion. From the horrific, cold truth of sex trafficking, to the heart-breaking compassion of organ donation. Marcus had taken real risks, filming in dangerous territory, interviewing victims and exposing the ruthless, powerful gangs that terrorised and controlled the vulnerable. He had followed the plight of a child desperately needing a heart transplant, covering the emotional scenes before his operation and the joyful ones at its success.

On the face of it, his latest documentary may not seem as hard-hitting as his previous ones. However, Marcus wanted it to be the catalyst that highlighted the glaring inequalities between the rich flourishing in their country estates, to the poor families living off food banks. Poverty was on the up. Homelessness was rising. Marcus was determined to emphasise the stark contrast of the two, as well as depicting Treweham village's quintessential charm. He had his work cut out, but Marcus revelled in the whole process of documentary making.

Finula tentatively poked her head round the cellar door. She, more than anyone, knew not to disturb Marcus when he was working, but he had been at it since early morning and she was bringing him down some lunch.

'Can I come in?'

Marcus turned away from the screens to face her. The sight of her made a welcome break. 'Course you can.'

Finula handed him a coffee and a sandwich.

'Thanks, darlin'.' It was good having her live with him. Normally he would work well into the evening without stopping and give himself a splitting headache. Now he'd learnt to expect Finula bobbing in with refreshment throughout his day, not to mention a scrumptious dinner of an evening, where they'd relax and share a bottle of wine by the wood burner. Life was good, very good, and it was all down to this gorgeous, fiery redhead who he had thankfully stumbled across whilst visiting Treweham.

'How's it going?' Finula pointed to the screens.

'Good. I'm on schedule.' Marcus bit into his tuna crunch sandwich and realised how hungry he was, but then he hadn't eaten since 6am. When he was in the thick of producing, he totally lost track of time. He was lucky to have Finula.

She looked at him with concern. 'Marcus, you look tired.'
'I am tired.'
'Then take a rest!'
'I will, soon. Let me just finish the fine cut.'

Marcus' talents lay in the selection and sequence of each scene, from its proportions, structures, rhythms and emphasis. The fine cut would pay attention to the details of each and every shot. Once that was agreed between himself and the editor, the sound designer and music composer would join them. Sound effects and music would be created and added to the final cut, which, according to the schedule, would mean the documentary would be aired in the autumn.

'Marcus, we get married in three weeks' time.' She looked pointedly at him.

'I'm well aware of that, Finula.' He gulped his coffee back. 'All the more reason to get the fine cut out of the way, then I can relax and enjoy the honeymoon.'

Finula eyed him with affection. He really was a handsome devil, she thought. He might be tired, but his rakish, dark stubble and twinkling, green eyes made her melt, together with his soft, Irish accent.

Marcus caught her gaze. 'Come here, you.' He patted his lap for her to join him. Finula walked over to him and sat on his thighs. Marcus wrapped his arms round her and kissed her cheek. 'Don't worry, Finula, just a few short weeks and I'm all yours.'

30

Sebastian stared at the review in front of him. He felt like he'd been punched in the stomach. Words hit him, assaulting his senses, "slight hobble", "tremoring with nerves", "lost his touch". All of this from *The Times*, which had less than twelve months ago hailed him as the new Laurence Olivier. Sebastian gulped; his mouth had dried up. Surely it wasn't that noticeable? Then he remembered the critic from the opening night, who was renowned for her direct, damning opinion and wasn't afraid to pack a punch. He dully realised that it was now his turn to be the recipient of her sharp tongue.

He wanted to slap her, hard, and sue the bloody *Times*. How dare they? How dare they sully his precious production and *his* acting ability? He was Sebastian Cavendish-Blake, the gifted, acclaimed actor of the Shakespeare Theatre! *Yes, but only as Richard III*, goaded a nasty, malicious voice inside him. Who could criticise his "hobbling" when playing the role of a crippled king? Sebastian's eyes filled. Was this the end for him? Just when he had made it to the pinnacle of his career, was he about to have it all snatched cruelly away? A tear spilled out and ran slowly down his face. He'd never felt so helpless.

Then another sinister thought struck him – Tobias. What if he'd seen the review? Feeling the need of his brother's support, Sebastian made the decision to tell him everything, now. He'd had enough of the secrecy, as if it was something to be kept hidden. Why? He realised how much he missed Tobias' wise words and counselling. His brother had always been there for him throughout his life. Now more than ever he needed him.

Tobias was in his study when Sebastian knocked quietly at the door and entered. It didn't help seeing *The Times* spread out on his desk. Tobias just looked at him, saying nothing. Sebastian swallowed then spoke.

'Have you read the review?'

'Yes.' Again he just stared, waiting for him to continue.

'Tobias, there's something I need to tell you.'

'About time.' He wasn't making it easy for him.

'I've got multiple sclerosis.'

Tobias' face remained deadpan. 'When were you diagnosed?' he asked flatly.

'Just before Edward was born. I didn't want to ruin things by telling you.'

'For fuck's sake, Sebastian!' Tobias thumped his desk hard, making him jump.

'Don't be angry—'

'Does Marcus know?' interrupted Tobias.

'Yes… only just—'

'I see,' he cut in again.

'No, Tobias, you don't see,' Sebastian threw back forcefully. 'Just when things were finally going well for you, with Megan and a baby on the way, I didn't want my diagnosis to add a dampener. I certainly did not want

Mother fussing round me either,' he added. Then he moved closer to the desk. 'Listen, Tobias, this came as a shock to me, I… I needed time to get my head round it.'

'How could you keep this to yourself?' Tobias asked, seemingly incredulous at his little brother's secrecy. They *never* kept things from each other.

'I was always going to tell you, but in my time. This isn't about you, Tobias, it's about me and how *I* deal with it.'

Tobias sighed and nodded his head, as if weakly understanding the situation. 'Are you going to tell Mother?'

'Yes, in time.'

'How are you feeling?' Tobias' face was etched with concern.

'In truth, fine. Apart from the obvious limp and fatigue, which comes and goes. Other than that, OK.'

'Will it get worse?'

Sebastian shrugged. 'Can't say. Sometimes symptoms don't, then again they could gradually worsen.'

'Right.' Tobias nodded his head again. Then he pointed to the paper on his desk. 'This, by the way, is bollocks.'

Sebastian laughed. 'I'm glad someone else thinks so too. It's not that obvious is it?'

'No.' Tobias shook his head. 'Your own brother didn't realise, did he?' he said sardonically.

'Do you think I should give up acting?'

'Absolutely fucking not,' Tobias answered immediately. 'Get out there and show them what you're made of. You're a Cavendish-Blake for God's sake.' Again, Sebastian laughed. Hadn't he thought the very same just moments before?

31

Flora was in the paddock with Phoenix. She'd just ridden him at full pelt down the all-weather wood-chip gallop and felt invigorated. Phoenix was still whooping up all the attention from the yard staff after his brilliant win. It was as if the horse knew he was the current star attraction.

She noticed a black Jaguar pull into the yard and park outside the office. Instantly she recognised it, especially when seeing the private registration plate "RoP3R" – Graham Roper. Quickly, she rode Phoenix out of the paddock and safely back to his stable, out of the way. The last thing she wanted was Roper seeing Phoenix, and especially in such good shape. Then again, he'd already seen how well Phoenix was looking from the point-to-point, she acknowledged with trepidation.

Dylan too had seen the car park right outside his window. Deciding to fight fire with fire, he got up to answer the door, rather than let the man stride into his own office. Not bothering with the pleasantries, Dylan spoke.

'What do you want?' He glared at Roper.

'The rest of the money you owe me for my horse.'

'It's not your horse and I don't owe you a penny,' replied Dylan icily.

Roper gave a harsh laugh. 'That horse is worth far more than the pittance you paid for it,' he spat, 'and what's your partnership called? The Last Laugh? We'll see about that, you swine.' Roper's face was blood red and angry.

'That horse was in dreadful condition.' Dylan's voice was dangerously quiet and controlled, though deep down he was feeling anything but. 'Phoenix was covered in whip lashes, he had swollen legs and was shaking with fear.'

Roper shook his comments off with a huff. 'I don't spoil horses the way you do.'

'I look after my horses well, Roper, unlike you. Tell me—' he leant forward to face him squarely '—have you ever been reported?' Roper, for the first time, looked taken aback. Dylan made good use of the silence. 'It's about time the authorities were informed of your mistreatment of animals. We took photographs, of the state Phoenix was in,' Dylan lied, but his threat seemed to be hitting home. 'I'll see to it that you no longer have any horses, Roper.'

At this Roper lunged towards Dylan, but he was too quick and easily dodged his throw. Dylan then straightened and threw his fist smack into Roper's face, bursting his nose.

'Ahh!' Roper clutched his face, which was now covered in blood. Dylan then booted him off the doorstep, sending Roper staggering backwards to land on the bonnet of his car.

'Now fuck off and don't ever step foot on my yard again.' Roper fumbled for his car keys and frantically opened the door and locked himself in. Within seconds he was speeding down the dirt track leaving a cloud of dust behind him.

Flora had seen the whole thing from the corner of the yard and came running to Dylan.

'Dylan! Are you all right?' Dylan looked at Flora, then burst into laughter. Flora stopped for a moment, then seeing Dylan shaking with hilarity, couldn't help but join in. Minutes later when they'd both calmed down, she asked, 'Do you think that's the last we'll hear of him?'

Dylan, finally gaining composure, replied, 'Oh yes, I doubt he'll be in a hurry to return.' Then, catching her eye, they both burst into hysterics again.

32

The alterations of the bedrooms at The Templar were making good progress. Together, Daniel and Christie had painted all but two, which were currently occupied. Daniel had moved out of his large family room and into the smallest at the back, which happened to be next door to Christie's. It had felt a little strange hearing each other potter about at night, only a wall apart. Dermot, making the most of the situation, often teased Christie, asking how her "next door neighbour" was, whilst chuckling under his breath. As predicted, they had both agreed easily on the colours of the rooms whilst studying the many charts containing every possible shade.

'Nothing too dark, we want a sense of space,' advised Daniel, flicking through the brochures Christie had collected.

'Definitely, how about this Aged Ivory?'

'Yeah, that'll give a real rich, warm feeling.' Then he pointed to a page he had open. 'What about Piermint Green, for a fresh, spring look?'

'Love it – that would go lovely with this fabric.' She bent down to pick up a material swatch. 'What do you think?'

'Good, matches well.'

'I'm going to make the curtains.' Christie had decided to try and make savings wherever possible.

'Hmm, I'd go for fabric blinds, sit them in the window, again giving more space. Plus, you'd be using less material.'

Christie looked at the heavy curtains draped either side of the small bedroom window. They were in one of the rooms at the rear of the property, which gave panoramic views of the lush, jade hills. It did seem a shame to cover the sides of the window with fussy curtains instead of leaving it open to take advantage of the stunning scenery.

'You're right. Again.' She grinned, so glad of his input.

Christie had thoroughly enjoyed working with Daniel these past few days and knew she'd miss him terribly once the bedrooms were finished. She also knew he was eager to start work on Keeper's Cottage and was pleased for him. Part of her wanted him to stop longer at The Templar, and had half hoped he'd extend his stay whilst working on his cottage; but that wasn't his intention. Daniel's parents didn't live too far away and it made sense for him to stay there, especially when he had Emily. Also, Daniel was keen to live on site at some point. His parents owned a campervan, which he intended to use during the week, when he didn't have Emily.

Christie had learnt a lot about Daniel during their time working together. Snippets about his ex-partner often crept into his conversation and from what she'd gathered, she didn't like the sound of her. Daniel, despite his easy-going outward appearance, was in fact a troubled man under the surface, Christie had come to realise. It was blatantly obvious how much he loved his daughter and the effect it had on him when separated from her. He was also successful in his career. That didn't surprise her, when seeing how creative and motivated he was. The fact Daniel had branched out to form his own business, and was making a huge success of it, reflected on the man himself. It also sadly left him open to others taking advantage.

Christie admired the way he provided for Emily, but couldn't help thinking how his ex was coining in. From what she'd gleaned, Daniel's house was actually providing a roof over Emily's mum and boyfriend, without either of them paying him a penny. Then she realised that technically, The Templar was half Stephen's too and an uncomfortable sensation swept over her.

'I promised myself some time off work to find a home and get settled,' Daniel had explained one afternoon whilst busy moving furniture. 'I've just completed quite a big project with a regular client and he wants me to start another in a few months' time, so it's worked out well.' He'd told Christie about the outbuilding at Keeper's Cottage and his plans to transform it into a studio to work in.

Whilst Christie was happy for him, she couldn't help but wonder about Emily and exactly how she fit in. When Daniel first arrived at The Templar he'd mentioned looking for schools for her. Would she no longer be living with her mum? It was all a little confusing, but Christie obviously couldn't pry about such personal matters. She longed to know more about him, but sensed he was restricting himself in some way, which she slightly resented, given what she had disclosed about her and Stephen that night of the play.

One night, through the dividing bedroom wall, she swore she heard Daniel crying. Startled, she pressed her ear to the wall. Yes, he definitely was, making Christie frown with dismay. It was a bit frustrating; one minute they were rubbing along easily, laughing and enjoying each other's company, then out of the blue, he would turn introvert and go quiet on her, deep in thought, as though he had the worries of the world on his shoulders. It was those times that Christie wanted to ask him, let him open up to her, about what was troubling him. Once or twice she suspected he'd come close to telling her, but no, he'd suddenly clam up or change the subject. With only having two more rooms to paint, Christie knew she was running out of time.

Dermot interrupted her thoughts as he stuck his head round the bedroom door.

'This is looking good. Well done, the pair of you.' Christie smiled, pleased he was coming round to the idea of her renovating the bedrooms.

'Any chance of a cuppa, Dermot? We're dying of thirst here,' asked Daniel as he rolled the walls with Elephant's Breath paint. Bits had splattered on his face.

'Will you just look at yourselves,' cried Dermot, noticing Christie too was covered in splashes of paint. 'Finish up here, and I'll have a nice dinner for two waiting for you both. You deserve it.'

Daniel eyed Christie. He couldn't think of anything better than an evening sat opposite this beautiful woman.

'Sounds good to me, Dermot,' he replied, then arched an eyebrow at Christie.

'Me too. Dermot, you're on. Give me an hour – I need to soak in a hot bath first.' The thought of Christie soaking in a hot bath yards away from him roused Daniel's insides.

'Right you are,' called Dermot as he made his way back downstairs.

★

It was no surprise they were sat an hour later at the most secluded table for two, candle lit and with a bottle of champagne chilling on it. Dermot was pulling out the stops tonight, thought Christie with affection. Daniel poured the champagne and handed her a flute.

'Cheers. Here's to The Templar,' he toasted.

Christie clinked her glass against his. 'Cheers, and thanks again for all your help.'

'My pleasure.' He smiled. Christie wanted to leap across the table and kiss him. They shared a delicious cooked roast beef dinner and relaxed comfortably together. Christie became aware of Dermot glancing over and started to giggle.

'What's so funny?' asked Daniel bemused.

'Dermot – I'm sure he's playing cupid.' The champagne had loosened her tongue. Daniel stared into her eyes, making her stop still.

'Does that bother you?' he asked quietly, still looking into her.

'Not at all.' She matched his gaze. Neither of them spoke for a while, acknowledging what had been said. Daniel leant forward. Christie met him and their lips touched. It was the softest, most gentle of kisses, but such a connection. Daniel wanted her so much, he yearned for his skin to touch hers, to have that warm, comforting reassurance lying next to him.

'Stay with me tonight,' he whispered.

Together they discreetly made their way upstairs. Christie automatically opened her bedroom door. Daniel quietly followed behind her. His eyes darted around the room, which was softly lit by a bedside lamp. Stars shone in the dark night sky and the faint smell of honeysuckle wafted through the open window. He turned to face her. She looked striking and serene, totally at ease. So was he, knowing full well this was where he wanted to be.

'Christie,' he murmured, pulling her to him. She enveloped him in her arms, wanting more than anything to hold him. His lips found hers and they kissed hungrily, urgently, whilst undressing each other. Christie's eyes devoured his toned body, then travelled down to his solid erection.

He in turn, drank in her smooth curves and firm breasts. He picked her up with ease and placed her gently on the bed. His mouth sank into her cleavage and he licked those freckles that he had so ached for. His tongue then covered her breasts before sucking hard, making her gasp in pleasure and run her hands through his hair. Daniel feverishly ran his hand down her body, over her thighs and nestled in between. Christie felt herself open as he separated her and began to gently probe. She arched her back as Daniel's touch became more intimate, seeking more of her. She was greedy for him.

'I want you,' said a voice she hardly recognised as her own. Daniel groaned and slid between her legs.

Gradually he edged himself into her and gave a guttural moan as she clenched him. She felt hot and slick as he moved inside her, sending him wild.

Christie's senses were swamped with emotion, feeling him glide in and out of her. She wanted him inside her and never to stop. He pushed harder and faster and cried out as she tensed and gripped him before releasing a shudder. He in turn let go and his climax surged from him. They both clung to each other in silence, then Daniel rolled onto his side and propped his head up, looking down at her.

'Daniel, can I ask you a question?' whispered Christie.

He frowned. 'Yes.'

'I heard you crying the other night through the wall. Why?'

Daniel froze. He'd been rereading the solicitor's letter with the details of the court hearing. Taking a deep breath, he sat up.

'Perhaps it's best if I show you.' He then stood to dress himself.

Christie wondered what he was about to do and lay there in silence. 'Just a minute.' He left the room and returned soon after. 'Here, read this.' He handed her the letter. Christie sat up and scanned the writing in front of her. Oh my God. It was a custody hearing for Emily. It was scheduled for next week.

'Oh, Daniel,' she whimpered. Her eyes met his.

'Emily could be taken from me, Christie. She could end up in Liverpool with her mum and that tosser boyfriend of hers.' His voice cracked with emotion. Quickly Christie got up and hugged him.

'It'll be OK,' she soothed, whilst inside her heart was breaking for him.

33

Megan had just bathed Edward and was gently tucking him into his cot.

'Night, night, darling,' she said softly as he gurgled away, kicking his legs. The moment she put his dummy in, his eyes became heavy and he slowly closed his eyelids. Within minutes he was sleeping, with his tiny chest steadily rising up and down. She stared, besotted at her beautiful bundle of joy. Creeping slowly backwards, so as not to wake him, she quietly opened the nursery door and closed it silently behind her.

Tobias was in their drawing room, pouring himself a brandy. He'd had a long day, meeting with his project manager to discuss the various works his building company was undergoing, which included now the restoration of Keeper's Cottage. He was keen to include Daniel and had arranged to see him in a few days' time.

'Fancy a drink?' he called over his shoulder.

'Just a tonic water thanks.' Megan sat down, glad to finally have a rest. She couldn't believe how tiring it was looking after a baby, but she was resolute in not having a nanny as Tobias had suggested.

'There you go.' He sat down next to her on the chesterfield and put an arm round her shoulders.

'Everything OK?' Megan asked, knowing there was something on her husband's mind.

'Just thinking about Sebastian.'

Megan wrapped her arm round his middle and hugged him hard. 'I know,' she sighed. Megan had been initially shocked when Tobias had told her about Sebastian's illness and had cursed herself for not seeing it. So how must Tobias be feeling? 'Thank God he's got Jamie, as well as us.'

'Yes, Jamie's good for him,' agreed Tobias. Then, changing the subject completely, he told her, 'Marcus is staying with us the night before the wedding.'

'Really?' Megan asked surprised, assuming he would be staying at The Templar.

'Well he can't stay with the bride the night before and I thought it would be good to have the three of us together.'

'Yes, it would.' Megan pictured the eve of her wedding day with Finula and her mum back in Gran's cottage. It all seemed so long ago now, although it really wasn't. Having Edward had taken so much out of her, it was hard to imagine what life was like before him. Each day she could see him growing more and more like his daddy, with his dark, tufty hair and green twinkly eyes, speckled with amber flecks. She chuckled to herself. Was there any of her in their son?

Tobias smiled. 'What are you thinking?'

'Just how like you Edward is.'

'Maybe our daughter will look as pretty as you,' he replied.

Megan turned her head sharply. 'You don't want another so soon, do you?'

'Well… there's no harm in practising…' He bent his head down to kiss her. Megan responded, instantly folding her arms round his neck. Then a cry came from the nursery. They stopped and waited to see if he would stop. He didn't. 'I'll go to him,' said Tobias sighing, leaving Megan grinning to herself. Another baby could wait.

34

'So, Finula's staying in room 3 and the rest of the rooms will definitely be complete by next week? I don't want me family having to rough it,' teased Dermot.

'Excuse me!' exclaimed Christie in good humour. 'I think you'll find those bedrooms are absolutely spot on and your family will be nothing but impressed by The Templar!'

He laughed. 'To be sure they will.' All the rooms had been painted now and Christie just had to add the finishing touches. The pieces she and Daniel had bought in Gloucester looked fantastic, really giving them charm and definition. Even Dermot had to concede they were a huge improvement on the old, slightly tired-looking décor that he never would have thought to change; but that's what a fresh pair of eyes did for you, he'd told her, and a young pair at that.

He'd gently enquired about her relationship with Daniel, once he'd left to return to his parents. Christie was discreet, although she suspected Dermot knew more than he was letting on. He may be getting older, but he was no fool, she'd learnt. Christie also thought it was sweet of him to care, which he obviously did. It clearly hadn't bothered Daniel: the fact that Dermot was trying to match-make, judging by the way he had casually sauntered down to breakfast the following morning after he'd stayed the night with her. She suspected Dermot had an inkling as to what had gone on but was keeping it to himself.

For Daniel it seemed business as usual as he had chatted away to Dermot, not in the least affected by having shared Christie's bed. He'd been very open and tactile with her, which made Christie tingle inside. It had been a long time since she'd been made to feel special. Her heart again cried out for him when he had to leave to go to his parents. The court hearing was tomorrow. She'd hugged him hard before he left.

'I'll be thinking of you,' she'd told him huskily.

'Thanks.' He'd given a sad smile. There had been a weighty pause. He'd slung his rucksack over his shoulder. 'I'll be in touch.' He'd kissed her full on the lips, in front of Dermot who'd been by the reception area. Then she'd watched him go, hoping and praying he'd get the outcome he desperately wanted.

Her thoughts constantly turned to Daniel and what he was about to face. She could only imagine the emotional trauma he was suffering.

'So, just to recap,' Dermot said now as he squinted to look at the A4 sheet of paper containing Finula's instructions, 'the cases of champagne will be delivered next week. The flowers are ordered. The wedding cars are booked. All the rooms will be spick and span, ready for the guests.'

'Yes, Dermot. Stop panicking. I have done this before you know,' Christie reassured him.

'Well I haven't,' retorted Dermot, looking slightly flustered, 'and it's *my* daughter we're talking about.' Then his face looked crestfallen. 'What if it rains?' He turned to look at the back lawn through the window.

'It won't,' said Christie with certainty.

'But what if it does?' Dermot was beginning to look even more agitated.

'Dermot, the long-range weather forecast says blue skies and sunshine for goodness' sake,' she cut in, a tad impatiently. Honestly, there was Daniel about to go to court to fight for his daughter and here was Dermot faffing about a bit of rain! Dermot blinked, quite taken by surprise at the tone of her voice. Immediately sensing this Christie apologised. 'Sorry, Dermot, I didn't mean to snap.'

Dermot looked thoughtfully at her. 'When is Daniel returning to Treweham?'

Christie looked down. 'I'm not sure. He has business to attend to.'

'I see,' he replied nodding sagely.

'I've finished the wedding cake and stored it safely in Tupperware.'

'Very good.' Marcus was on his laptop at the kitchen table.

'I've wrapped my dress and it needs to be laid flat on the back seat with nothing placed on it.'

'OK.' Marcus still didn't take his eyes off the screen.

'Marcus, are you even listening to me?'

He looked up. 'Yes.' Then he returned to the laptop.

'Marcus, have you sorted out your morning suit?'

'It's in hand.'

'What's that supposed to mean?' she asked, hands on her hips.

'It means that Tobias is sorting out all our suits – mine, his and Sebastian's – so we're matching.'

'Have you actually organised anything at all for your own wedding?' The frustration in her voice made him smirk.

'The honeymoon?' he offered.

'You've booked a couple of flights to Ireland. Anything else?'

'I've been busy,' he replied half laughing, 'and anyway you said you wanted to go to Roscommon.'

'I do!' she was quick to reply. 'But I just feel like that's all you've contributed. I've done everything else.'

'I'll turn up on the day and look breathtakingly handsome,' he batted back with a wicked grin, then closed his laptop. 'Come on.' He grabbed a bottle of wine out of the rack. 'Let's unwind in the garden with this.'

Finula instantly relaxed. Sitting in the pretty cottage garden overlooking the majestic Shropshire hills with a glass of full-bodied red wine was just too tempting.

'Let's.' She smiled.

35

'Are you sure you don't want us there, as moral support?' Daniel's mum looked searchingly at him. He shook his head.

'No thanks, Mum. I think it'd be better if I went alone. You and Dad would just be sat about waiting.'

'That doesn't matter, son, we could still be there for you.' His dad reassured him.

'Thanks, but really, I'd rather do this alone.'

They both nodded their heads, understanding yet anxious.

Daniel was wearing a suit, as instructed by his solicitor. He imagined Alana Frost donning something very similar today in court: black and formal. He felt like he was going to a funeral. They had arranged to meet in her office beforehand and walk the short distance to the court together. Alana had wisely suggested this, rather than have him wait in the court foyer, where Jenna and her representation would be. The less contact he had with her the better. He could barely bring himself to look at her now.

As predicted, Alana Frost appeared pristine and very business-like. Wearing a dark, tailored suit and carrying a large file bulging with papers, she gave Daniel the once-over.

'Good. You look the part,' she stated in clipped tones,

looking him up and down, 'and remember, don't interrupt if I'm speaking, or anyone else for that matter. Signal and whisper, or write any queries or comments down, yes?' She looked piercingly into his eyes.

'I understand,' replied Daniel. Then gulped.

'No matter what's being said,' she continued in the same no-nonsense nature, 'and believe me, there'll be things said you won't like.'

His head shot up. 'Like what?'

'All sorts. They'll dish the dirt – but,' she said firmly, 'so will we.' He believed her. On balance, despite the astronomical fee she was charging him, he knew he'd be unable to do this without her. He didn't doubt that Jenna would also have hired a good solicitor. His stomach churned; he felt positively sick with nerves. This was it. He was about to face the very day he'd been dreading. The culmination of what his body and mind had slowly suffered through stress and anxiety was about to be reached. Alana must have read his thoughts, as her face softened ever so slightly. She put a hand on his shoulder. 'Stay strong, Daniel. We're in this together,' then she gave a tight smile.

They were the first on the list, which meant a prompt start, the usher informed them as they entered the waiting room. As it was a family hearing, it was to be held in the Judge's Chambers rather than in an actual courtroom. Daniel's eyes darted round the waiting area. There she was, her back to him, talking intently to her solicitor. Next to her was that prick JonJo. He wanted to wrap his hands round his neck. What the hell was *he* doing here? This concerned him and Jenna, not her boyfriend. Alana caught him staring and quickly nudged him.

'Remember, you must keep your cool,' she said quietly. 'He won't be allowed into the hearing.'

'James and Connor,' called the usher. That was them. Both parties made their way to the Judge's Chambers. Daniel's gaze burnt into Jenna's back as he silently followed her. They were all seated round a large table, where the Judge sat at the top. Their file was spread out before him, with various notes made in the margins. At least he'd read the reports beforehand, thought Daniel bleakly. Then Alana coughed and opened the hearing.

'Your Honour, my client is seeking full care and control of his daughter, Emily Louisa James.' The rest became a slight blur to Daniel as he was forced to sit back and listen to all his family life being scrutinised and assessed. Alana outlined the input and influence Daniel had had on his only child. She highlighted the time, care and attention he had willingly poured into his precious little girl's life. She spoke of his achievements in his career, which enabled him to provide very well financially for Emily.

At this point, Jenna's solicitor interjected that Daniel's career was indeed successful, which inevitably meant he would not be able to look after Emily full time, to which Daniel urgently whispered details of his intention to work from home and the proposed studio in his garden at home.

Then it was Jenna's turn. God, listening to her solicitor, you'd think she was a saint. His stomach started to churn again at how she was a "stay-at-home mum" and couldn't possibly leave her little girl. Never had a problem constantly dumping Emily on him or his parents, he thought with spite. Rage surged through him at how "Emily had taken to her boyfriend, who was a doting stepfather to be." What? *They were getting married?* His blood boiled, then he remembered Alana's counsel. He was deliberately being provoked. Him losing his temper would be playing straight into her hands. He looked across at her, sat primly straight-backed, hands neatly folded on the table, like butter wouldn't melt. No mention of the drunken nights out, the girly weekends away, the shagging behind his back.

He picked up a pen on the desk and wrote clearly on a piece of notepaper for Jenna to see "Mention her drinking" then passed it to Alana. He enjoyed seeing the flicker of horror flash over her face and sat back with satisfaction. Jenna, in retaliation, whispered something in her solicitor's ear. The Judge spoke next.

'I'm going to adjourn for thirty minutes,' he said decisively.

'Yes, your Honour,' both solicitors answered and they all rose to their feet. Outside, in the waiting area Daniel took Alana to one side.

'You need to tell the Judge about her drinking,' he hissed urgently.

Alana looked at him. 'Listen, Daniel, I'll use ammunition if and when we need it. So far Jenna's being sensible.'

'What?' he squeaked.

'The only negative comment was your working full time, whereas she doesn't.'

'Yeah, because I'm bloody well providing everything,' he rasped.

'Keep your cool,' she ordered, looking sterner than ever, making him shrink back. He was on the verge of tears and forced himself to be composed. His head turned to the corner of the room where JonJo had an arm round Jenna. Bastard. They were soon called back into the Judge's Chambers. The Judge gave direction to both representatives, stating he had read all the reports, listened to both parties and was about to give his summing up, followed with his order. All sat still, waiting with bated breath.

The Judge summarised all he had concluded from the case. He gave acknowledgement to both parents, stating they clearly loved and cared well for their daughter. He emphasised how important it was for each party to co-operate as much as possible, especially regarding future access, reiterating communication was key for the sake of their child. Then he gave his order. Emily was to remain living her mother, with weekend access to her father. Holidays would be shared equally. Flexibility and any adjustments to arrangements would have to be consented by both parties.

No! *No, no, no.* Daniel closed his eyes. A whooshing noise filled his ears. Alana discreetly put her hand on his lap.

'I seek leave to appeal, your Honour.'

'Granted,' replied the Judge. There was a short silence, then all rose from their seats and vacated the Chambers. Jenna practically ran down the corridor to the waiting area.

He turned to Alana. 'I can't go in there.' The last thing he could stomach was watching her and JonJo celebrate taking his child.

'We'll wait till they've gone.' She sat him down on a bench near the doorway. He was shaking. 'Give me a couple of weeks to work on the appeal.' She tried to console him.

Daniel was numb with shock. His first instinct was to get home to his parents, then realising how devastated they would be, he decided he couldn't face that. He got up and went to the gents, where he vomited the anger, hate, frustration and sheer injustice of it all down the toilet.

36

Dylan was busy entering Phoenix for his next race. He'd chosen to do so when Flora was out of the office, knowing full well the repercussions that would follow. Whilst they were blissfully living together, Dylan was still very aware of what had become the elephant in the room. Neither had spoken about Phoenix racing again and who would be riding him, but both knew it had to be addressed. Dylan was prepared to put his foot down as the owner of the yard, yet was reluctant to do this, knowing the impact it would have on Flora. He'd much prefer to persuade Flora not to race again, but truly couldn't see how, knowing how geared up she was.

It was as if they both knew this could be a real problem in their relationship, professionally and emotionally. Yet still it seemed neither would budge. Flora was out there now, flying through the air, hurtling Phoenix over the fences, whilst Dylan was registering Joshua as the jockey for Phoenix's next race – and this time he wouldn't move until the email came through confirming receipt of his entry.

He had to admire her tenacity though; if nothing else it proved her grit and courage. She reminded him of himself when he had first started out on the circuit; but this was different, this was Flora. The very thought of her being injured, especially as a result of his racing yard, turned his blood cold. Then an idea came to him. The more he thought about it, the more appealing it became, so much so, he cursed himself for not having thought it before. Feeling rather pleased with himself, he picked up his mobile and scrolled for his favourite restaurant.

'Hello, could I book a table for two this evening?' Well, he thought smiling widely, if a job's worth doing, it's worth doing properly. Yes, he'd wine and dine Flora, get her in the mood, then give the performance of his life in the bedroom, then, when she had fully succumbed to him and was at her most obliging, he would coax her with his suggestion of having a baby. He'd long wanted to start a family with Flora and had hinted at it too. Flora had warmed to the idea, but nothing concrete had been decided. Well, now *was* the time. They'd be a happy family – he knew that. Plus, Flora wouldn't want to race if she was pregnant. Everyone was a winner, surely?

Flora had been too tired to stay long with Phoenix, which was most unlike her. Needing a rest and a hot drink, she walked the horse back to his stable and made her way to the office. Dylan had just completed registering Phoenix and Joshua for the next race when she entered. Excellent timing, thought Dylan.

'Fancy a coffee?' he asked, as casually as he could.

'Thanks.' Flora sat down with a thud and put her head back.

Dylan eyed her whilst making them both a drink. 'You OK? You look a little pale.' He handed her a cup.

'Just tired, thanks.' She took a sip and screwed up her face in revulsion. 'Ergh, what's in this?'

'Nothing, just the usual coffee.' Dylan frowned. Flora put it down then leant her head back against the sofa again and closed her eyes. 'I've booked a table at Angelo's tonight,' he told her.

'Oh, Dylan, I don't think I'm up to it.' She looked at him regretfully. 'Do you mind? I'm exhausted.'

'No, course not. I'll cook dinner, shall I?' He could see his romantic plans for the evening slowly slipping away.

'To be honest, I don't feel like eating anything.' It was true. A sickly sensation had suddenly gripped her.

'You sure you're all right, Flora?' Dylan sounded concerned, then not waiting for her to answer, he said, 'Come on, we're going home.'

Flora sank into a hot bubble bath and relaxed, though that nauseated feeling refused to budge. Then it dawned on her, whilst stretching out amongst the glittering bubbles – her period was late. She sat up abruptly. Taking a deep breath, she tried to clear her panicked brain and calculated when her last one had been. A week before the point-to-point. Flora remembered throwing up a few times in the run-up to the race with nerves and tension, such was the state she'd been in. She had obviously flushed the contraceptive pill out of her system.

Oh God. Making herself stay calm she wisely decided to buy a pregnancy testing kit to be absolutely certain, before dropping the bombshell on Dylan.

37

Tobias made his way through the woods on the Treweham Hall estate to Keeper's Cottage. He had arranged to meet Daniel there, to discuss the renovation works. On arriving he noticed a campervan was parked up under the trees. He frowned, then saw Daniel come out of it and walk towards the crumbling stone cottage.

'Hello, Daniel.' Tobias joined him. He was initially a little shocked at the sight of him. Daniel clearly hadn't slept well, with bruised-looking bags under his eyes and he badly needed a shave.

'Hi,' Daniel replied, then turned to look at the dilapidated building. A part of him wasn't sure about this anymore. Since the court hearing, all his enthusiasm had been sapped from him. All the desire and eagerness of making a fresh start and a new home for him and Emily had been extinguished – the fire had simply gone out of him. His parents had endeavoured to reignite a spark of hope, telling him to stay strong and positive for the pending appeal, reminding him that he still had Emily at weekends and holidays; but what good was that when she'd be in Liverpool?

Jenna was planning to move with JonJo that very week. She certainly wasn't letting the grass grow under her feet, he'd thought scornfully, clearly confident that he wouldn't have a hope in hell regarding the appeal. It all seemed pretty pointless now, pouring time, money and energy into a project that wouldn't be his child's full-time home.

Then again, the voice of reason within him advised, *you need somewhere to live, and where better than Treweham?* The place certainly ticked a lot of boxes. For a start Christie was there. Christie, the kind, supportive strength he so wanted and needed. She had showed nothing but care and sympathy when he had called at The Templar late that morning. Daniel had outlined the whole sorry event at court and she'd sat listening with tears in her eyes. There was nothing she could say – what could anyone say to make him feel better? It was futile; instead she hugged him hard and let him cry. Christie had encouraged him to continue with the plans for Keeper's Cottage, maintaining it would still be a home for him and Emily, even if Emily was to be based in Liverpool.

He knew it made sense and would give him something to focus on, but right now all he could contemplate was his beautiful daughter being driven up the motorway and away from her family, to a place that was totally alien to her. He wanted to scream his objections. For the first time ever, he felt real violence towards both Jenna and that dickhead boyfriend of hers. He fully understood crimes of passion and what drove otherwise decent people into cold-blooded murderers. Right now he'd shoot the pair of them – no problem. He hadn't slept, he hadn't eaten, he couldn't think straight and was functioning like the living dead. No wonder Tobias Cavendish-Blake had looked slightly alarmed by his appearance.

'Well, you've certainly got your work cut out here.' Tobias nodded towards the derelict building. Daniel just stared at it. 'You still want to do this?' he asked quietly. Daniel turned to face him. It would be so easy to simply say "no" and walk away, but his inner strength refused to let him. Grit and determination surged through his veins.

'Yes. I'll show you the plans I've done so far.' He went to the campervan and took out a folder. Then he pulled out the drawings he had drafted. Tobias eyed them carefully, listening to Daniel's proposals. He was pleased that although Daniel was slightly extending the footprint, the design was still in keeping with the original build, using the same stone and materials. Tobias nodded in agreement, as Daniel talked through estimated time schedules and costs.

In short, he'd been impressed with what he had seen and didn't doubt that Keeper's Cottage was in good hands. Tobias sensed a lack of keenness though, especially compared to Daniel's previous manner, when he was bursting with gusto. After hearing all the plans, Tobias smiled.

'Excellent. I think you've just about covered everything, Daniel, and your vision is spot on.'

For the first time Daniel smiled and seemed to lighten up a touch.

Tobias pointed to the campervan. 'I take it you're camping here during the works?'

'Yes, I'd prefer to be on site.'

Tobias suddenly felt a pang of sympathy, picturing him all alone here in the woods, with only a pile of stones for company.

'Come for dinner this evening. Megan would love to hear your plans.'

Daniel's head shot up in surprise. 'I…' he stammered, seeming unsure and taken aback by the invite.

'Really, we'd enjoy your company,' insisted Tobias.

Daniel's shoulders relaxed. 'Then yes, thank you.'

'Great, just call up at the Hall when you're ready. We usually dine about sevenish?'

'That's great. Thanks.'

Christie was relieved to see Daniel in slightly better spirits when he entered the bar. Although still looking somewhat dishevelled, he had a bit more spring in his step.

'I'm invited to dinner at Treweham Hall,' he'd told her, whilst gulping back a well-earned pint. He'd been clearing all the overgrowth surrounding the cottage, in particular the ivy covering the outbuilding. He'd been pleasantly surprised at the size of it and thought it would make an ideal work studio, especially with added skylights in the slate roof. Daniel couldn't help but be encouraged by what he'd seen and the potential of the whole place. It was going to be exactly what he'd wished for, despite Emily not being there full time.

'Well, you'd better scrub up then,' said Christie with a wry smile.

Daniel laughed. 'I suppose so. Any chance I could use your bathroom? The campervan has a shower, but I'd love to soak in a hot bath.' His muscles ached from all the bending, stretching and carrying he'd been doing for the last few hours. Adrenalin had pumped through his blood whilst replaying the court hearing in his troubled mind. Now his body was crying out for a rest.

'Of course, help yourself.' Then she gave a sly grin. 'You know the way.' Those pale, blue eyes looked into hers, making her chest thump uncontrollably.

'I sure do.' He smirked.

Within an hour, Daniel had returned looking more like his usual self, freshly shaved and with that sage aroma she'd grown to love.

'Have a good evening,' Christie said, whilst still serving behind the bar.

'Thanks.' He leant over and kissed her full on the mouth like it was the most natural thing to do. She caught Dermot smiling with approval.

Walking up the sweeping gravel driveway, Daniel couldn't help but feel in awe of the place. Treweham Hall was a huge, impressive sandstone building. Virginia creeper climbed the walls and stained-glass windows twinkled in the early evening light. He was greeted by a sombre-looking butler who seemed to be expecting his call. Once inside, his architectural mind appreciated the marble flooring, intricate wood-carved staircase and stone pillars. The butler directed Daniel through the mahogany-panelled hallway, which showcased various family portraits to what was described as 'His Lordship's private quarters.'

It felt surreal to Daniel being a guest in this environment. He only hoped his attire was suitable; surely they didn't dress formally for dinner did they? If so, his grey chinos and white shirt would have to suffice. His worries were soon quelled when he saw Tobias and his wife Megan, who was holding their baby.

'Mr James to see you, Sir.'

'Thank you, Henry. Daniel, come and join us,' called Tobias. He was still wearing black jeans and a polo shirt.

Megan smiled up at him. 'Hello there, I'm just about to put this young man to bed, then I'll join you.'

Daniel smiled, thinking what a nice, down-to-earth couple they were.

Soon all three were sat in a small dining room overlooking the south wing gardens of the Hall. Daniel felt at ease as he told Megan his intentions for Keeper's Cottage. She seemed genuinely interested.

'Well, here's to you and Keeper's Cottage, Daniel.' She raised her wine glass.

'Absolutely,' agreed Tobias, raising his glass too.

Such kindness. Daniel swallowed the lump in his throat and blinked back the tears threatening to spill. 'Thank you,' he replied, then took a huge gulp of wine.

38

'Finula, we can't fit any more in.' Marcus slammed the boot down.

'Oh, I was just going to—'

'No more,' he cut in firmly, 'seriously, it'll be a miracle if this thing sets off – it's packed to the rafters.' Impatience was clear in his voice. Little wonder, Finula had been up since 6am, packing and fussing over what to take to Treweham. After what seemed like an age of planning and arranging to Marcus, the wedding would finally be upon them in a few short days.

They were staying at The Templar for a few days beforehand to meet Finula's family who would also be there. Marcus' aunty and a couple of cousins from Ireland were the only members of his family attending the wedding and were stopping in nearby accommodation. Secretly, if Marcus had had his way, he and Finula would have just gone away quietly and come back married, without any of this fuss. No chance of that though, not with his future father-in-law. Whilst he loved Dermot dearly and Dermot treated him like a son, Marcus sometimes longed for the quiet life whilst visiting him, instead of the full-on bonhomie that he knew to expect. It was good to know how welcomed they'd be, but it could be a little too over the top at times.

He imagined the pre-wedding celebrations in the pub, Dermot slapping backs, ordering drinks, roaring with laughter, introducing him to everyone and him having to play the dutiful son-in-law, when all he really wanted deep down was a quiet affair with just his wife-to-be. He looked at Finula and saw the stress etched in her face. Was it really what she wanted? A touch of resentment niggled at him. Had they been perhaps a little bullied into this family wedding?

His concerns soon evaporated once they were on the road and within distance of Treweham. He could sense the anticipation build inside Finula.

'I can't believe the wedding's about to arrive,' she said excitedly, sitting forward in her seat. 'It's been ages since I've seen my aunties and uncles.'

Marcus turned sideways for a moment. 'Looking forward to it then?' He smiled.

'Of course! Aren't you?'

'Having a sexy redhead for a wife – you kidding?' he joked.

He realised his previous misgivings had been selfish. He couldn't possibly have expected Finula to have a wedding without her father and family. It wouldn't have been fair at all, and, a voice inside instructed him, it was one day. Once he and Finula were married, they had the rest of their lives together. At this point Marcus made a conscious decision to throw himself into it and accept Dermot's hospitality with the good cheer in which it was intended.

True to form, Dermot was there at the front entrance to

welcome them. Marcus' heart squeezed when seeing Finula hurry out of the Range Rover and rush into his arms.

'How you doing, Marcus?' He beamed, which poked Marcus' guilty conscience.

'Fine, Dermot.' He smiled widely. 'And yourself?'

'Never better, busy, but never better.' He guided them into The Templar. On entering the bar, Finula's eyes instantly homed in on the marquee being erected on the back lawns, through the patio doors.

'Oh, Dad, it's going to be fab!' she exclaimed. Marcus felt another stab of guilt.

'To be sure it is, Fin, nothing but the best for my daughter,' he replied proudly. Then he turned to Marcus. 'I believe you're stopping at Treweham Hall the night before?'

'Yes—' Marcus nodded '—probably best,' and he gave a wry grin making Dermot throw his head back in laughter.

'Good man ya'self!' he exclaimed. 'Best not to get under the bride-to-be's feet.'

Marcus gave a tight smile in response. Finula by this time had moved to the patio doors to get a better view.

'I think I'll just—'

'They know what they're doing, Finula,' warned Dermot. 'Leave them to it.' He really didn't want Finula attempting to tell Christie, who was overseeing operations outside, what to do. He'd wisely learnt both girls had minds of their own and he didn't fancy a clash of opinions.

'Come on, Finula, let's get unpacked,' coaxed Marcus, knowing full well what Dermot was trying to avoid. Finula hesitated, then he quickly added, 'Your dress, it'll need hanging before it creases.'

'Oh my God, you're right!' gushed Finula, then rushed back to the car.

Outside on the lawns, Christie was having a nightmare. To top it all, she'd seen Finula hovering by the doors out of the corner of her eye and willed her to stay away. The last thing she needed was an extra pair of critical eyes. Luckily, Daniel had offered a hand, bugger all use Dermot would be once his relatives arrived. Playing number-one host was all well and good, but certain things needed doing, and they weren't all one-man jobs.

This served as a warning to Christie. How would she fare once Dermot left The Templar? A sense of foreboding settled in her, making her more tense. She looked across at Daniel who was carrying tables and positioning them according to the plan she had drawn up. Christie noticed he seemed a little less edgy, probably due to him being so absorbed with the works at Keeper's Cottage. Also, Emily had rung him several times since moving to Liverpool, however temporary that may be, as Daniel had told her the appeal was due to be listed imminently. Judging by his raised spirits, he obviously thought the outcome would be favourable. She sincerely hoped it would.

Jenna, it appeared, was playing nicely and being reasonable. She had put Daniel's mobile number in her phone under "Daddy" and taught Emily how to ring him whenever she wanted. Often Daniel's mobile would ring when he was busy on site working, but he always made time to speak to his little girl. He was also due to pick Emily up next week and he'd booked a couple of nights at The Templar, as Emily had wished for. Christie too, was looking forward to seeing her again and could only imagine how hard it must be for Daniel.

She caught his eye and he winked back, making her heart skip a beat. They had shared another night together since his return to Treweham and it still felt rather clandestine, trying to hide it from Dermot. Silly really, she thought, they were both grown, consenting adults and it was after all her pub. Even so, she was reluctant for all the staff and locals to know just yet, wanting to set the right tone as the new owner of The Templar; and technically, she was still married. That sense of foreboding reared its ugly head again.

39

Flora had woken again with the same sickly feeling. It rose gradually up her throat and she only just managed to make it into the bathroom in time. After vomiting, she splashed her face with cold water. Her reflection in the mirror told her how white she was. She was glad Dylan hadn't been there to witness her morning sickness.

A whole week had passed since she had bought the pregnancy testing kit. After opening it with shaking hands, Flora had read the instructions, but had put off actually following them. She was scared. A baby hadn't really figured in her plans at the moment, what with only being twenty-one and having a busy career running the training yard. Yet, the more she contemplated the idea, the more Flora warmed to it. She had tried to imagine what sex it would be, how it would look and what it would be called. Part of her was desperate to do the pregnancy test and know for certain, another part of her wanted oblivion, not to have to deal with it all.

Then there was Dylan to consider. How would he react? Flora knew he had loosely tiptoed around the subject, but she'd never taken him seriously, especially when the yard took up most of their time. Then another thought occurred to Flora – racing. She knew she wouldn't be in condition to race Phoenix over the jumps if she was carrying a child. Even she conceded that would be irresponsible of her.

There was so much to contemplate, Flora was beginning to feel overwhelmed. Deciding once and for all to know for definite, she took the kit hidden in her make-up bag from the bathroom cabinet and followed the instructions. She sat patiently on the side of the bath and waited for the white stick to tell her what her future held. Again, she was relieved that Dylan had got up early to meet a prospective client at the yard. She needed time out – alone – to think.

After what seemed an eternity, she took hold of the white stick. A clear blue line stared back at her. Flora blinked and reopened her eyes. It was still there. She was pregnant. Confirming what she already knew deep down, Flora put the stick back in her make-up bag and decided to take a warm, relaxing bath. It didn't matter if she was late getting into work; she just needed time to adjust.

Flora let her body unwind and took long, deep breaths. Her thoughts were sprinting, but inside a sense of reassurance filled her. Getting used to the fact she was pregnant, she found herself making life adjustments in her mind. Obviously racing was out, most probably riding too. She would have to be extra careful in the yard and not lift anything too heavy. Then there was childcare to consider. Flora didn't want to be totally away from the yard, yet didn't like the thought of handing her baby over to a minder either.

Her head spun. She needed to tell Dylan – this wasn't just her problem – then she quickly reprimanded herself. It wasn't a problem, she thought with a tinge of guilt, it was just unexpected.

Dylan had had a busy morning. After meeting an owner who was more than impressed with his yard, he had secured another client, taking it to full capacity. He'd need more staff, he thought, and would ask Flora to advertise. Then realising the time, wondered where she was. Flora wasn't normally late. He was about to ring her mobile when she walked into the office.

'Hi.' She smiled.

'Hello, you, I was just about to ring you. Everything OK?'

How to answer that? mused Flora. "Perfectly fine, by the way we're having a baby." Probably not. She almost laughed to herself.

Dylan saw her lips twitch and frowned.

'Yes, fine.' She smiled again.

Dylan, sensing now was perhaps the opportunity to revert to his plans of wining and dining Flora, seized the moment. 'Let's go out tonight. Fancy Angelo's?'

Flora nodded her head. 'Yes, let's.'

Dylan and Flora found themselves seated in a romantic, secluded area at a candlelit table for two. Flora said no to the wine and opted for a mineral water instead, which had surprised Dylan slightly. After enjoying a beautifully cooked dinner and chatting over coffee, Dylan decided to make his move.

'Flora.' He took her hand over the table and held it. 'I've been thinking.' He looked lovingly into her eyes. 'Do you think…' He paused, wanting to get this right. 'I really want to…' then he stalled again.

'Want to what?' asked Flora, beginning to suspect where this was heading and smiling at the irony.

'To...'

'Start a family?' Flora supplied.

Dylan looked a tad shocked. 'Yes,' he confirmed.

'That's handy then.' She grinned, loving the confusion in his face.

'Sorry?' Had he heard her right?

'Dylan, I'm pregnant.'

He stared at her for a moment then his face broke into a huge beam.

'Flora, that's wonderful!' He leant across the table and kissed her hard, making her laugh, partly with relief. Then his face sobered. 'I want to do this properly – let's get married.'

'Oh... but my parents are still away...' Her face fell at the thought of a wedding without them.

'Where are they now?'

'Rome.'

'Then we'll go there, get a licence,' he answered.

Flora's head shot up. 'Really?'

'Well, there's no shortage of churches there.' He grinned.

'Oh, Dylan!' Her hands flew to her face with joy.

Dylan smiled at her response. 'I take it that's a yes then?' he teased.

'Yes. It is.' They kissed again over the table, a slow, loving kiss that went on forever, not caring in the least who was watching.

40

'Here's to a long and happy marriage.' Sebastian raised his glass. Tobias and Marcus joined theirs.

'Cheers,' they replied.

Marcus was enjoying his stay at Treweham Hall, secretly glad to get away from the full-on celebrations at The Templar, and the wedding wasn't until tomorrow. As he'd predicted, Dermot had taken his hospitality to a new level – which his family had lapped up no end. Whilst it was good to see everyone enjoying themselves so much, Marcus was now glad of a bit of peace with just his two brothers. He was touched that they'd organised a stag do, however intimate, and really appreciated the time with them. Having only just discovered he actually had two half-brothers months ago, they all had a lot of catching up to do.

Tobias, very thoughtfully, had brought family photo albums to show Marcus, while he had talked about his childhood in Roscommon, and his mother, who he had nursed before she had died of cancer. It was the first time Marcus had really opened up. Apart from confiding in Finula, he hadn't discussed his private life before, choosing instead to throw himself into his career as a TV producer.

'How's the documentary coming along?' asked Sebastian.

'Good. We're on schedule.' Marcus nodded, taking another sip of his favourite Jameson Irish whiskey.

'So, it's still to be aired in the autumn?' asked Tobias.

'Yep. We'll be good to go,' confirmed Marcus firmly.

All three brothers sat and contemplated for a moment, knowing the effect the documentary would have on them all. The Cavendish-Blakes, an ancestral family dating back to the twelfth century, with connections to the Knights Templar, was about to announce that the late Lord Richard Cavendish-Blake had actually sired his firstborn son out of wedlock, to a girl who worked in the kitchens at Treweham Hall some thirty-two years ago. Albeit Richard hadn't ever known this, the repercussions were about to be faced – on national TV.

Each brother, especially Marcus, knew what to expect. He had seen how Tobias had been practically plagued by the press throughout his life and dully realised his own would suffer the same intrusion. It was inevitable. He was only glad that his marriage to Finula was taking place before any of the revelations could cause such an invasion of his privacy.

'I suggest we all watch the documentary here, at Treweham Hall, together,' Tobias stated.

'Yes, so do I,' agreed Sebastian.

'Fine by me,' chipped in Marcus. Not a bad idea, he thought; at least he'd be protected from the media inside this enormous fortress. Then he half laughed to himself. This "enormous fortress" was in fact his family home.

41

The first thing Finula did on awakening was look to the window. With relief she saw sunrays shining through the gap in the blind. As if needing further confirmation, she pulled back the bed sheets and went to open the blind. Yes, beautiful, clear blue skies thank God. Her gaze wandered to the marquee on the lawn. Already the staff hired for the day were busy about their duties, carrying flowers, tablecloths and cases of champagne. Finula's stomach fluttered with butterflies. It was finally here, her wedding day. There was a knock at the bedroom door.

'Come in!' she called.

Dermot poked his head round. 'Do you want breakfast in bed, Finula?'

'I'm not sure I could eat breakfast, Dad,' she replied rubbing at those butterflies, which refused to go away.

'You'll need something to line your stomach,' he gently warned. 'How about scrambled egg on toast?'

'OK then, thanks.'

Dermot nodded and went back downstairs.

Finula heard the church bell chime. It was nine o'clock. She'd slept remarkably well considering the nerves inside her, which were gradually building up. She smiled, remembering

Megan and Tobias' wedding. She hadn't felt anxious at all, and the nation's press had been out in full force then. This was different though, this was *her* wedding day. She tried to picture Marcus, waking up in Treweham Hall and wondered if he was having breakfast in bed. She giggled at the mental image. Would he be showing any sign of jitters? Doubtful, she thought, but that was why she loved him so much; they were polar opposites, her the fiery redhead, he the cool, composed rock.

Finula turned to see her wedding dress, hanging patiently, along with a pair of white satin shoes, neatly tucked underneath on the floor. Megan was due to help her get ready at 11am, leaving plenty of time for the wedding at 1pm. Willing herself to stay as calm as possible, she ran a hot bath and put on the soothing CD she had bought. It contained "Sounds of Nature" to relax the mind, such as waterfalls and wind chimes. Marcus had howled with laughter when he'd seen it, saying he'd prefer a stiff drink.

Maybe Marcus had had one stiff drink too many last night. He woke with a thick head, rubbed his eyes and wondered where the hell he was, before rational thought kicked in, along with a throbbing headache. Jeysus, that was some stag do. Setting off tame, he, Tobias and Sebastian had had a few drinks whilst chatting, then the cards came out and one drink led to another. At three in the morning, Tobias had had the sense to send them all to bed. And what a bed it was, noticed Marcus, his head turned upwards to the floral canopy of the four-poster. He hardly remembered getting in it.

Water, he needed water. His mouth felt like sandpaper. He looked sideways. There on the bedside table was bottled water and a glass. He hurriedly leant over and poured himself a drink. By the bottle was a box of aspirin. How thoughtful. Had the butler supplied them? Probably used to looking after his brothers this way. He chuckled to himself, then swallowed a couple and finished off his glass of water. After a few minutes, he was beginning to feel better and his head began to clear. Rubbing his hands together, he looked forward to the hearty breakfast, which they were all to share in the great hall.

He was the first down. Marcus stalled initially at seeing all the silver platters lined up on the sideboard, then decided to just help himself. He really didn't want any staff waiting on him. After piling his plate high with bacon, sausages, eggs and fried bread, he sat at the long oak table running down the great hall and stared round the enormous room. Portraits glared down at him. It was a touch unnerving, especially as one or two showed definite resemblances to himself.

Not for the first time, he contemplated how different his life could have been, if his mother had not bolted from Treweham Hall. Would he have been any happier, being brought up in these surroundings? He didn't think so, not when he knew the price his brothers had to pay for belonging to such a prestigious, ancestral line. He was a private man. Again his thoughts turned to the documentary and how it would change his life forever. He was interrupted by Megan, who was carrying Edward, his godson.

'Good morning!' she breezed. 'How are you feeling?'

'Fine,' replied Marcus smiling. Tobias and Sebastian

followed, along with their mother Beatrice. Marcus stole a glance at Beatrice, never feeling quite easy in her company. Hardly surprising really, considering he was the illegitimate, firstborn son of her husband. Both had been polite and civil to each other, but that was all. There were unspoken boundaries between the two.

'So, Marcus—' Sebastian slapped his hands together '— ready for blast-off?'

'As ready as I'll ever be,' he replied, casually tucking into his breakfast.

Megan smiled to herself, knowing full well the state Finula would be in compared to Marcus' nonchalance. She quickly ate her breakfast and checked her watch. 'I'd best be off now,' she told Tobias.

'OK.' He moved Edward's high chair closer to him.

'Any message for Finula?' she asked winking at Marcus.

'Yes, tell her she's the luckiest woman alive,' he retorted with a wink back, making them all laugh.

After much fussing and flapping, Finula was finally ready to go and looking absolutely radiant. The vintage, sleeveless wedding dress in ivory silk could have been tailor-made for her (as opposed to the charity shop buy it was). The smooth material fitted her curves beautifully and the long, ivory gloves she wore elegantly complimented her slim arms. Megan had painstakingly wound Finula's auburn locks round long curlers to create ringlets, which cascaded down her back. Finula wore a tiara that contained an emerald as the centre stone and had chosen to carry her late mother's pearl rosary beads, which she'd woven shamrock into. Her make-up was light and fresh, but still showed the freckles that Marcus loved.

'Finula, you look amazing.' Megan's eyes started to fill.

'Don't you start.' Finula laughed. 'It'll be bad enough when my dad sees me.'

'True,' agreed Megan. 'Right, I'll have to dash back.' Megan had already showered and done her make-up; all she had to do was change and join the others.

Finula composed herself. It was 12.30pm. She could hear everyone scurrying about The Templar before making their way to the church. After ten minutes there was a silence. She knew her dad would be waiting downstairs for her. With a deep breath she made her way to the top of the landing.

There he was gazing up at her. Immediately his chin wobbled. 'Finula, you look beautiful,' he choked. 'If only your mammy could see you now,' then he took out his handkerchief and wiped his watery eyes.

Finula swallowed hard. 'Don't, Daddy, you'll set me off.'

Daddy? It had been a long time since she'd called him that. He understood her vulnerability and willed himself to be strong for his girl.

'I'm so nervous,' she told him, gliding down the stairs.

'Well don't be. There's a man waiting in that church who loves you as much as I do,' he said encouragingly. 'Now would I be giving you away if that wasn't so?'

Finula smiled. 'No, of course not,' then she pulled her shoulders back and stood tall.

'That's my girl.' Dermot hooked his arm for Finula to hold and together they walked through the hallway, to cheers and claps from all The Templar staff, eagerly waiting to see the bride off. Christie quickly ran to them both before they got into the wedding car.

'Good luck, enjoy every minute and we'll be waiting for you, with the champagne flowing!'

'Thank you, Christie.' Finula gave a dazzling smile and waved at everyone.

Marcus was stood next to Tobias on the front row. Behind them sat Sebastian, Megan with Edward and Beatrice. His heart started to beat faster when the organ music struck up and all stood to greet the bride. Megan turned to see Finula and Dermot slowly walk up the aisle then leant forward and whispered in Marcus' ear. '*You're* the luckiest man alive.'

That made him smirk. How right she was, though, he thought, when Finula joined him before the altar. His eyes pierced her. God, she looked like a Gaelic queen. He was speechless. Finula too was blown away by this tall, dark, handsome man standing proudly in a grey morning suit. Their eyes locked and they held hands.

Dermot just about managed to keep it together for the full length of the service. Sebastian, true to form, gave a wonderful reading from Mark, Chapter 10, where Jesus teaches about marriage and welcomes children, with all the expression and drama one would expect from an actor. When the priest announced them husband and wife a loud cheer and applause echoed round the church.

Walking down the aisle with his new bride on his arm, Marcus had never felt such completeness. He turned to Finula who was now looking peaceful and serene.

'I love you, Mrs Devlin.'

'You better,' she replied grinning.

They were greeted with more cheers and applause, plus

confetti as they walked hand in hand into The Templar. An Irish folk band played merrily on the lawn as guests chatted and circulated, ate canapés and sipped champagne. Dermot was in full flow, constantly ensuring everyone's glass was full. He was thoroughly looking forward to making his speech and didn't have to wait too long before Christie announced dinner was about to be served and they could all take their seats. After enjoying a banquet of carrot and coriander soup, roast beef and Yorkshire pudding, and Baileys Irish cream cake, the guests sipped coffee as they listened with anticipation whilst the groom spoke, followed by the best man. As expected, they were touching, genuine and peppered with humour. But then up stood Dermot, all eyes on him.

'Well, when I set eyes on Finula today, the very last thing I wanted to do was give her away…' And on he went, with humorous tales of her childhood, how together they'd coped with the loss of her mammy, how proud he was of her and how pleased he was with her choice of husband. It was met with a warm round of applause and Finula's eyes swam with emotion.

She looked round the marquee, now softly lit with tea lights. Here, under this canopy, was every single person she loved. This had to be the happiest day of her life.

42

Christie took a well-deserved mid-morning break. It was now a couple of days since the wedding and all the family guests had gone. In fact, all the rooms except for two were vacant. It was a relief to be a little less hectic and have a more tranquil environment. Even Dermot had calmed down and seemed glad of a bit of peace and quiet; well, he wasn't getting any younger, he'd remarked. No, Christie had reflected, he wasn't and soon he would be leaving The Templar altogether to enjoy his well-earned retirement.

Once again, Christie's apprehensions bubbled to the surface when contemplating this; after all, it wasn't exactly what she'd bought into was it? When she had taken on The Templar, it was supposed to be a partnership with Stephen, not going solo. Then, realising she really didn't need a partner like Stephen in any event, concluded she was most likely better off on her own. That said, it would be nice to have a second opinion, that reassurance another partner would give. Christie appreciated how fortunate she was to have had Daniel's input. The bedrooms were a triumph, really adding character to the upstairs.

After finishing her coffee, she decided to pay him a visit on site. Every credit to him, he was there every day overseeing and working alongside Tobias' team of builders. Often he would carry on after they'd finished for the day, and then either shower, change and have his evening meal in The Templar, or sink into Christie's bath and soak his aching body.

Walking along the public footpath through the Treweham Hall woods, she soon came to the clearing where Keeper's Cottage stood. Already, the footprint of the house could be seen and the external stone walls were being built up. There Daniel was, wheel-barrowing sand, ready to put in the mixer. It was strenuous work and a hot day, which is why he was only wearing shorts and no top. Christie's eyes devoured his toned, muscular body and her stomach gave a flip. He noticed her walking towards him and his face lit up with a smile.

'Hello there, what brings you here?' He wiped his forehead with his arm.

'Just thought I'd see how it was all coming along.' Christie turned to look at the building. 'It's looking impressive, isn't it?'

'It will, once all the external walls are finished and the roof frame goes up.'

'You're making good progress,' she remarked, watching all the busy workmen.

'We are, fancy a quick drink?' He nodded towards his campervan. They both made their way out of the sun and inside.

Christie was surprised at how spacious it was, as Daniel poured them both a cool lemonade. He plonked himself down on the two-seater settee next to her.

'It's quite quaint in here,' she said, taking in the décor.

It was all there, just on a smaller scale, along with the cute kitchenette, with its little sink and draining board, oven and fridge.

'I know.' Daniel smiled. 'Emily loves it in here.' There was a charged pause. 'How about a camp-side supper tonight?' Daniel suggested, taking Christie by surprise.

'That sounds like fun. What should I bring?'

'Just your lovely self.' He looked at her seductively, then added, 'And a bottle of wine.'

'You're on.' She met his gaze, then ran her eyes down his bare chest and taut, flat stomach. What could be better than sharing a camp-side supper with this man under a starry sky?

So, as planned, Christie found herself walking back through the woods carrying a bottle of wine in the balmy early evening. Daniel had set up a barbeque. It smelt heavenly as she made her way across to him.

'Hmm, that looks good.' Burgers and sausages were cooking nicely, while barm cakes and a salad were set out on a small picnic table. Christie sat on one of the deckchairs, whilst Daniel poured her a glass of wine.

'Cheers, it won't be long.' Daniel looked quite domesticated in his jeans, T-shirt and apron.

'Thanks.' Christie took a sip of the crisp white wine that Daniel had been chilling in a bucket. This was the life, she thought, relaxing in the great outdoors. She looked at Keeper's Cottage and noticed even more progress since that afternoon. She glanced towards Daniel, concentrating on turning the food over on the grill. She'd wager he'd have the cottage ready in no time, judging by his drive and commitment. Plus, it was giving him something to focus on, instead of mulling over Emily. Christie daren't ask when the appeal was, that's if a hearing date had even been set yet. Within a few minutes he was handing her a plate with perfectly cooked sausages and burger.

'Help yourself to salad.' He sat down opposite her and took a mouthful of wine. He'd definitely caught the sun, giving him a healthy, golden glow, instead of that pale complexion he'd had days ago. Yes, the outdoor life certainly suited him.

Daniel caught her assessing him and smiled to himself. He could tell by her appreciative expression she liked what she saw, and likewise. Who could resist her sexy curves in that sundress, showcasing her cleavage and her long, shapely legs? He longed to run his fingers up her elegant neck and into her shiny, brunette hair. He took another swig of wine and tried to cool himself; hell she turned him on.

The two of them enjoyed chatting and just relaxing in the still night air. As dusk fell, the sounds of the woods came alive with owl hoots and the rustle of branches.

'This really is a beautiful spot,' remarked Christie absorbing the atmosphere.

'It sure is,' agreed Daniel. This was the most comfortable he'd been in ages. 'Come inside, I'll make us a coffee.'

Christie followed him into the campervan. She too was feeling chilled, especially after the frantic few days they'd all had at The Templar. She looked at the back of him as he made them a drink and once again admired his broad shoulders and muscular arms. On impulse, and perhaps good spirits, she crept up behind him and put her arms round his waist.

'Hmm, very nice.' He turned around to face her and hugged her further into him. Christie's head rested on his shoulder.

'I love your smell.' She kissed his neck and Daniel could feel himself start to respond. With a groan he ran both hands into her dark curls and moved her head to face him. His lips sought hers and they kissed softly at first, then it deepened into an urgent passion as they pulled at each other's clothes, both eager to touch bare skin. Daniel led Christie to the far end of the campervan. The moon shone through the widows, illuminating the bed tucked at the back. He threw back the covers and gently pulled Christie in to join him.

She ran her hands up his hard thighs, then felt his cock harden and pulse under her palm. She slowly rubbed up and down his shaft, making him moan with pleasure, until he couldn't take anymore. Holding her hips with each hand, he positioned her to straddle him and then gradually guided himself into her. Christie cried out and gripped him as he started to move inside her. She felt hot and slick as he edged further and probed deeper. Christie matched his rhythm and her body moved in unison with Daniel's until they both reached a shattering release.

Christie moved to lie next to him, with her head on his chest, and together they fell into a blissful sleep.

43

Daniel awoke in the early hours of the morning to his mobile ringing. Drowsily he leant over the bed to see it on the floor. Jenna's name was flashing. Immediately he jolted and became wide awake.

'Jenna?'

'Daddy... I can't wake Mummy up.' Daniel froze. His heart stopped for a moment.

'Emily, where are you?' he asked, desperately trying to stay calm when inside he was crashing.

'At the house in Liverpool.'

'Where's JonJo?'

'He isn't here... and Mummy won't wake up...' Emily started to cry, breaking him even further.

'Listen, Emily, it's all right, I'm going to get someone to you... Don't cry, Sweet Pea. You get back into bed and take Mummy's phone with you.'

'But Mummy...'

'You do as I say, Emily, good girl and I'll ring you back in a few moments. Go now. I'll stay on the phone till you're back in bed.' Daniel imagined little Emily clutching the phone as she went back into her bedroom and climbed into bed. His chest was hammering. 'Are you in bed, Emily?'

'Yes,' said a small voice.

'Emily, is anyone else there?'

'Just me, Polly and Snuggles.'

Daniel closed his eyes. 'Well you give them a big hug and wait for me to ring you back – good girl.'

'OK.'

Christie was rousing and heard the tail end of the conversation. Rubbing her eyes, she saw Daniel punch out a number urgently on his phone.

'What's happening?' she asked drowsily.

Daniel turned sharply. 'Emily's on her own and can't wake Jenna up.'

'Oh no…' Then she heard Daniel speak to the emergency services, giving clear, concise information and the address in Liverpool for the police to attend to. Christie got out of bed and dressed. How could she help? After Daniel had finished his call, he rang Emily back. It was heartbreaking listening to him trying to calm Emily, when he himself was in such distress too. After twenty minutes, which seemed like an eternity, Emily opened the door to a police officer, whilst all the time Daniel was on his mobile guiding her. Once Daniel had spoken to the attending officer he quickly dressed.

'I've got to get there.' He was frantic.

'I'll drive you,' Christie replied. 'You're in no fit state.' Together they ran back to The Templar. After waking Dermot to tell him what had happened, Christie and Daniel got in the car, bolted to the motorway and up to Liverpool.

'If she's pissed, I'll kill her.' The shock had worn off now and Daniel was gradually getting angrier by the minute. 'And where the fuck's that JonJo? Emily's all alone there!'

Christie momentarily put her hand on his lap. 'Don't panic, stay calm, Daniel,' she soothed.

'Stay calm?' he squeaked. 'That's what my fucking solicitor said, and look where that's got me!' he thundered, then stopped. 'Sorry, Christie.'

'It's fine, honestly.' Then to her horror, Daniel started to cry. His shoulders shook as great, racking sobs escaped from him. All the pent-up tension was being released and Christie let him get it out of his system. Thank God he wasn't driving. Eventually Daniel quietened. 'Emily's in safe hands now,' Christie softly reminded him.

'I know, the police officer was brilliant.' Then, taking out a piece of paper with the station details on, he gave Christie the directions to where Emily had been taken.

'Was there any news on Jenna?' asked Christie, suddenly realising that she hadn't asked, such was her concern for Emily.

'No,' he answered flatly. To be honest, she was the last thing he cared about at the moment. All he could feel towards Jenna was pure fury. *How dare* she get into such a state, leaving Emily so vulnerable? He was incensed with rage. One thing for sure, he was going to fight tooth and nail to have Emily living with him. This incident was definitely going to be addressed at the appeal hearing.

Finally, Christie pulled into the police station car park. Daniel shot out of the car and ran to the enquiry desk. It was now 5am and daylight was breaking. The police officer on reception knew to expect Daniel and immediately took him into a private room.

'Emily, where is she?' he asked anxiously.

'She's safe in the other room, Mr James.'

'But... I need to see her,' he pressed.

'Mr James, I'm afraid there's something you need to know first, before you see Emily.' The officer sat him down.

Daniel looked into her serious face and once again he froze. 'What's happened?' he asked quietly.

'Mr James, Emily's mother has died.'

'What?'

The police officer took a steady breath. 'Jenna had been drinking, heavily, and choked on her own vomit.'

Daniel sat still, not believing what he was hearing.

She continued, in a grave voice, 'There are signs of bruising, on her face.'

'What? He bloody hit her?' he rasped, still in disbelief. This was turning into a hideous nightmare. He felt sick. 'Where is he?' he asked in a steely tone. He wanted to kill him. He *would* kill him, if he clapped eyes on the bastard.

'We're out searching for him. In the meantime, Emily is waiting for you.'

'But... what do I tell her?' His shoulders started to shake again with emotion.

'Listen, we'll do all we can. There are child counsellors who will help.'

'Yes... thank you.' Daniel gulped, then turned to face the officer. 'I'm taking her home – she doesn't belong here.'

'I understand.' She nodded comfortingly.

'I want to know the minute you find him.' He looked sternly at her. 'And find out what exactly's gone on.'

'Yes. You'll be informed.'

★

Of course Emily had been fast asleep when the argument started. She hadn't heard her mummy tell JonJo she'd been having second thoughts about the move to Liverpool and their relationship. Emily had slept through the insults that had been hurled from JonJo and then the punches that followed. She hadn't witnessed her mummy gulp back the wine in shock and desperation, as he slammed out of the front door, or seen her crying hysterically on the bed in a drunken state until she started to choke, uncontrollably, on the bile that gushed up her throat.

All Emily did know, as her daddy had religiously drummed into her, was to ring him if she ever needed him. No matter what, wherever she was, whatever time it was, she *must* ring him; and that's what Emily had done.

44

Like in any village, the devastating news of Jenna's death spread like wildfire. Although the residents of Treweham had never known Jenna herself, they'd grown fond of Daniel over the weeks he'd lived there and most had seen his cute little girl at The Templar. Dermot had given himself the task of discreetly informing the regulars who visited the pub, whilst Christie had reserved the family room for Daniel and Emily once they were ready to return to Treweham. At the moment Daniel had taken Emily to his parents, needing to be around family. Christie's heart cried out when she had been with them at the police station in Liverpool. Emily was pale, clearly in shock and clinging to her daddy, whilst Daniel had been quietly subdued and also shaken by the events.

During the days that followed Jenna's death, Daniel had to obviously make contact with her family and also ring Alana Frost, his solicitor. It had crossed his mind that Jenna's parents may try to claim Emily, but Alana had eased any worries and was in the process of overseeing the necessary legal paperwork, giving him, as Emily's father, full care and control. That in itself was a comfort in this whole sorry mess. A part of him had felt guilty. Was it right to feel such relief when Jenna hadn't even been laid to rest? Of course it was, his parents had told him. He was only human, and look what Jenna had put him through. Being dead didn't make you a saint.

Daniel had contacted the police on several occasions, eager to know if JonJo had been found. He had and was being questioned. That's all they could or would tell him. Daniel had gone back to his house that he'd shared with Jenna. Putting his key in the latch and it not turning told him the locks had been changed. He shook his head. She'd even locked him out of his own home. A cutting voice inside told him that JonJo would have a key, but he punched his fist through the window on the back door and let himself in. He'd buy new locks himself and replace the glass.

Looking round the kitchen, it was as if life was ticking along perfectly normally. Emily's colouring book and crayons lay on the table, Jenna's bracelet on the windowsill, along with her hand cream, even pots stacked on the draining board. Daniel frowned. This place didn't look as if it had been left permanently. The faint stale smell was the only indicator that it hadn't been lived in for a while.

He opened the windows to get some fresh air in, then went upstairs. He noticed a few DVDs scattered on the floor by the TV. Glancing down, his face twisted with distaste at the violent films that lay there, all for Emily to see. Once again, the urge to kill JonJo filled him. Would he be at the funeral? Half of him wanted him there, to confront him; then the other side reasoned it wouldn't be the time or place to kick the shit out of him.

Taking a deep breath, he climbed the stairs to the master bedroom. The very same bedroom Emily had been conceived in. A sorrowful, empty sensation washed over him and his eyes filled with tears. Such a waste. They had been happy once, but that seemed a long time ago now. He pictured Emily as a baby, snuggled in between them in that huge, king-size bed. Then that cutting, taunting voice returned. *They'd* have been in there too, having sex, whilst Emily slept next door. The revulsion was almost too much to bear.

He turned to leave the room and suddenly noticed Jenna's bathrobe hanging on the back of the bedroom door. Instinctively he leant forward to smell it. There it was, the distinctive musky scent she'd worn. Daniel didn't feel anything. No emotion at all. He then went into Emily's room and cleared it. Most of her toys and clothes were still there, which again made him think that the move to Liverpool hadn't been a final decision. He filled the bin liners he'd retrieved from the kitchen with all Emily's possessions, telling himself that was the main purpose of his visit. He was done with dissecting the past. It was the future he needed to focus on.

His thoughts led to Keeper's Cottage, his and Emily's new home, to Christie and Treweham village. All this eased his troubled mind and it was at this point he took out his phone and searched for a local estate agent. This house was going on the market. It was time to say goodbye.

Tobias had learnt the sad news from Dermot who had rung him to explain why Daniel would be away from Keeper's Cottage for a few days. Tobias, moved by what he had been told, made the trip to the site to inform the builders.

After announcing to the small team of workmen what had happened, there was a short, respectful silence.

'Poor little kiddie,' one murmured, to everyone's agreement.

'I suggest, gentlemen, that this job remains our number-one priority.'

'Aye,' they all said.

'So, in Daniel's absence, I will project-manage. Any queries come to me, although I'm sure you all know what you're doing.' They all nodded. Tobias surveyed Keeper's Cottage. He was impressed. The external walls were all up now and the roof was almost completely secured. 'I say we finish the outside structure by the end of the week. Get the windows and doors in early next week and then begin the electrics and plumbing works. I want to start the internal walls in a fortnight.' There was a pause. He looked at them. 'I'll pay overtime if need be, but I want this wrapping up. Daniel and his daughter need our help.' This was greeted with more approving nods.

45

Flora was engrossed behind the computer screen. Dylan smiled to himself, knowing full well it wasn't anything to do with work that was catching her attention. Every now and then he would hear a gasp in awe, or a dreamy sigh escape from her. He loved that she was so excited about their upcoming marriage. Since proposing, Flora had done little else than trawl through glossy wedding brochures, or wade through numerous wedding websites. Even Phoenix, her beloved horse, was taking a back seat.

He had to admit, though, Rome really was the most magical of settings for a wedding. The most appealing thing about it, for Dylan, was that the location was far away from any prying eyes that could ruin their special day. Like Tobias, he'd had more than a taste of the media's presence, albeit on a smaller scale; even so, it was enough to be ever wary of their potential to invade his privacy. And privacy was exactly what Dylan wanted on his wedding day to Flora. It was far too special to be sprawled all over some trashy magazine. He'd done his bit with that, when he and Flora appeared in *Hi-Ya* magazine months ago, not to mention being exploited in another kiss-and-tell article from a former lover.

This was personal. It was him, Flora and their unborn baby. Just thinking about it made him warm inside; he couldn't be any happier.

Another intake of breath came from Flora. 'Oh, Dylan, look at this!' She clasped her hands together.

Dylan, still smiling, made his way to stand behind her and look at the screen.

'We will provide the most romantic and exclusive Italian locations. Just relax in the knowledge you're in the safest of hands,' gushed Flora, whilst pointing to the stunning rooftop terrace of an opulent luxury hotel, giving panoramic views of Rome.

'Hmm, looks impressive,' agreed Dylan.

'We are creating an emotion,' continued Flora reading from the website, 'much more than an event that lasts one day.'

Dylan chuckled. They knew how to spread it on thick these wedding companies, and how to charge no doubt. Still, it didn't matter, as long as Flora was happy. He eyed her abdomen. Would she be showing by then? He hoped so, although he wasn't sure Flora would think the same.

'Thought about a dress yet?' he casually asked, as if she hadn't.

'Something loose and floaty, I think.' She grinned back. God she was pretty. He couldn't help but melt. Carrying his child seemed to make her more so. 'Anyway, there's lots to sort out before I can think of a dress.' She suddenly looked serious. 'My parents want a church wedding.'

'Do you?' Dylan would be content to get married anywhere to Flora.

'Yes,' she replied chewing her lip in thought, 'I think so.' Then she clicked away on the keyboard, bringing up another page. 'I like the look of this.' Dylan dipped his head further down to see it. *The church of St Lawrence at Lucina, standing in the modern piazza San Lorenzo in Lucina.* A stunning Baroque-style chapel filled the screen. It struck Dylan as being the most romantic place to marry. For a moment he was speechless. 'Well?' pressed Flora.

'Perfect.' He gulped.

'It was built on the remains of a Roman noblewoman's home, named Lucina.' Flora was again reading the blurb.

'Lucina,' whispered Dylan.

Flora looked up at him. 'Lucina,' she echoed, 'what a beautiful name.' She gazed wistfully over his shoulder.

'That's just what I was thinking.'

46

'How's the little mite bearing up?' Dermot asked Christie as he passed through reception.

'Not bad. She looks so pale and tired, poor thing.'

'Well, she's had one hell of a knock,' he replied shaking his head. Just then, Daniel came down the stairs and joined them. He too looked exhausted. 'You OK, son?' Dermot looked compassionately into Daniel's eyes.

'I'm getting there, thanks, Dermot.' He then turned to Christie. 'I need to enrol Emily in a school as soon as possible.' Now that it was a given she would be living with him in Treweham, it was essential that he register her with the local primary school. Luckily, he had been assured that it was a particularly high-ranking one with a good reputation. One less thing to worry about, thought Daniel. He was gradually coming to terms with being a single parent. At times the enormity hit him, then in his quieter moments he realised he could make all the decisions without having to fight or convince Jenna. He also wouldn't have to tolerate any unsuitable boyfriends that his daughter would encounter. From now on it was just him and Emily; that in itself was comfort enough.

His parents had been a brilliant support, actually offering

to move nearer to his new home in Treweham, but he'd gratefully declined the offer. He really didn't want to have to rely on anyone anymore. Daniel had been truly touched by the huge effort made by all the workmen at Keeper's Cottage. Knowing that Tobias had instigated it had also moved him. He'd been moved, too, by all the kind words and backing offered by the locals, especially as he was new to Treweham. Dermot and Christie had shown nothing but concern for him and Emily on their return to The Templar. Christie, especially, had attended to their every need, but also had the insight to know when to back off and give them space.

All in all, he felt at home – that this was the place they were meant to be. As to be expected, Emily was a touch nervy and very clingy with him. She struggled sleeping at night and fretted if she was ever left alone, even for a moment. It broke Daniel's heart seeing her little body tense at the slightest noise or sudden movement. Emily was continuing to see a child counsellor, and as advised, it was all a matter of adjusting. Daniel was confident she would, given the amount of time Emily had actually spent with Jenna.

On reflection, Daniel realised his daughter had lived between him and his parents probably more than with her mummy. She never once asked after JonJo, which was a relief. He, in turn, didn't ever mention him. There was no need; he was well out of the picture, thank God. The bastard hadn't even shown up at the funeral.

Daniel's stomach contracted when picturing Jenna's coffin being carried up the church aisle. He had chosen not to be a bearer; it just didn't seem right. Her father and brothers were given the task. Instead, he sat at the back, his eyes darting across the pews, trying to decipher which of the mourners could be JonJo. In between recalling the happier times with Jenna, his ears would tune in to what was being said on the altar. "Devoted mother" struck a chord, and not a good one.

He'd refused point blank to take Emily. A funeral was no place for a four-year-old. His parents had agreed and had taken Emily out for the day instead. As Jenna's coffin had been slowly lowered into the ground, still he found no emotion forthcoming. He was numb, devoid of any feeling. He made the effort to talk to her parents, who had confirmed that JonJo had not attended. He didn't push for further information; he was past caring now. All he'd wanted to do was go home; and Treweham was home from now on.

Daniel had been staggered by the progress on Keeper's Cottage. Even he hadn't expected to find the outside structure complete. He'd been amazed. Now he had to concentrate on the internal layout. Again Tobias had proved more than helpful, offering suggestions and advice. Daniel was impressed with his team of workmen and the relationship Tobias had with them – no wonder his company was as successful as he'd heard.

Then there was Christie, whose voice alone warmed his heart. She was as beautiful on the inside, as she was on the outside. Emily had run into her arms when first seeing her at The Templar. Christie had picked her up and hugged her hard, bringing a lump to his throat. From then on, every opportunity Emily had, she'd be scurrying to Christie's side. Daniel wondered if it was female company she missed.

Christie was always pleased to see her, giving her odd jobs to keep her occupied, like helping set the tables or to tidy reception. Once or twice, Emily had insisted that it was Christie who read her bedtime story, while Daniel had sat surplus to requirements on the edge of the bed.

Whilst he was desperate to visit Christie's bedroom, he wouldn't run the risk of Emily waking up alone. Definitely not. So, any snatched opportunity they had for a kiss and cuddle they took, whether it be in a secluded corridor, or empty bar. Once or twice they'd come close to Dermot interrupting, but had just laughed it off.

Daniel was keen to have his own place and move into Keeper's Cottage. Having Tobias on side and pushing things forward was a bonus. Emily needed stability, a proper home, and he was anxious to be in the cottage before she started school at the beginning of September.

'The school in the village has an excellent reputation,' Dermot told him.

'Yes, I believe so.'

'Where's Emily?' asked Christie.

'She's just fallen asleep. I'd better go back up.'

'Listen, I'll take her out this afternoon, give you chance to sort the school out,' she said.

'Would you? Thanks.'

Dermot looked on with an approving smile. It was good to see how they blended together. He was further pleased that Daniel was going to be a permanent villager. The time for his departure was fast approaching, now that Finula's wedding had taken place. He was reluctant to leave Christie just at the moment, given the situation with Daniel, but he couldn't stay forever.

47

Finula and Marcus had loved honeymooning in Ireland. Staying in Roscommon had meant seeing where Marcus had been born and grown up. Finula had cooed over the sweet, whitewashed cottage where he and his mother had lived, with breathtaking views of the mountains. It was hard trying to picture his childhood there, in such a humble home with magnificent, dramatic backdrops, when really, by rights, he had belonged in Treweham Hall as the firstborn to Lord Richard Cavendish-Blake.

Not that it bothered Marcus – the opposite in fact. The last thing Marcus wanted was attention, especially the kind that having an ancestral, aristocratic family would bring. Secretly, he was glad to have been out of the limelight, but what really rankled him was the way his mam had had to struggle to keep them both. Many times he had contemplated what would have happened if his mam hadn't bolted and escaped to Ireland. But it was no good; he'd never know and it didn't do any good pondering over what might have been. The good thing was that *he had* found his true home, and his brothers.

He and Finula had rented a cottage in his home village of Kilsalla and explored the area. Marcus had enjoyed showing Finula where he had gone to school and the local pub, where he'd taken his first pint. Here, he was well known and regarded as somewhat of a celebrity due to his award-winning documentaries. The locals had welcomed Finula with open arms, at first mistaking her for one of them, rather than coming from England.

He had taken her to the Sacred Heart church, where his mam was buried and they had laid flowers by her tombstone. Finula had been so impressed inside the church, with its lovely mosaic work throughout and gold gilt décor, its ornate altar and vaulted ceiling. Never had she felt so serene and peaceful. They had climbed Ireland's famous "Holy Mountain" Croagh Patrick, giving them the most amazing view of Clew Bay. Hand in hand they had wandered through the crumbling ruins of Roscommon Castle and marvelled at its history.

All in all, they had had a ball, a real rest from the nagging pressures of everyday life and just enjoying each other's company, but now the honeymoon was over. It was time to go home. Finula felt like sobbing, having to leave such a beautiful, charming place that had struck a chord in her heart.

'Do we really have to go?' she pleaded, knowing full well the answer. Of course they did.

Marcus gave a wry smile. 'Darlin', we can always come back.'

'Yes, yes we must.' She felt suddenly appeased. After all, it would be nice to head off back home to Shropshire. To be fair, she'd missed the lush, rolling hills of the place and was rather looking forward to settling down to married life in their quaint, black and white timbered cottage. She glanced at her new husband. My, what a handsome brute he was, with his black, wild curls and green, twinkling eyes. The sun had caught his skin, giving him a healthy glow.

He was busy packing his suitcase for their departure the following morning. He turned to face her and winked. 'Come on, Fin,' he coaxed, 'it's not the end leaving here. It's just the beginning.'

How right he was.

48

Tobias and Megan sat having breakfast, whilst baby Edward slept peacefully in his Moses basket. Tobias had been filling Megan in with the progress on Keeper's Cottage. She had been horrified at what Emily had been through and wanted to help in some way.

'I can't stop thinking about Daniel's little girl,' she told him whilst pouring another cup of tea.

'I know,' sighed Tobias, 'but we're doing all we can,' he tried to reassure her.

She chewed her lip in thought. 'Maybe we should invite them over here to the Hall, give them a change of scenery. I could give them a guided tour and we could have dinner together. What do you think?'

Tobias nodded his head. 'Yes, good idea. I'll speak to Daniel later – we're due to meet up this afternoon.'

Megan was pleased with her suggestion and pondered how to make it special for Emily.

When Tobias had invited Daniel later that day, he had been happy to accept, knowing Emily would love it.

'Could we bring Christie too?' asked Daniel. 'I know Emily would love her to come.'

'Of course, you're all welcome.' Tobias smiled, then turned to Keeper's Cottage. 'Have you chosen the kitchen yet?'

'Yep, I've ordered it, plus all the bathroom fittings.' Daniel had thoroughly enjoyed flicking through various websites on his laptop, showing Christie what he had bought. Christie's reaction told him he'd chosen well and had made him even more eager to get on and move in. Emily had been enrolled at school, which meant that he had a month to finish the cottage before she started the new term. Daniel was confident, as was Tobias, that they would manage it.

Daniel also needed to start thinking about work, ever mindful of the job he'd been commissioned to do. Hopefully, it would all fit together time wise. Even if his studio wasn't quite ready, he would have to temporarily work in a spare bedroom. He was beginning to feel more positive as time went on and thankfully Emily seemed to have settled too. Daniel was ever grateful of the way Christie helped with Emily, and loved the way the two bonded together, which was why he'd wanted Christie to come with them to Treweham Hall.

Christie had been delighted at the invite, often wanting to have a tour of the Hall, but never getting the time to do it.

'You all go and have a lovely time,' Dermot had told them. He was conscious that he wouldn't be at The Templar much longer, so was happy to man the fort and give Christie some time out.

The following day all three of them set off late afternoon to Treweham Hall. Emily gaped in awe at the size of the sandstone fortress with four corner turrets, giving it a castle-like appearance.

'Does the queen live here?' she asked.

'No, Sweet Pea.' Daniel laughed. 'Lord and Lady Cavendish-Blake live here.'

Emily looked blankly at him.

'We call them Tobias and Megan,' said Christie smiling.

'I used to have a friend called Megan,' replied Emily, making Daniel and Christie exchange looks.

After walking down the long, gravel driveway to the huge wooden front door, Daniel lifted Emily up to use the brass knocker. Henry the butler soon answered and ushered them in. Emily's eyes widened at the space and décor, as did Christie's.

'Hello!' Megan came rushing up to them with a breezy smile. 'Tobias will join us later,' she explained then lowered herself to Emily's height. 'Would you like to look round?'

'Yes!' Emily jumped excitedly on the spot, eager to explore.

'This way then.' She grinned. 'Let's start in the music room.' Megan led them through the marble-tiled hall and up the sweeping staircase. Emily was taking in all the portraits on the landing, while Christie admired the intricate woodcarvings on the banister and covings. It really was a magnificent place. Entering the music room, Emily rushed to the Steinway piano in the corner.

'Can I touch it?' she asked.

'Of course.' Megan lifted her onto the piano stool and played Chopsticks, a very basic piece she'd learnt as a child herself.

Emily giggled.

'Here, you help me play.' She patiently showed Emily which keys to press.

Daniel watched Emily's face in concentration and thought he would buy a piano for their home. She obviously was enjoying playing and seemed to pick it up quickly.

'Hey, you're good!' Megan laughed, making Emily beam up with pleasure.

Christie couldn't help but admire Megan and the way she was handling Emily.

Next they visited the chapel. 'This is where Tobias and I got married,' Megan told them, 'and where Edward was christened.'

Emily turned to her. 'Where is Edward?'

'He's with his daddy – they'll be joining us in the dining hall.'

'Where's that?'

'Come, I'll show you.'

All four of them went back downstairs, through the oak-panelled passageway and into the dining hall. A long mahogany table ran down the centre of the room, with ten chairs seated each side. A silver candelabra burned brightly in the middle. A spectacular chandelier hung from the ceiling, its cut glass flickering light on the pale silk walls.

'Is this where you eat?' asked Emily in awe.

'Sometimes – only on special occasions, like today.' Megan smiled. Just then, in came Tobias holding Edward. Emily immediately ran to him.

'Ooo… look, Daddy, a baby!' she gushed.

Tobias laughed as Edward reached out to touch her.

'Be careful, he likes pulling hair,' he warned.

There was a slight knock on the door. 'Dinner is served, Sir,' Henry announced rather piously, making Emily giggle again. Daniel shot her a warning look.

Soon they were all sat round the huge table enjoying roast chicken with all the trimmings, followed by syrup pudding and custard. Emily lapped it up, all the time gazing at baby Edward in his high chair. They chatted easily, mainly about the renovation of Keeper's Cottage and life in Treweham. Christie talked about her career in the hospitality industry, which particularly interested Megan. All in all it was a great success and had given Daniel and Emily a much-needed lift.

On their walk home back to The Templar, Daniel carried a now very sleepy Emily. Christie wrapped her arm round his back and nuzzled into his neck.

'Hmm, that's nice,' he whispered.

Christie couldn't remember feeling so happy and content. But all that was about to change.

49

Christie passed reception the following morning to collect the post. As she sorted through the various envelopes one made her stop dead in her tracks. She'd recognise that neat, small handwriting anywhere. It was Stephen's. Her mouth went dry and her hand trembled a little opening it. She was alone on reception, but didn't want to run the risk of someone passing by and witnessing her reading a letter which, her gut feeling told her, wasn't going to be good news. Instead she hastily made it to her room. All the while her heart was beating fast in anticipation.

It had been five months since Christie had last had contact with Stephen. It seemed a lifetime ago now – so much had happened in that space of time. Sitting on the bed she took out the letter and forced herself to stay calm. After momentarily closing her eyes and taking a deep breath, she read it.

Dear Christie,
 I hope this letter finds you well. I know it may come as a surprise – me writing to you like this. I often think about you and how you're doing there in The Templar.

Christie, I'm sorry for the way things ended between us, but I really didn't have a choice, and I still don't. You see, Sophie is due to have the baby next month and with her not working, money's tight. Very tight. There's no way of saying this gently, but I need my share of the pub. I know I said you should go for it, but the reality is, I can't afford to let you have it all. The Templar is half mine, well in name anyway, and I need my share back.

I'm so sorry to do this to you, Christie, but I'm desperate for the cash and I have a family to think of now. I hope you understand. Perhaps it's time to finalise things between us. I've taken advice from my solicitor, who says the quickest way to divorce would be for you to start proceedings and file for one under the grounds of my adultery. I've enclosed details of the solicitors for you to liaise with.

I know you're living your dream, Christie, and I'm sure you're doing a fantastic job, but please understand my predicament. If you could let my solicitor know when I can expect the finances to be sorted out, that would be helpful. At least that way I can make plans.

Very best,
Stephen.

She stared at the letter, numb with shock. On refection, something like this was always in the pipeline, but to have it now, delivered to her like this, shook her to the core. So, Stephen wanted out. Well, he was never really in, was he? Even so, it angered her the way he still called all the shots. It was *him* who decided to go, after getting the girl in the office pregnant, and now *he* was deciding to pull the rug from under her feet and claim half of The Templar – so much for the contract he'd promised.

The divorce he was welcome to, she thought bitterly, and yes she would file for one, stating his adultery. He could fucking well pay for it too. She was damned if she was going to put a penny towards the costs. As for "the finances to be sorted out" he could wait. If he thought she was going to rush and come up with the coffers (though God knows how) he had another think coming. How on earth could she afford to buy him out? He must know it was impossible. They'd borrowed to the max as it was. He obviously assumed she'd sell and move on. Never.

Christie gripped the letter and only just resisted tearing it up. After months of hard slog and bonding with all the staff and locals, gradually putting her stamp on the place and making it her own, her dickhead of a husband was about to take it all away from her. The bastard. Yet despite all the injustices, common sense told her he could, because as unfair as it seemed, it was still technically half his. Did she really expect him to give his share for good? Deep down Christie had known it was too good to be true, and that it had been his guilt talking. Another thing he'd done for himself, easing his guilty conscience by letting her go and fulfil her dream, taking his share of the money.

At the time she'd been happy to do it, just relieved that she could still go, however daunting it seemed. Now though, reality was kicking in and Stephen couldn't afford to appease his shame any longer – a girlfriend and a baby needed paying for. She pictured him now, excited about becoming a father. That really pissed her off the most, especially after the way he had reacted when it became apparent why they couldn't conceive. Oh, nothing to do with him, all Christie's fault – well look how he had soon knocked Sophie up!

She was furious. Why had everything gone right for him and not her? Spitefully, she didn't want him to have a son, who would play rugby just like him, father and son together. No, let him have a daughter who ran rings round him. Then she laughed at her own childishness. Did it really matter? They'd both moved on. She thought of Daniel and Emily and her shoulders relaxed. No, the real issue here was money and how she could manage to keep The Templar. The thought of having to let it go filled her with remorse. And what would she do? Where would she go? The whole scenario sickened her. It was *so* unfair. Tears of anger and frustration ran down her face.

Later that evening when the bar was slowly emptying, Christie approached Dermot.

'Can I have a word please?'

'Sure.' He motioned towards a table in the alcove.

Christie passed him the letter. 'Dermot, I got this from Stephen this morning. Read it please.'

Dermot's eyes darted over the handwriting. He handed it back with a serious look. 'Do you have the funds to buy him out, Christie?' he quietly asked.

Christie suspected he already knew the answer. 'No,' she replied, then gave a big sigh. 'I don't know what to do.'

'Doesn't look like you have much choice.' Dermot looked sympathetically into her eyes. 'I'm so sorry,' then he added, 'Is there no one else who could help out?'

'My parents you mean? I don't think they have that

kind of money and I wouldn't want to ask them. They're retired now.'

Tell me about it, thought Dermot. Would he ever feel free to leave The Templar? Finula's wedding, Daniel's situation and now this. Without wanting to appear too harsh, he really was ready to leave and put his feet up. He wasn't getting any younger, after all, and he had already stayed longer than he had planned.

'Sometimes, Christie, things happen for a reason. Would you always want to be in Stephen's pocket? Knowing he could pull the plug on you at any time?'

'You mean like he just has?' she replied flatly.

'Better now than in a few years… when perhaps you're more involved…' He struggled with the words.

Christie sighed again, utterly defeated.

'What am I going to do, Dermot?' she asked weakly.

Dermot patted her shoulder. 'Just take your time and give it some thought, Christie.'

50

From the moment Flora stepped off the plane she fell in love with Rome. It was hard not to fall for all its historic charm, bursting with culture and style. Dylan was happy to soak in the sun and relax, realising it had been literally years since he'd had a proper foreign holiday. Together they had strolled hand in hand down the quaint, cobbled streets and through the warm, amber monuments. They had sipped espresso in characterful old coffee bars, zipped through passageways on Vespa mopeds and emerged into vibrant crowds, buzzing with passion.

After dusk the sights were even more magical, watching Rome light up with life. Dylan was sipping a cool tonic water from the hotel balcony, taking in the breathtaking rooftop views. He deliberately avoided any alcohol, wanting to appear his best for Flora's parents. They were about to meet for the first time that evening, two days before the wedding. Dylan was slightly apprehensive regarding his future in-laws. Well, hardly surprising considering he had moved their daughter into his home and got her pregnant without so much as casting eyes on them. He hoped getting married in Rome, where they were, would win them over.

Flora seemed unperturbed when Dylan had voiced his

concerns. She was just so excited to see them and enjoy their time together. To her relief, the wedding planners were on the ball. She felt able to unwind and let them take care of everything. And a happy Flora meant a happy Dylan, even though it was costing him an arm and a leg.

'Ready to go?' called Flora through the balcony doors.

'Here goes,' he muttered and threw back the rest of his drink.

The evening was a success on the whole. Flora's parents were delighted to see her and had welcomed Dylan with open arms, well her mother anyway. Dylan sensed a slight coolness with her father, which he understood under the circumstances.

Whilst Flora and her mum talked animatedly together, her dad leant forward and spoke to Dylan. 'How long have you known Flora?'

Dylan swallowed. 'A few years,' he lied, making her dad frown.

'Funny, she's never mentioned you before.'

'Please know, Mr Tudor, I intend to love and look after your daughter and future grandchild very well.' He felt about sixteen years old, but it appeared to do the trick.

'Good. Good.' He nodded and sat back in his chair looking somewhat relieved.

51

Daniel was due back on site full time. Whilst he was staying at The Templar with Emily, it was heaven to spend some much-needed time with her, and Christie had been a tremendous help, but now he really had to get on with finishing Keeper's Cottage. He had arranged with his parents to take Emily to their place. They'd been desperate to see their granddaughter and son after everything that had happened. Although Daniel regularly assured them they were fine, they had asked to have Emily for a short while, which would give him the opportunity to press on with the build. Emily was obviously excited to see her grandparents as she chatted over breakfast.

'Are Grandma and Grandpa going to live with us in our new home?' she asked.

'No, Sweet Pea, but they'll come and stop sometimes.'

'Oh.' She looked crestfallen. Daniel, hating seeing her disappointed, paused, then made a decision that he had been toying with for some time.

'Emily, I've been thinking, would you like to get a dog, once we're settled in our new house?' Watching her face light up melted his heart.

'Daddy, yes!'

Daniel smiled. 'Well, when we're all moved in we could get one.'

'Let's!'

So it was with good cheer that Emily said goodbye to Dermot and Christie, giving them each a big hug.

'Have a safe trip,' said Christie as she walked with them to the car.

'Will do. I'll be back early evening,' he told her, expecting her to give him a knowing smile. It would be the first night they'd had together for some time now. Instead, Christie just nodded. He frowned. Was there something wrong? Dermot had seemed rather subdued too.

Within an hour he arrived at his parents' house. There they were, both standing by the front door with big beams, waving away. Bless them, he thought. Where would he be without them? Emily dashed down the footpath and flung herself at them. It was good to know she was in safe hands. For a fleeting moment that sickening anxiety flared through him, then as easily as it came, it dampened. That was all in the past now.

'Hi!' he called, carrying Emily's suitcase and rucksack full of toys.

'Hello!' His mum hugged him, before Emily took her hand to go inside.

'Son, we've had a call from Jenna's parents,' his dad said quietly. Daniel looked at him. 'They've got the coroner's report. The police have also been in contact with more information.'

'Oh, I see,' Daniel replied, motionless.

'They've asked to see you.'

'But…'

'They think you should know, as Emily's father, exactly what happened.'

Daniel had wanted to know at the time, but now he wanted to put it all behind him.

'I don't want to see them, Dad.'

'I understand, but it could give you real closure, Daniel.'

'I'll ask them to send me the coroner's report. Did they mention JonJo?'

'Yes. He's been charged with GBH and is due to appear in court anytime soon.'

Daniel's blood ran cold. Not just for Jenna, but at what Emily had been living with. He never wanted to hear his name again. Forcing himself to act as normally as possible, he went inside to join Emily and his mum.

'Emily tells me you're getting a dog.' His mum was busy putting fairy cakes on a plate.

'We certainly are.' Daniel smiled, while an excited Emily ran to him and wrapped herself round his legs.

'I can't wait, Daddy!'

'Not long to go, Emily, but let's get the new house ready first.' He lifted her up and squeezed her tight. He breathed her in, this beautiful, precious daughter of his.

Christie had had a busy morning. After sleeping on it, she had woken with a determined resolve to take control of her life and deal with the matters in hand. First of all, she had contacted a firm of solicitors and instructed them to issue a divorce petition, under the grounds of her husband's adultery and had given them the details of his solicitor. Secondly, she had made an appointment to see the bank manager who had overseen the loan she and Stephen had taken out when buying The Templar. To be honest, she didn't hold out much hope of an extension, but she was going to ask anyway. What had she to lose?

Christie had wanted to reply directly to Stephen, but he hadn't given his home address, just his solicitor's. He could even have moved for all she knew. Another flicker of annoyance prickled her; again, he was calling the shots, knowing where she lived, but not disclosing his whereabouts. The postmark on the envelope told her he was still in Chester – that's all she knew. But then, did it really matter?

A voice inside told her to just get rid of the loser. He was beginning to irritate her now more than anything. Gone were any sentimental what-could-have-been thoughts she'd once had. All she felt for him now was a bitter realisation of what he really was – a selfish bastard. How had it taken her so long to see it? Probably comparing him to Daniel had made it obvious. The difference between the two was startling. All Daniel cared about was his daughter's happiness, whereas Stephen only cared about himself. It would be interesting to see how much he compromised once becoming a parent. Would he forfeit his rugby and the boozy nights out with his mates? He certainly hadn't when he'd been married to her. Good luck to Sophie – she'd need it.

Then she gave another sigh. All this resentment wasn't helping. The issue of where this left her was what she must concentrate on. Christie simply couldn't let The Templar go without a fight, refusing to accept that one day, very soon, she may have to hand over the keys to another proud owner. She felt queasy with despair.

52

Dylan and Flora held hands tightly as they stood outside the church of St Lawrence at Lucina. It was quite a humble building by Rome's standards, with its terracotta front, small stone pillars and neat chrome railing. Located in the modern piazza San Lorenzo, a typical Roman pedestrian area with open-air cafés and restaurants, meant that quite a few locals were interested in the young couple about to enter their church to marry.

And what a striking couple they made. Flora looked beautifully elegant in white. Her wedding gown had a sheer floral lace bodice, with a subtle stretch, and had a silk chiffon skirt that flowed to her ankles. Her hair had gypsophila woven through it, resembling a floral crown and she carried white roses. Dylan cut a dashing figure in his smart navy-blue suit. Together they stepped into the cool church to be greeted by the priest. Flora's parents sat on the front row of the wooden pews. More of the local Romans sat dotted in the benches behind them, eagerly awaiting to see the young couple marry. It touched Flora that they wanted to be there to witness it.

The church, although modest from the outside, was magnificent inside, with its Baroque-style side chapels and huge Reni painting of The Crucifixion taking pride of place above the main altar. Ornate paintings covered the arched walls and a high wooden ceiling with elaborate carvings hung over them. Shafts of sunlight blasted through the windows above, lighting up the glorious marble altar. Dylan was once again struck by the place and gulped back the emotion.

The priest led them up the aisle and stepped onto the altar, while they followed and stood before him. The priest spoke good English and after greeting all present began the order of service. They exchanged their vows gazing into each other's eyes, causing a few tears from the small congregation. When the priest announced them husband and wife a gentle ripple of applause echoed through the church. After kissing his bride, Dylan turned and guided her back down the aisle, never so proud. He'd done it. He and Flora were married. He was a husband and a dad-to-be. The feeling of euphoria gushed through his blood; truly he had never been so happy. He turned to face Flora – she too was beaming with joy.

'Dylan, we're married,' she said with glee, not quite believing it as they stepped out into the warm sunshine.

'And it's the best thing we've ever done.' He bent down for another kiss, creating a cheer from the onlookers sitting in the piazza.

Soon they were whisked off to a deluxe five-star hotel in the heart of Rome. Its rooftop restaurant with unrivalled views of the entire city proved the ideal venue for the reception. There the newlyweds and parents sat, eating a delicious wedding breakfast, toasting futures and basking in happiness.

As twilight set in, Dylan and Flora stood in each other's

arms admiring the spectacular view before them. St Peter's Basilica lit up majestically in the background.

'It's amazing, isn't it?' Flora remarked in wonder.

'It is. No wonder it's called the eternal city.' Seeing Flora frown he explained, 'Because the Romans considered it so great, it could go on forever.'

'Ah, I see.'

Dylan held her closer to him. *Just like my love for you,* he thought.

'Let's take a picture.' Flora reached for her phone on the table. Her parents had left, leaving them alone to enjoy their wedding night together. She held it out and captured the pair of them with the wonderful backdrop.

'Send it to everyone. Let them know we're married,' said Dylan.

'Yeah, let's.' Flora laughed as she shared the photo and the caption, *"Just got hitched!"*

Dylan chuckled. 'Now let the fun begin.'

Tobias was the first to open the message.

'What the…' His eyes widened in shock.

'What?' said Megan, scurrying over to see his phone.

'It's Dylan and Flora – they've got married,' he replied still staring at the picture of his mate looking relaxed, wearing a slight smirk and a twinkle in his eye.

'Oh my God!' gasped Megan. 'Oh, don't they look lovely.' She took in Flora's pretty, sun-kissed face and her blonde waves entwined with gypsophila. They both looked utterly in love. Megan dipped her head closer. 'They're in Rome. Look at the background view.'

'So they are,' replied Tobias. 'The sly old dog never mentioned any of this.'

And so it went on throughout the evening, as family and friends learnt of the happy news.

Dylan and Flora's phones buzzed with messages from well-wishers, but they would all have to wait until morning before being opened. For the bride and groom lay in bed, after passionate lovemaking, in each other's arms, sound asleep.

53

Finula heard Marcus end the conversation on his phone. Excellent timing – their evening meal was just about ready. Entering the kitchen Marcus smelt the lasagne and garlic bread and his stomach gave a grumble. He hadn't eaten since 11am that morning and had been tucked away, busy working in the studio down in the cellar. Finula, knowing he had a deadline to meet, had let him get on with the final touches of the documentary. Now, at last, it looked like he and his co-editor had finally reached the end of the project.

'Hmm, this smells delicious, Finula.' Marcus pulled out a chair and sat readily at the kitchen table and poured them both a glass of red wine.

'Was that the BBC on the phone?'

'It was. I've confirmed the documentary's complete and they've given me the date.'

'You mean when it's to be shown on TV?' Finula's voice was lit with excitement.

'Yep. The 1st of October.'

'Oh, I can't wait to see it!' Finula placed two steaming-hot plates of lasagne on the table and sat opposite him. She picked up her glass. 'Here's to the documentary.' They clinked glasses. Despite his wife's enthusiasm, there was a part of him that couldn't let go. That niggling sense of foreboding wouldn't disappear. Whilst he knew the documentary had been produced to a very high standard, it was the content that worried him. His *personal* family history was going to be the catalyst of its success; and with that came the inevitable exposure. In his heart of hearts, he wanted to stay as he was: Marcus Devlin, award-winning producer. His private life had been just that, private. He had lived a blessed life, nestled in the Shropshire hills, appreciating the peace and tranquillity. Converting his cellar into a high-spec studio meant he was still able to operate from home, in between visits to London.

All that could change. Once the media got wind of his ancestry, they'd plague him, just like they had his brothers, Tobias in particular. His mam's history would be dug up and exposed, for all to see and judge. Thank God she wasn't here to experience it – she'd never have coped with the press and unwanted attention. He wasn't sure he could. His imagination ran riot. He envisaged a team of reporters camping outside his house. He looked at Finula sipping her wine nonchalantly. How would she manage with the sudden intrusion?

A dark dread began to simmer inside him. Should he ever have agreed to the interview? But the truth would out in any event and it was the best solution to put the family's spin on it first. His mind then pictured being shadowed, never being able to leave his front door without a microphone being shoved in his face, or a car following behind him. At least Tobias and Sebastian had a bloody great fortress to hide in, with security to boot. What did he have? A humble cottage on a hillside, where any number of people could get at them. He was totally uncovered.

He glanced out of the kitchen window to the garden. Only a small, stone wall separated them from the surrounding countryside. Anyone could easily see in, especially with a long-lens camera. The more he contemplated it, the more anxious he became. Suddenly his appetite left him. Finula, sensing his mood, stopped eating.

'You OK, Marcus?' He looked into her concerned face.

'Finula, I think we should go to Treweham when the documentary's aired.'

'Good idea, let's all watch it together,' she agreed smiling, not fully picking up on his reservations.

'I also think we should stay with Tobias and Sebastian at Treweham Hall.' He wanted a piece of that security, which meant not staying at The Templar.

'Yeah fine.' She shrugged, thinking it was only natural he should want to stay with his brothers. 'I suppose Dad will have moved out of The Templar by then anyway.' Marcus eyed her again. She really didn't have any idea what was going to hit them. He remembered how carefree and happy they'd been on their honeymoon and so wished it could stay that way. Maybe that was the answer – to live in Ireland? But why should they have to run away? And he doubted Finula would want to be so far away from her dad. Hopefully, once the revelation had settled, he'd be left in peace and could carry on as normal, although a persistent uncertainty wouldn't let him believe that.

He was going to talk to Tobias. He'd be able to advise him; after all, he'd been chased by the pack hounds most of his life. How he wished he could turn back the clock. But then, he'd never have met Finula, and gazing at this sexy redhead before him he retracted the thought.

'Sure you're OK?' she asked again.

'Yeah, just tired.'

'Well, you've finished the documentary now.' She smiled. 'It's time to sit back and relax.'

He gave a tight smile. If only.

54

Christie sat in the corridor outside the bank manager's office. It was just as she'd remembered: pale grey walls, pale grey carpet and pale grey seats. Even the staff looked pale and grey. How depressing. This wasn't doing much for her mood. The last time she'd been here, Stephen sat next to her, full of interest, just like her, both wanting to hear the news that their dream could at last become a reality. Only it had been her dream. Not Stephen's. Even now, Christie found it difficult to believe how her husband had abandoned her so spectacularly. It was bad enough having to cope with managing The Templar alone, but for him to have got another woman pregnant too? Having a baby had been the one thing that Christie had so badly wanted. It was a double hit, a real smack in the face.

And so here she was, forced to ask for more money, on top of the already hefty loan, in an attempt to pay Stephen off. How did the guy sleep at night? She certainly didn't. Last night had seen her toss and turn with worry, fretting about today and what she must face. Daniel had been a brick when she'd told him. He too had read Stephan's letter and looked at her solemnly. Christie had told him the kind of money she had to raise to get Stephen's name off The

Templar deeds. Daniel's wince hadn't exactly filled her with confidence.

She glanced at the sign on the bank manager's door, which read "Mr Jolly", and nearly laughed out loud at the irony. Was Mr Happy next door? She doubted it. That said, Mr Jolly had given them the answer they'd both wanted before. He'd read their financial plans, agreed with their cash flow forecasts and approved the investment. Job done. It was music to their ears! Would it be this time? Christie doubted that.

'Mrs Newbury?' A lady with long, sandy-coloured hair in a powder blue suit appeared from behind the door. Christie sat up surprised.

'Yes?'

'This way please.' She smiled. 'I'm ready for you now.'

'Oh, right. It's not Mr Jolly I'm seeing then?' she asked, whilst entering the office.

'I'm the new manager – Mrs Wright. Mr Jolly left last week.'

'Oh, I see.'

'Sorry, the name on the door's being changed shortly,' she explained, then looked at the set of papers in front of her. She sat back and rubbed her hands together. 'So, let's talk about your proposal.'

Christie took a deep breath and outlined everything. Absolutely everything. Her emotions had got the better of her and she gave it all. The phrase "too much information" rang in her ears, screamed in fact, but she was past caring. It felt more like a counselling session than a bank manager's appointment, as Christie unleashed all the pent-up hurt and anxiety building up inside. Mrs Wright just sat there unperturbed, nodding calmly in all the right places.

'So you see, I'm... desperate,' Christie finished somewhat lamely and looked to Mrs Wright for all the answers.

After a moment's pause she sat forward. 'Christie, me giving you what you're asking for would lead to desperation. Believe me—'

'But—' interrupted Christie.

'No, please hear me out.' The manager held her hand up. 'I can't agree to extend your loan, not in the current climate. You can't do this alone, Christie, you need a business partner, someone who has the money to pay him off.'

'There is no one,' Christie replied quietly.

'No one who you know as yet. Put the feelers out, someone out there could easily see The Templar as a thriving business and be willing to invest.'

Christie sat listening. Originally, she had thought selling The Templar would mean her having to leave too, but this way meant it was more a case of finding a business partner. She looked up into Mrs Wright's face.

'How long have I got... you know to find someone?'

'As far as the bank's concerned, there's no problem as such. It's more a matter of how heavily your husband is going to lean on you. In the eyes of the law he owns half the pub, and can push for a sale if not bought out.'

All this was only confirming what Christie knew in the depths of her troubled mind. Hearing it out loud was giving her clarity and a clearer vision.

'But what if The Templar takes ages to sell?' Like dragging your feet kind of ages. Well she'd be the one who was expected to oversee the sale wouldn't she? She couldn't envisage Stephen donating the time with a new baby.

Mrs Wright gave a sardonic smile. 'That would be unfortunate, for your husband.'

'But it could happen. I mean, I couldn't help it if The Templar didn't get any takers.'

Mrs Wright's lips twitched slightly. 'Like I said, it would be unfortunate.'

55

Daniel was shattered, but happy. All the team had done a tremendous job and Keeper's Cottage was almost complete. The rooms were bare, empty blank canvases for him to make his mark on. The kitchen and the main bathroom were fully fitted and tiled. The interior design needed concentrating on: choosing colour schemes, light fittings, blinds and rugs. Daniel didn't want carpets; instead he would varnish the wooden floorboards for a real country feel.

Before he went ahead and ordered all his soft furnishings, Daniel wanted a second opinion. He thought about bringing Christie here and discussing what he had in mind. She had already liked his choice of kitchen with its thick oak units, brass handles and granite worktops, its butler sink and big silver taps. Christie had also loved the roll-top bath and green Victorian tiles in the bathroom. It pleased him that they shared similar tastes.

The only hesitation he did have in bringing her here, to show off his new home, was her sudden predicament. That swine of a husband had well and truly landed her in it. Then, on reflection, he did see his point of view as a father, and wanting to provide for his family. Even so, it was leaving Christie in deep water. The Templar was her life, her ultimate ambition, and he couldn't bear to see her leave Treweham. The very thought dampened his good mood slightly.

Forcing himself to stay positive, he went upstairs and into the master bedroom. It was a large room with a big sash window overlooking the back garden. His outbuilding, which would soon be his studio, was fully visible now. He couldn't wait to get cracking on that and finally have an ideal workspace. He intended to install bi-folding doors to maximise the light and create a sense of space. He was also going to install a wood burner to keep it warm and dry.

Daniel envisaged meeting clients in his studio and was keen to set a professional impression. He was looking forward to really building up his clientele, and working closely with Tobias as he had had opened up more business opportunities. Tobias had been impressed with Daniel's work and having his recommendation wouldn't do him any harm.

His next project was transforming an old warehouse into a block of swish apartments. Originally, he had considered actually buying one of the apartments himself. At the time the idea seemed to have ticked a lot of boxes: good location, near his house where Jenna and Emily lived and low maintenance. How things had changed. Just then, as if on cue, his mobile phone rang.

'Hello.'

'Hello, Mr James, it's Hepworth and Hayes estate agents here. I'm ringing to let you know that we have a viewer for your house.'

'Oh, right.'

'He seems quite keen and has asked if he can see it today.'

'I can't make today.'

'How about tomorrow?' Daniel paused. He could make the trip back and show some stranger round his old house, but did he want to? Somehow the thought of wandering through the home that he, Emily and Jenna had once been happy in didn't appeal to him. It was like dragging himself back into the past and reopening old wounds. He suddenly realised that it would never, in fact, be a good time to step foot inside that house again.

'Actually, it might be better if you could show him round. I'm a bit tied up here.'

'Yes, that's no problem. Like I said Mr...' She looked at her notes. 'Jones is keen, so we'll probably arrange a viewing later today.' The name rang like a death knell inside Daniel.

'What's his first name?' he asked flatly.

'Err... Michael. Is there a problem?' If she'd answered John or JonJo, there most definitely would have been, but maybe he was being a touch paranoid. And anyway, he very much doubted that tosser could afford a four-bedroom detached house with an acre of garden. Not unless he'd won the lottery – and had all charges dropped. 'Mr James? Are you still there?' The estate agent sounded puzzled.

'Yes, sorry, that's fine. Show Mr Jones round.'

'I'll let you know straight away if he makes an offer.'

'Good. Thanks. Bye.' He hung up. He'd gone from feeling euphoric to dejected. Would it always be like this? Would the past constantly taunt and take over him? He had contemplated further counselling sessions, but then dismissed the idea, thinking he was on the mend. Being so busy with Keeper's Cottage, looking after Emily and seeing Christie had kept him cheerfully occupied. Then, just when he was buoyant, back came the dark, depressing mood that threatened to swamp him. It was early days, he told himself, just like his parents had said. He and Emily had been through a lot and it was going to take time. On impulse he pressed Christie's number. He had a need to hear her voice. She'd told him about her appointment and he'd been thinking of her.

'Hi,' she called through the loudspeaker. She was driving home from the bank.

'Hi, how did it go?' he asked tentatively.

'No go, I'm afraid.' She sounded tired and fed up. 'The bank manager was nice enough, but wouldn't lend me any more. I'm not surprised to be honest,' she admitted in defeat. Neither was Daniel, but he didn't like to say.

'Listen, when you get back I'll take you out for dinner,' he said attempting to cheer her up.

'Thanks, but I'm not that hungry.'

'Oh, I see.'

'Where are you?'

'At Keeper's Cottage. It's almost finished.' He couldn't disguise the glee in his voice.

'I'll meet you there. I'd love to see it.'

'Really?'

'Of course!' Christie laughed. Despite obviously feeling low, she sounded genuinely pleased for him. 'I'll be there in half an hour.'

Once Christie had arrived, Daniel was bursting to show her round. He could hardly contain himself and Christie couldn't help but be infected by his excitement. The place was as wonderful as she'd imagined. Daniel's flair for design was brilliant, making the most of the space, keeping it airy and bright with skylights and an open-plan design.

'It's fabulous, Daniel, it really is,' she said in awe, gazing round the kitchen.

'Thanks. I just wish, you know…'

'What?' She turned to look at him.

'That things were good for you too.' He looked into her eyes. They looked a little red and swollen. Had she been crying? A lump formed in his throat.

'I may have to sell The Templar.' Her voice cracked as she spoke.

'Oh, Christie, come here.' He pulled her into him and hugged her close. Why did life have to be so hard?

56

'Congratulations!' cheered all the staff at Delany's Racing Yard. Flora and Dylan had laughed when stepping out of their Range Rover onto the yard with bunting swooping across the stables. Flora was touched that they'd made such an effort to celebrate them getting married.

'Oh thanks!' she said, then laughed again when seeing Phoenix had even been dressed up with a pink sash across his body and a balloon saying *"Just married"* tied to his saddle. Josh was at the ready with the champagne and flutes were handed out. A loud cheer sounded when the cork shot out.

'To Dylan and Flora!' he shouted and all joined in.

Tobias and Megan pulled into the yard.

'Well, you're a dark horse, Delany,' said Tobias as they approached them all. He and Dylan shook hands, whilst Megan hugged Flora.

'Congratulations. Flora, you looked absolutely lovely.' She beamed.

'Thanks,' she replied, pouring them both a glass of champagne.

'And in Rome, how romantic!' gushed Megan, turning to a grinning Dylan.

'Well you know me, Megan, ever the Romeo,' he teases,

then quickly looked at Flora. 'Only with Flora, of course.' That made everyone laugh.

Next to arrive were Gary and Tracy Belcher. The yard staff had told them too of the celebratory welcome. Tracy ran over to Flora.

'We couldn't believe it when we saw your photo!' She smiled, giving her a quick squeeze. Gary thumped Dylan heartily on the back, nearly knocking him over.

'Well done, mate.'

'Thanks, Gary,' replied Dylan, regaining balance.

'Oh look at Phoenix.' Tracy pointed to the horse, which they jointly owned.

'I know.' Flora couldn't wait any longer – she had to go over to him. Patting his side, she whispered gently to him. 'Hello, old boy, how are you?' Phoenix nudged his face into her shoulder and neighed. His nostrils flared a little. Something was different about her. Flora sensed his intuition. 'I can't ride you, Phoenix, not for a while.' She spoke quietly, stroking his mane. She looked into his beautiful, brown eyes. They seemed to be questioning. 'But you're still my number-one boy.' She kissed his nose.

Dylan had clocked her. He had been anxious about how Flora would be with Phoenix and hoped that she wouldn't ride him whilst pregnant. Not wanting to lay the law down, he had quietly waited to see how she would react when seeing Phoenix on returning from Rome. Looking at her now, he was pleased she hadn't climbed onto his saddle. A feeling of relief swept through him.

'I swear she thinks more of that horse than me,' he joked, nodding his head towards them.

'Nonsense,' said Megan giggling, 'she adores you.'

'I adore her,' he replied, staring at his wife.

Tobias caught his expression of complete contentment and felt pleased for his friend. He could hardly believe it; Dylan Delany, the most notorious of his friends, had finally settled down. His previous comment was so true, Dylan had been a Romeo, making him and Seamus Fox, their close friend since childhood, look like saints in comparison; and now look, Dylan was married, just like the rest of them. He'd never seen him so happy.

57

'It's good. Very good. As expected,' said the bigwig from the BBC sat opposite Marcus. He'd been called to see the chief executive producer in London to discuss the documentary being aired in the autumn. Marcus nodded and averted his gaze. He always found praise difficult to take. 'Must admit though, the revelation you dropped was a bit of a shocker,' he continued with a wry smile.

Marcus remained silent. He knew to expect this kind of reaction and was dreading it. After a short silence, feeling obliged to say something he spoke. 'Yes, it came as a shock to me too when I was told.'

'Hmm, by your mother—'

'Yes, by my mam,' interrupted Marcus with force. He wasn't prepared to talk about her, not in this situation, here with a virtual stranger.

'Yet there's only one reference to her in the documentary,' he pressed, clearly not picking up on the vibe Marcus had sent. 'Could you not have elaborated a little more, shown photographs of her and you in your childhood?'

'No. Absolutely not.'

The chief executive's head turned sharply, finally getting

his drift. He stared at Marcus' defiant face, knowing any suggestions he may have had would be non-negotiable.

'Right,' he replied, realising when he was beaten. He'd been warned about Marcus Devlin and what a prickly fellow he could be. Still, if tolerating a temperamental, obstinate TV producer meant obtaining a first-class documentary into the bargain, then so be it; because this documentary was red-hot. A real show stopper. The ratings would soar; he was totally convinced. It had everything, not just the twee country setting, but the rich and varied characters within the idyllic lifestyle, making it not so twee and idyllic. It had stark contrast, depicting the homeless and poor families' plight living off the streets and food banks. It contained age-old traditions, which hinted to a darker, mysterious side of village life; vendettas between residents, rivalry between the classes, and ultimately the bombshell announcing the documentary's own producer was in fact the illegitimate son of the late Lord of the Manor.

It didn't get much better than that. No, putting up with an awkward young man like Marcus Devlin was well worth it. He had talent and that's all that concerned him. The last thing he wanted was this gifted chap to take his work elsewhere. Who knows what else he could come up with? One thing *did* concern him, or at least baffled him though. Shifting in his chair he coughed and stared directly at Marcus. Sensing his unease, Marcus returned the stare.

'What?' he asked bluntly.

'Marcus, have you considered how this is going to affect you?'

Had he ever. Truth be told, he hadn't thought about much else lately. To the point where he had contacted Tobias to voice them. They'd both agreed that he and Finula staying at Treweham Hall for the foreseeable future was the most sensible course of action.

'Yes, I have,' he answered, still looking him in the eye. Well, what was he to do about it now? The documentary had been made, submitted and was being aired in a few short months. What options did he have but to press on and brace himself for the media onslaught?

'And... you're quite happy about the intrusion this will inevitably cause?' The chief executive frowned. It perplexed him, how a private, introverted man like Marcus Devlin notoriously was, would agree to disclose such personal details. It didn't add up. Marcus intrigued him; he wasn't the norm.

'No, I'm not happy about the attention this will bring.'

'Then why did you reveal your parentage?' he shot back, getting a touch tired of Marcus' manner.

'Because it makes good TV.'

'At the cost of having your life changed so dramatically?' he replied incredulously. Marcus too, was growing a little impatient at this fecker who was digging far too deep for his liking. The honest answer to his question would be that it had been revenge originally that had driven him to these lengths, so intent had he been to blacken the Cavendish-Blake name. Marcus believed his mam had been cast away, pregnant and shamed, only to learn that in fact that hadn't been the case. Far from it. Diaries of the late Lord Cavendish-Blake proved that he had been totally oblivious of his firstborn son. His mam had bolted and fled to Ireland in despair.

Once the truth was out, Marcus' revenge had died, along

with any plans to discredit what had since become his family. But he was damned if he was telling all this to the man sat opposite him – bigwig or not.

'I know what to expect. I'm prepared.' He gave a cool look. 'Now, if that completes everything, I've a train to catch.' He stood up.

The chief executive slowly looked him up and down. Who did he think he was? A skilful TV producer who had just made him an explosive piece of viewing, he reminded himself. 'Yes, thank you, Marcus.' He managed a rigid smile, while standing to shake hands. 'All the best.'

Marcus gave a curt nod and strode out, never looking back.

58

'Good news, Mr James, an offer's been made,' the estate agent trilled.

'The asking price?' replied Daniel.

'Err... not quite.'

'How much has he offered?'

'Three eighty.'

'No. I want the full four hundred,' he stated flatly. A few weeks ago he'd have snapped the offer up, but not now. An idea was forming in his mind, which meant he'd need every penny available. There was a brief pause; obviously his tone had surprised the estate agent, who had been led to believe his client had wanted a quick sale.

'Right... I'll get back to Mr Jones and let him know.'

'Yes. Any other viewers?'

'Not yet, but it's appearing in the centre pages of our property post as you directed.'

'Good. Bye.' Daniel hung up. He didn't intend to be quite so abrupt, but he was on a roll to get things going. Since having his idea, he'd become focused. Once Daniel set his mind on something there was no room for manoeuvring, he had to have total control and see it through. It was this level of determination that had made his business the success it was. Having the house valued had made him realise just what he had been prepared to sacrifice for Jenna. It had put matters into a sharper focus and made him sit up. There had been every chance of Jenna returning to live in that property, he was convinced; and if that JonJo had followed her, there they would have been, tucked up nicely in *his* house, again.

His blood boiled. How had he not seen it earlier? His mind cast back to the last time he'd been in there, JonJo's DVDs scattered on the living room floor, his used razor on the bathroom windowsill, the unmade double bed. The very same bed he and Jenna had bought together, a king-size sleigh bed. His hand curled into a fist. Potentially, he could have provided them both with a roof over their heads until Emily was eighteen. It beggared belief.

Events had changed his outlook. Obviously he'd never been happy about JonJo living with Emily, let alone in his own property, but he'd seen it as a means to an end. At least it meant that Emily would still be near to him. Daniel had been prepared to subsidise them, in order to keep Emily close by. But now it had all moved on. Jenna was gone. His eyes filled. He wasn't sure what to feel anymore: hurt, anger or sorrow. Probably a mixture of all three he concluded.

It was time to get practical and stop being maudlin about the past. The first thing he needed to do was empty the property. He didn't envisage any of the furniture fitting in well at Keeper's Cottage, and besides he wanted a complete fresh start. He'd be glad to sell the lot, especially that bed. His thoughts were interrupted by his mobile ringing again. It was the estate agents with an update.

'Hello, Mr James. Mr Jones has upped his offer to three eighty-five. He gave the usual reason for not wanting to offer the full asking price, that the house needs redecorating and some money spent on it.' With that he couldn't argue; the property did need a little TLC. Jenna had hardly looked after the place.

'Offer him the furniture, see if that makes any difference,' replied Daniel. With a bit of luck he could be shot of the whole lot and still get the asking price. It was worth a try.

'Will do.'

'Thanks. Bye.'

Within a quarter of an hour, the estate agent rang. Mr Jones had offered a further three thousand, but gave a clear indication three eighty-eight was his final offer. Daniel took it. His instincts told him to accept and be rid of it. Considering what he had paid to build the house, he'd made a very good profit. Plus he wouldn't have all the hassle of clearing it. Job done. Time to move on.

Now he had to concentrate on furnishing Keeper's Cottage, especially Emily's room. He missed her terribly. Although he spoke each day to her and she sounded happy enough at his parents', he wanted her with him, where she belonged. Ever mindful of the start of school term in a couple of weeks, he realised time was of the essence. He didn't fancy another night in the campervan. He felt the need to celebrate selling his house. The workmen had long gone, finishing off the final touches. Now all the rooms had been plastered, the skirting boards and architraves fitted, the doors hung. Keeper's Cottage stood waiting for Daniel to make his mark, to make it his own.

★

Christie had had a busy day. Business had picked up and all the rooms were currently full. Being so busy had left her with very little time to think about a business partner. She had outlined her meeting with the bank manager to Dermot, who had listened carefully. She knew that her days with him were numbered, but couldn't bring herself to actually broach the subject. Christie didn't want to see Dermot go – he was a part of The Templar as much as the fixtures and fittings. But go he must. He couldn't stay indefinitely – that she knew.

The prospect of running The Templar completely solo daunted her slightly. Without the added worry of paying Stephen off, she would probably have seen it as a challenge, but a positive one. Now her mind spun with worries of the future. So different for Daniel. She smiled, recalling his buzz when showing her round Keeper's Cottage. Christie was genuinely pleased for him. He more than most deserved it. As if reading her thoughts, he entered reception.

'Hello there.' Good God those pale blue eyes and dimpled cheeks could brighten anyone up, she thought.

'Hi.' She smiled.

'Busy?'

'Very, we're full.'

Daniel leant over the reception desk seductively. That heavenly sage aroma hit her senses. 'That's a shame. I was going to ask for a bed for the night.' He gave a smouldering look.

Christie yearned for him. It seemed like ages since they'd spent the night together, each wrapped up with the necessities of everyday life. She knew Emily would soon be returning to Treweham, which would occupy him even more. Christie had enjoyed long, relaxing baths in the evening after a hectic day in the pub, but longed for Daniel's warm, firm body lying next to hers. Instead he'd been working flat out, well into the evening until dusk, then collapsing on his camper bed.

Not tonight. Daniel had other ideas. So did Christie – she needed comfort, and not the tea and sympathy kind.

'I'm sure I could fit you in somewhere.' She gave a wink.
'Sounds good to me.' He chuckled. 'How about dinner?'
'Should be OK, we're fully staffed.'
'Great. There's something I want to run past you.'
'Sounds ominous.' She eyed him thoughtfully.
'Nothing to worry about.' He leant over and kissed her lips.

That evening Christie took extra care with her appearance. Wanting to look her best and enjoy the evening, she wore a figure-hugging black dress, which flattered her curves perfectly and rested above her knees, showing off her long, slim legs. The neckline hinted just a glimmer of cleavage, finishing off the job nicely. Applying a small amount of make-up made her eyes shine and gave her a rosy complexion. She assessed her appearance in the full-length mirror. Not bad.

Daniel too was looking pretty hot in his pale jeans, showcasing his firm thighs and white open-necked shirt. Christie couldn't help but notice the heads he turned when entering the bar. She'd put them in the far corner, by the leaded window out of the way. Once they'd ordered and Daniel had poured the wine, he pulled his chair closer and spoke.

'You look beautiful, by the way.' His eyes bored into hers, making her heart start to pound.

'Thank you.' She smiled. Despite trying to stay relaxed, curiosity was burning inside her. She sat patiently waiting for him to continue.

'Christie, I have a proposition.' He gave her a serious look. 'I've sold the house Jenna and Emily lived in.'

'Oh, right.' She was surprised and wondered why he hadn't told her before.

'Which leaves me with a considerable sum of money.'

Christie sat still, listening. All the while her heart continued to pound.

'I'd like to invest it.'

'I see.'

'In The Templar.' Daniel stared at her, waiting for her reaction.

'You mean buy Stephen out?'

'I mean buying a stake in your business and offering him three hundred thousand pounds to see the back of him. I suspect technically he could get more, but would it be enough to tempt him, especially if he could have the money soon and not have to wait for a possible sale?'

Christie chewed her lip in thought. There was so much to consider and this suggestion had taken her unawares.

'Maybe… he did sound desperate.'

'From what you've told me, he's getting a good enough deal.'

Christie nodded in agreement; after all, she had stumped up the bulk of their savings towards The Templar. Daniel was right: to offer Stephen that kind of money was indeed reasonable, but would he see it that way? Unfair as it was, Stephen could easily dig his heels in and hold out for more, even though her money had provided the lion's share.

'His baby's due shortly. He will need the money.' Christie's eyes narrowed in thought. Could a glimpse of light be flickering in this gloom?

'Give it some thought.' He closed his hand over hers.

59

Tobias clipped Edward into the straps of his buggy. 'Come on, Edward, let's go see Uncle Sebastian.' Edward jibber-jabbered in baby talk, then blew a raspberry, making Tobias smile with affection. His son was growing by the day. Megan was right: Edward resembled every inch of him. Already his black, tufty hair was growing and his green eyes sparkled with mischief. He tried to grab his daddy's hair, but Tobias backed off in time. 'Oh no you don't, you little tinker.'

Tobias pushed the buggy through the estate, earning them lots of admiring comments from the staff tending the grounds. Edward lapped the attention up, gurgling and beaming up at all the smiling faces cooing over him. Tobias walked along the footpath past Keeper's Cottage and paused for a moment to inspect the building. Yes, they'd all done an extremely good job there, he thought, taking in the solid, stone cottage with its new wooden sash windows and oak door. Once the outside space was cleared and landscaped, it would look even better.

Tobias continued through the clearing to reach The Folly. The *A Midsummer Night's Dream* production was now drawing to a close, which meant hopefully he'd see more of his brother. He couldn't help but worry about him, knowing Sebastian wouldn't be flattered to hear that. Tobias knelt down and pulled Edward out of his buggy. 'Let's see where he is.' Entering The Folly, all was quiet. Expecting it to be full of the cast and the usual flurry of activity, he carried Edward through to the sitting room where he thought Sebastian would be. He was, fast asleep in the armchair. Tobias walked forward to him. Sebastian slowly opened his eyes. Tobias spoke quietly. 'Hi, stranger, I thought we'd come and pay a visit.'

'Hi.' He sat up and rubbed his eyes. 'I was just catching up on some sleep.'

Tobias looked thoughtfully at his brother. To all intents and purposes he appeared fine, but then, why shouldn't he? Since learning of Sebastian's condition, he'd researched MS and realised it didn't always mean the worst.

'It must take it out of you,' Tobias replied, then quickly added, 'I mean the play, night after night.'

'It does, but it's not every evening and tomorrow's the last performance. To be honest, I'll be glad of a break,' he admitted, stretching languidly.

'I'll bet.'

'And how's my favourite nephew?' said Sebastian, reaching out to hold him. Edward giggled with glee at being held by him. 'Aren't you the most adorable little chap?' He pressed his cheek against Edward's and kissed his forehead. Edward gurgled and chatted back with a gummy smile. Tobias sat in the armchair opposite them.

'Can I ask you something, Sebastian?'

'Yes, of course,' he replied never taking his eyes off Edward wriggling in his arms.

'How are you really feeling?'

Sebastian turned to face him now. 'Apart from feeling tired, I'm OK. I went to see the consultant last week and he seems happy enough with me.'

'What did he do?'

'He examined me, to see if there are any differences, but everything's the same – no change apart from the limp.'

Tobias nodded. 'So you're still not on any medication?'

'No. Another brain scan would indicate any further lesions, but up to now I don't warrant one.'

Tobias sat and listened. There was a long pause. What could he say?

Sebastian, sensing his unease spoke gently. 'Listen, Tobias, I don't want you to worry.'

'Easier said than done,' he replied. His eyes started to fill.

'Please, Tobias, don't.'

'Sorry.' He coughed. Then changed the subject. 'Marcus and Finula will be staying at The Hall, for the documentary.'

'Good, it'll be great having him around.' Sebastian smiled, looking forward to seeing his eldest brother.

'Yes. He's anxious about the reaction to the documentary.'

'Don't blame him.'

'And the intrusion it'll bring.'

'Welcome to our world,' Sebastian replied dryly. He was still smarting over the rather nasty review he'd been given weeks ago. Like most actors, he took any criticism to heart.

'I think it makes sense, him being here, with us.'

'So do I – at least here we can lock the gates and hide away with some privacy. What protection has he got in Shropshire?'

'Exactly. None.'

'It's what Father would have wanted.'

Tobias turned his head sharply. Yes, he thought, it's what their father *would* have wanted: all his sons together, regardless of illegitimacy. Tobias was left in deep thought. For very different reasons, he felt compelled to protect both his brothers. The feeling stayed with him as he strolled back to The Hall. Edward was asleep in his buggy, looking blissfully peaceful. The need to protect increased. The seedling of an idea was beginning to take root.

60

Christie opened the letter addressed to her with trepidation. It looked official and she was dreading it being from Stephen's solicitors, pushing her for some financial indication. To her relief, it was from the county court, stating that her decree nisi would be announced in two weeks' time. Good, at least that side of things was ticking along nicely. The sooner she was divorced from Stephen the better. Would he remarry Sophie straight away? So what if he did? Christie knew that there had to be some sort of arrangement regarding money before the decree absolute was given. Even more reason why Stephen would start to pile on the pressure. She could almost feel the net closing in on her.

Once again she thought of all the hard work she had poured into The Templar. The bedrooms were a triumph, thanks to Daniel. It was hardly surprising that they were full again. Looking back over the books from last year told Christie The Templar had never been so full, apart from when Lord Cavendish-Blake had married and the whole village was packed with reporters and journalists. Christie knew instinctively the place could be a gold mine when she first clapped eyes on it. She immediately saw The

Templar's potential. Stephen had agreed, seeing her vision and being swept along with her enthusiasm.

How things had changed, and in such a relatively short space of time, thought Christie as she glanced down again at the letter. It felt strange seeing her marriage dissolving in black and white on paper. It made it legal. This really was the end.

'This came today.' The ripped envelope containing a letter was plonked in front of him.

'You opened my mail?' Stephen asked incredulously.

'Yeah, why not?'

'Because, Sophie, it was addressed to *me*.'

'So, it concerns me too,' she batted back. 'Look, there's my name.' A podgy finger pointed to the title "co-respondent" where her name did indeed appear.

'That's not the point. Don't open my mail again,' he replied through gritted teeth.

'Sor-ry,' she said with sarcasm. 'Good news though isn't it, about the nisi coming through soon?'

Stephen remained silent. Was it? His eyes moved sideways and assessed her. Sophie was heavily pregnant now. Being small made her look even bigger and swollen. Her ankles, wrists and face were bloated. She walked slowly, with great effort, and she constantly panted. His eyes moved down to her huge stomach and a part of him feared she'd never be able to push it out. *Him* out. He quickly corrected his thoughts. His son. This was why he was sat here, with this letter in his hand.

Looking at Sophie though, his mind couldn't stop

comparing her to Christie's svelte body. How he missed that; a twitch in his trousers made him shift guiltily. But it wasn't just physical, Stephen dully realized. Christie was practical, excellent at managing money, well at managing anything really. She had been the "sensible" one between them, leaving him to act the lad with his mates while she sorted everything out. How it had all changed.

'I said, it's good news isn't it?'

'Hmm.' He pretended to read the letter in concentration.

'We'll have to start planning our wedding.'

Stephen looked up and blinked. 'Pardon?'

'Well, once your divorce comes through, you'll be free to marry.' A puffy, pale face stared at him.

'I'm not sure we'll be able to afford it.'

'I thought you said you'll get a decent settlement?' The alarm in her voice was evident. She glared at him accusingly.

'Yes... but—'

'When's it coming?' she interrupted with force. What had happened to that sweet, caring girl he used to know? Where had she disappeared to and more to the point, who was this... this demanding, imposing woman who had replaced her? Memories of how she had enticed him with her beguiling looks, offered comfort and support when things hadn't been great with Christie seemed just a blur now.

At first he had been more than happy to confide in her, found himself unwinding at work, when at home he'd felt pressured by Christie's expectations. Now he could see that his wife had ambition and drive. Not like Sophie, who had made it clear, in no uncertain terms, she was going to be a "stay-at-home mum". The chances of her even working part-time to help tide them over were remote.

He couldn't picture being in this position with Christie. Far from it. She would be horrified at his debts that were racking up. They didn't seem to worry Sophie though; she was adding to them by the day. Every evening on his return from work, she'd be showing him the latest "can't do without" item.

'Do we really need to buy these clothes yet? They're aged twelve months.'

'He'll be in them before we know it.' She'd smiled, patting her bump. Stephen shook his head in despair. Was there no stopping her? In the end he'd retrieved his credit cards. Sophie couldn't be trusted to use them sensibly. On doing so, he suddenly realised how Christie must have felt. He too, had spent money foolishly, selfishly even. At least Sophie had been buying for their baby.

Often he would think of Christie, imagining her there in her pub, tucked away in the Cotswolds. He could have been there too, running The Templar and making it a thriving success, coining it in, when instead…

'I said, when's the money coming?' Sophie's loud voice made him jump. He closed his eyes.

'Soon.'

'It better, 'cos there's no way my baby is doing without.'

He opened his eyelids to find her face shoved in his. His son, he reminded himself, he had to think of him.

61

'So, ladies and gentlemen, that concludes our tour of Treweham Hall. Please feel free to take refreshments in the tearoom and thank you for visiting.' A small round of applause followed. Megan gave a smile and bowed her head in thanks. Thank God that was over. The last tour of the summer season couldn't come quick enough for her. It had been hard work having to balance being a tour guide and see to a baby. Tobias had been right, perhaps she had been too quick to return to work, but she'd been desperate to get back into a routine and she'd loved giving the tours last year. Now all she wanted was to relax with a cup of tea and put her feet up. She hoped Edward was ready for his afternoon nap. Climbing the stairs and heading towards their private quarters, she heard Tobias talking to a man from the maintenance team in the passageway.

'Yes, Sir, they could easily be opened up and renovated.'

Tobias was pointing to two open doors at the bottom end of the corridor. 'Good, then I want to start work immediately.'

'Yes, Sir.'

'But not a word of this to Dowager Cavendish-Blake.'

'Of course, Sir, we'll be discreet.'

Tobias turned to see Megan approaching and smiled widely. 'All done?' He opened his arm out and pulled her into his side.

'Yes. I'm ready for a sit-down. Is Edward asleep?'

'I left him with Mother – he'll be fine. Come on, let's have a drink.' They entered their drawing room and Tobias poured himself a brandy. 'You eaten yet?' Megan shook her head. Tobias rang down to the kitchen and ordered tea and sandwiches. Megan was still getting used to being waited on, but when feeling as drained as she did, she was glad of the help.

'What were you discussing in the corridor?' she asked.

'I'm having the rest of the wing restored.'

Megan frowned. Surely they had enough room. Tobias read her thoughts. 'Not for us.'

'Then who?' she asked surprised.

'I want Marcus and Finula to have a base here.' He slung back his drink.

It did make sense for Marcus to have his own rooms at The Hall; after all, it was his family home too.

Tobias came and sat next to her. 'Megan, you remember the commotion our wedding caused?' His voice was gentle, as if pre-warning her.

'Do I ever,' she sighed. It had been one of the most traumatic times of her life. Nothing could have prepared her for the level of invasion they had encountered.

'It's going to happen again, Megan.' He took her hand and kissed her lips. 'But this time it's Marcus who's coming under the cosh. As soon as the documentary announces his parentage, they'll be back.'

'You mean the media?'

'Yes, just like the wedding. Treweham will be crawling with reporters. I'm upping security. Marcus and Finula can't stay in Shropshire alone.'

Megan digested the information. Part of her began to feel afraid. 'Edward—'

'Edward will be fine,' he cut in immediately. The last thing he wanted was his wife afraid in her own home. 'We may have to be extra vigilant. At least the tours are over now.' Tobias wouldn't have allowed them to run whilst the documentary was aired. He was also glad The Folly Players had now finished their production. He hated having to live like this, like they were prisoners. However, experience told him that time would pass and they would soon become yesterday's news.

He looked into Megan's anxious face and was keen to comfort her. Sometimes he almost felt guilty marrying her into his family and subjecting her to this attention. 'Hey—' he lifted her chin '—there's no need to worry.' He kissed her again.

She wrapped her arms round him, as if needing reassurance. She ran her hands through his hair and the kiss deepened. A fire sparked inside and he could feel a need surge through him. His fingers slowly pulled loose the fastening on her wraparound dress, to reveal her shapely body. A sharp intake of breath left him as his eyes devoured her full bosom bursting out of white lace cups. He groaned as he dipped his head to taste them, his tongue flicking at the rose pink nipples.

'Tobias,' Megan groaned, as if losing herself. She ran her hands up his shirt and over his back. He pressed hard against her, wanting more, but knowing their lunch would soon be arriving. To hell with it – urgently he unzipped his jeans and eased himself out. 'Tobias... we can't,' whispered Megan faintly.

'Oh yes we can.' His voice was thick with lust as he gently edged down her lace knickers. Within moments he was inside her. Megan clutched his shoulders as his body thrust further into her in rapid movements. It was hot, fast and exciting, making him climax quickly.

Megan heard footsteps on the landing and quickly rewrapped her dress as Tobias adjusted his attire. Slightly out of breath he turned to the young girl carrying the tray. 'Just leave it on the table, thanks.'

'Certainly, Sir.' She put it down and left the room.

'That was close,' Megan hissed, face flushed. Tobias winked and began pouring the tea.

62

Flora opened the package with excitement. This was the wedding album that she had been expecting. The wedding planners in Italy had promised a swift delivery and Flora couldn't wait to see the photographs of their special day. She gasped at the cream leather album with their names written in gold across the cover. Turning the first page she beamed with delight at seeing herself and Dylan on the steps of St Lawrence at Lucina – she looking a tad nervous, Dylan looking completely composed, not to mention devastatingly handsome. He smiled lazily into the camera like a true pro. But then, he was used to cameras flashing and snapping at him.

Flora's mind spun back to when she had first met him, in the stables on the Treweham Hall estate, where she had worked. It seemed like she'd known him forever now, but in fact it had only been a year and a half since he had first introduced himself with his winning smile, which Flora had completely fallen for. The moment she had looked into those blue, mesmerising eyes she had been smitten. Flora had obviously known who he was. Dylan Delany had been her idol since pony club. She had applied to be a groom at Treweham Hall in the hope of meeting him. Everybody knew he was Tobias Cavendish-Blake's friend.

When she did actually stumble across him, he had proved to be everything she had fantasised about. For Flora, it had been love at first sight. For Dylan, it had taken a little longer. He'd soon realised where his loyalties lay after straying elsewhere, albeit in a drunken stupor, not to mention the old flame who had hovered too close for Flora's liking. Loyalty had been new to Dylan, never having experienced it before. Up until meeting Flora, he had woven in and out of relationships, ducking and diving any form of commitment.

Now Flora knew he couldn't envisage life without her. Flora understood him, understood his world, unlike any of his previous girlfriends. She was a horsewoman and helped him run his training yard with ease and efficiency. In a nutshell, Flora was his perfect match. And now look at them, thought Flora as she turned the pages of the wedding album. Large, clear images of them by the altar exchanging marriage vows, walking hand in hand down the aisle as husband and wife, in the piazza San Lorenzo square laughing with the locals, dining with her parents in the rooftop restaurant; but the picture that still stole Flora's heart had to be the selfie, which she had taken of the two of them on the balcony with the eternal city behind. That defined them. That was the photo telling everyone they had "just got hitched". Her thoughts were interrupted by her mobile ringing.

'Hi, you OK?' Dylan asked with concern. She'd been due at the yard over an hour ago.

'Yeah, fine. The wedding album's just arrived.'

'Ah, I see – bring it with you.'

'Will do, the pictures are fantastic,' she gushed.

'Well, what do you expect, with a fantastic-looking husband?' he replied with humour.

'I'm in them too,' she replied grinning. 'See you in a minute.' She shook her head at hearing him laugh down the phone. Then she glanced down at her tiny bump, which was beginning to show. Yes, a lot had happened since meeting Dylan Delany, her heart-throb, in the stables that day.

63

Entering their new home, Emily couldn't contain herself. Daniel smiled with real satisfaction at his little girl's delight. It was so good to see her happy and excited.

'Daddy!' she squealed as she ran into her new bedroom. It was a lot larger than her last one, but still decorated in her favourite ice pink, which she had chosen. The bed crown canopy hanging above her pink, quilted bed looked very princess-like, making Emily jump up and down.

'Do you like it?' he asked, folding his arms, sitting on the windowsill.

'Yes, yes, yes!' she claimed, her eyes darting round the room, taking it all in; a pretty kidney-shaped dressing table surrounded with pink gingham fabric, a pine wardrobe, book case and toy box. The wooden floorboards matched the rest of the house, with a large pink rug in the middle. A lump formed in Daniel's throat at seeing his daughter's reaction. She deserved this.

'What about all the other rooms?' He laughed. Emily had rushed straight to her bedroom and hardly taken any notice.

'It's all nice, Daddy.' She beamed, then asked, 'What about my old bedroom?' Daniel paused. The question had taken him unawares, however innocently asked.

'Emily, we won't be going back there. This is our new home now.' He looked at her carefully, gauging her response.

She looked out of the window, then back at him. 'Mummy's with the angels, isn't she?' she asked in a small voice.

Daniel had to clench his jaw. He went to pick her up and hugged her hard. 'Yes, Sweet Pea, Mummy's with the angels,' he replied gruffly.

'Can I see Christie?' She wrapped her arms round his neck.

'Of course you can. Let's go now.' He kissed the top of her head.

Christie had just finished in the kitchen, looking at the menus for the week, when Dermot stuck his head round the door.

'Someone to see you, Christie!' he called. Christie made her way to reception to see Emily and Daniel stood waiting for her.

'Hi, Emily!'

Emily ran into her open arms. 'Christie, Christie our new house is ready!' she burst out.

'I know, how exciting.' Christie laughed.

'Do you want to see it?' asked Emily.

'Oh—'

Daniel grinned. 'We'd like you to come for dinner tonight, wouldn't we, Emily?'

'Yes!'

'Then I'd love to.' She tousled Emily's hair.

'Daddy says we can get a dog.'

Christie looked at Daniel and raised her eyebrow.

'All in good time, Emily,' he said. 'Let's settle in first.'

*

That evening the three of them sat cosily round the kitchen table. Daniel had made them Emily's favourite: macaroni cheese. A feeling of contentment filled him as he cooked in his own new home. No more campervan stoves in a dark, cramped space, but a spacious, modern kitchen. His mum had kindly supplied him with the basic utensils and cooking dishes to help him out, till he was fully stocked.

Christie had brought a bottle of champagne to toast Keeper's Cottage, along with a small cake for Emily, to celebrate. Daniel had popped the cork in the back garden, making Emily giggle as it flew across the treetops.

'Here's to Keeper's Cottage!' he called, raising the champagne bottle.

'To Keeper's Cottage!' Christie cheered back laughing, holding Emily's hand by the patio doors. Emily couldn't stop smiling. Exhausted, but happy, her eyes became heavy and she gave a loud yawn.

'Come on, sleepyhead, time for bed.' Daniel picked her up and carried her up the stairs. For once Emily didn't argue; she was too tired and besides she was itching to get inside her princess bed.

Wandering through each room, Christie admired Daniel's taste. He really had captured the spirit of the old cottage, whilst giving it a new lease of life. The logs piled in a great wicker basket by the wood burner, the jute rugs, polished wooden floorboard, open stone walls, even the brass planters bursting with greenery – it all fit together seamlessly. He definitely had an eye for design.

'What do you think then?' he asked, entering the kitchen and joining her by the breakfast bar.

'It's amazing. You've done a great job.' She saluted him with her champagne flute.

'Have you thought any more about my proposal?' he asked.

'Yes. Are you sure about investing in The Templar?' Christie searched his face for signs of doubt. There weren't any.

'Absolutely sure. It'd be a sound investment.' He took a sip of his champagne and eyed her. 'Plus, it will be helping you out.'

'Daniel, don't do this out of sympathy.'

'I'm not. Like I said, it would be a good investment.' He stared at her. If she were to sell up and leave Treweham he would be gutted. Truth be told, he was prepared to put his money into The Templar for his sake, as much as hers. 'Do you think Stephen will take it?'

Christie sighed. 'I hope so. But who knows?' Despite all her good intentions of keeping positive, tears started to swell.

'Come here.' Daniel pulled her into him and held her close. 'Don't worry, it'll all work out,' he whispered.

They enjoyed the last of the champagne whilst sitting in the garden. When dusk fell, Christie got up to leave.

'Well, I'd better be going.'

'Thanks for coming – it meant a lot, to us both.'

'My pleasure.' Her lips reached his and they shared a slow, sensuous kiss. Daniel longed to sweep her up and carry her up the stairs too, into his new king-size bed, but both knew that wasn't appropriate tonight.

'See you tomorrow,' she said quietly and then made her way home.

Daniel watched her walk down the footpath and waved when she reached the end to join the main village road.

Christie had thoroughly enjoyed her evening at Keeper's Cottage. Humming to herself she went through the back way into The Templar to be greeted by a serious-looking Dermot.

'Christie, you have a visitor.'

'Who?' she asked surprised.

'Stephen.'

64

Christie's chest was pounding as she made her way to the bar. There he was standing with his back to her. She'd recognise that profile anywhere: tall, large shoulders, blond short-cut hair. It was rather disturbing how much like Daniel he was. Fortunately it was quiet; even so, Christie wanted him out of the way. She saw the dining area was empty and decided that would be the best place to talk. Something inside told her not to go anywhere too private. She turned to Dermot who was solemn-faced behind the bar. He nodded reassuringly, as if indicating he was there for her.

'Hello, Stephen,' she said as confidently as possible, with her shoulders back.

He quickly turned. 'Christie!' He smiled, appearing genuinely pleased to see her, which threw Christie a touch. 'How are you? You're looking great.' She didn't feel at all comfortable about the way his eyes looked her up and down.

She gave a non-committal shrug. Then choosing her words carefully, she said, 'I'm fine thanks. Do you want to come this way?' She led him into the dining area and pointed towards a settle in the corner. 'We shouldn't be disturbed there.' Christie wasn't in the mood for pleasantries. It had annoyed her that he had chosen to turn up unexpectedly. Once again, she felt wrong-footed by him, like he was still calling the shots. 'So, I take it you've come to talk money?' she asked directly, looking him straight in the eye.

'Well.' He shifted and attempted a shallow laugh. 'I wouldn't put it quite like that—'

'But that's why you're here,' she cut in.

Stephen gave a deep sigh and ran his hands through his hair. 'Yes. It is. Let me show you these.' He reached inside his jacket pocket and pulled out some photographs. 'I have a son, Christie.' There was no mistaking the pride in his voice. 'See, look.' He passed them to her.

Christie went numb. So, Stephen was now a dad. He had the son he'd always wanted. Her eyes were drawn to the tiny bundle, which she had to admit looked every inch of Stephen. The same shaped nose, blond hair and eyes. She swallowed, unable to speak. Stephen was too wrapped up, showing off his baby, to realise the effect this was having on Christie. 'The thing is, I... we really need the money,' he urged.

Christie stared at him. How she would love to tell him to fuck off. But Christie felt nothing. Zero. Even the pictures of him proudly holding his son didn't ignite a flicker of emotion. It was as if she'd never known him, had never shared any part of herself with him.

'Sophie's obviously not working at the moment.' Stephen refrained from telling her that Sophie had long since packed in work and was refusing to return. 'So things are tight... You do understand, don't you?' He looked longingly into her eyes. 'I'm so sorry, Christie—'

'Don't be,' she cut in.

Stephen frowned slightly. This was hardly going to plan. This wasn't the Christie he had been expecting. Surely the photos of his precious baby would prompt some kind of compassion? Apparently not, judging by this cold, almost indifferent woman sat staring, totally unmoved.

'Christie?' His frown deepened.

'Christie?' she mimicked sarcastically. 'What do you expect, Stephen? Do you think I care about you or your family? Do you really think I'm about to sell my business in a hurry to help you?'

Christie saw his expression turn. 'I think you'll find this is *our* business actually,' he said in a low voice.

'Yeah, the business you poured your heart and soul into,' she spat back. Anger was beginning to simmer inside her.

'Christie, I need the money,' he stated flatly.

'And what if I haven't got the money?' She stared him out. There was a pause.

'Then The Templar goes back on the market.'

'Well good luck with that, because you can sort it all out. I'm in no hurry to sell this place.'

Stephen was dumbfounded. He honestly hadn't been anticipating this. In his mind, Christie would take one look at his son and concede she had to act swiftly.

Christie had actually surprised herself. Although knowing Stephen was right – it was his pub too – an inner strength told her to make it difficult for him. How dare he turn up here, unannounced, and demand she either come up with the money, or sell The Templar? This, after gloating over the baby she had been unable to give him. The absolute cheek of the man.

'You can't stop the sale.' His voice was dangerously quiet.

'No, but I can drag my feet,' she replied in the same tone. 'Sophie could have a few more babies by the time this place sells.' She gave a sweet smile. 'Maybe more sons? You could have a rugby team before you know it.'

'Right. That's it. It's no use talking to you when you're like this. I'll be back tomorrow evening. One way or another this has to be settled.'

Christie sat in silence, refusing even to look at him. She'd handled it badly, but anger had got the better of her. That, and Stephen's arrogance. She watched him through the window as he got into a Mercedes. So much for being broke, she thought with spite. Then another thought crossed her mind; was he living beyond his means? He never was any good at handling money and with Sophie not bringing in a wage, perhaps he really *was* getting desperate. He certainly sounded it. Could Daniel's money be enough to tempt him?

65

Christie woke with a throbbing head. The sun was flickering through the bedroom blinds, with the promise of a lovely summer's day, but not for her. Stephen was coming that night. A low sickening sensation settled in the pit of her stomach. She had to speak to Daniel – and fast. After showering swiftly, she decided to skip breakfast and make her way to Keeper's Cottage. Before doing so she went into the bar to see Dermot. He glanced up, still looking sombre.

'Dermot, I need to see Daniel.' He nodded, knowing something was afoot. The sooner Christie sorted out The Templar, the better. Although it pained him to say it, he was more than ready to leave. There was only so much he could do, and if she was unable to keep the pub, then she had no choice but to sell it. He couldn't be expected to stay here working indefinitely, as much as he'd loved it.

'I see.'

'I won't be long.'

'Take as long as you need, Christie.' He gave a weak smile.

She practically ran all the way to Daniel's cottage.

Panting for breath, she rapped at the front door. She could hear Emily calling, then Daniel opened it.

'Hi.' He smiled surprised at her early call, then he frowned at seeing her in such a state. 'Whatever's the matter?'

'It's Stephen, he's here,' she said in between breaths.

'At The Templar?'

'No, no, he was there last night when I got back, but he left and said he'd return tonight.'

'Come in.' He ushered her inside. As soon as Emily saw Christie, she ran over to her.

'Hi, Emily.' She smiled, in an effort to act normal.

'Christie, are you having breakfast with us?'

'Emily, just finish yours, there's a good girl,' Daniel said.

Emily trotted back into the kitchen.

'He wants his money,' hissed Christie. 'He's got a baby boy now. Showed me photos of him.' She was talking rapidly.

'Calm down, come on, sit down.' Daniel gently directed her to the settee and sat next to her. 'Listen, don't worry, I'll be there tonight as moral support.' Christie looked a tad alarmed.

'Do you think that's wise?'

'Why not? We can put the offer of money to him straight.'

Christie sat still for a moment, considering. 'Maybe you could be within earshot and intervene if needs be?' She looked searchingly at him. She didn't want to antagonise Stephen any more than she had done, but then did like the idea of assistance. Stephen cut quite an intimidating figure. Having Daniel as backup was comforting. And after all, it was his money that was being dangled as the carrot.

'Yes, OK, if that's what you'd prefer,' agreed Daniel. 'What time is he coming?'

'He didn't say.'

'Right, I'll ring my parents and ask them to stop here with Emily.'

'Thanks, Daniel.' She covered his hand with hers.

'Daddy! I've finished!' shouted Emily from the kitchen.

'I'll get going.' Christie stood to leave.

Daniel quickly turned her face to his and kissed her lips. 'I'll be there, keep calm.'

Keeping calm was easier said than done, thought Christie as she prepared herself for meeting Stephen that evening. She deliberately chose to dress down, letting him know he wasn't worth making the effort for. Dermot had been filled in with the details and also assured her he'd be on hand for any unpleasantness. Wearing skinny jeans and a T-shirt, she made her way down. She scanned the area; there was no sign of him.

She spoke quietly to Dermot behind the bar. 'Is Daniel here?'

'In the dining room, sat in the far settle,' he replied in the same quiet tone. It had been agreed that sitting Daniel there would be the best place. The high-backed settle facing the window meant that he'd be hidden from the table in the alcove where Christie planned to sit with Stephen, yet he would still be able to hear everything. There had been no bookings till later in the evening so it would be quiet. Dermot, in his wisdom, had discreetly placed "reserved" signs on the tables until then, ensuring maximum privacy.

Christie looked at the clock – it was 6.30pm – then her eyes darted to the window and saw Stephen's Mercedes pull into the car park.

'He's here,' she urgently whispered to Dermot.

'You go and meet him. I'll let Daniel know.'

As Stephen entered the bar, Christie approached him with a cool expression. 'Hello, Stephen.'

He gave her an equally cool nod. 'Christie.' He followed her into the dining room. She made her way to sit at the table in the alcove. Glancing quickly at the settle knowing Daniel was there, she took a deep breath.

'You're right. We do need to reach an agreement,' she said clearly, looking Stephen in the eye.

'We do,' he butted in unnecessarily.

'I can offer you three hundred thousand pounds,' she stated flatly. Stephen paused. He appeared to be a touch taken aback. 'Technically, I know you think you deserve more.' This made him give a quick bark of a laugh. 'But I don't. And it's all I have to offer.'

'Where's the money coming from?'

'Does it matter?'

'Well perhaps it does, if this source can actually give a more realistic sum.' Daniel had heard enough. He rose from the settle, making Stephen jump slightly. With a foreboding look he moved towards them.

Stephen's eyes flew to Christie, then back to Daniel.

'It's coming from me.' He towered over Stephen, staring him out. 'And it's the final offer. Failing that, you'll have a long wait getting your greedy hands on any money.'

Stephen was secretly pleased to have had *an* offer, and yes, it was his greed that was chancing his arm. So, Christie had a new man in her life. It hadn't occurred to him that she would have found someone else. He'd assumed she'd still be missing him. On the face of it, three hundred thousand pounds was a decent sum of money, enough to certainly make things a whole lot easier at home with Sophie and a new baby. The thought of having to wait months and months to reach a final settlement was a daunting one.

He turned to face Christie. 'Yes. I'll agree to it.'

'Then I suggest you email your solicitor immediately.' Daniel spoke calmly and folded his arms. All the time he never took his gaze off Stephen.

Christie felt like punching the air, but forced herself to remain silent. Stephen looked at her. Was there sadness behind those eyes? She refused to be moved, even though her heart was pounding.

'I'll contact them tomorrow.' He scraped his chair back. Taking one last look at her he swallowed. 'Goodbye, Christie.'

'Goodbye, Stephen.'

Then he was gone. She would never set eyes on him again. The relief was unimaginable.

66

'You've made good progress,' said Tobias to his maintenance manager. The new rooms he was renovating for Marcus and Finula were taking shape.

'As you know, it's not too complicated a job, Sir, just a matter of sprucing up.' Assessing the freshly painted pale grey walls and high, white ceiling with decorative coving, Tobias nodded his head in agreement. He was particularly pleased with the huge stained-glass window, which had been painstakingly restored and cleaned. It made a real feature to the room.

'Is the bathroom complete?'

'Almost – let me show you, Sir.' Walking through the large sitting room, Tobias was led to an adjoining door, which opened up a small corridor. Off there was the bathroom and two bedrooms. Again the bedrooms had been painted and housed a huge double bed in the master and twin beds in the other. The bathroom was white marble tiled and had a grand, roll-top bath.

'Yes.' Tobias nodded again. 'I'm sure Marcus will be more than happy with his rooms.' Should bloody well think so, thought the maintenance manager tartly, given what had been achieved in such a little time.

'Very good, Sir.' He smiled pleasantly.

Megan's voice could be heard. 'Tobias! Are you there?'

Tobias walked back to join her. 'In here,' he called.

'Wow! Look at this,' she gasped at the newly refurbished room. 'You wouldn't believe it was the same place.' Her mind cast back to being shown a tired, dowdy, dark room covered in dust sheets. The stained-glass window had been blocked by wooden shutters. She gazed in amazement at it now as the glass panes sparkled with colour in the sunshine.

The manager smiled at her reaction. He'd always liked Lady Cavendish-Blake, finding her far more down to earth than her husband.

'Finula's going to love this,' she said half laughing.

Tobias grinned. 'Do you like it better than our rooms?'

'No, ours are beautiful too,' she was quick to reply and she smiled at the manager, not wanting to cause any offence. It would be strange knowing Finula was only next door to her. Megan was so looking forward to having her best friend stay at Treweham Hall. When Finula had moved to Shropshire after meeting Marcus, she had been heartbroken at seeing her go. They had always enjoyed each other's company and shared many a giggle. Now, it would be just like old times and she couldn't wait.

Together Megan and Tobias walked through to their own suite.

'It'll be nice having all three brothers together at the Hall,' she remarked.

'It will and I'm sure it's what Father would have wanted. Sebastian said so too.'

Megan turned to face Tobias. 'How is Sebastian? I haven't seen him for ages.'

'Fine. A little tired, but then the production's taken it out of him.'

'Good job it's finished then.'

'Too right. He deserves a long rest.'

'And where better to take it easy?' Megan replied staring out of the window overlooking the manicured grounds. She still had to pinch herself at times. Originally, she had moved to Treweham to live in her gran's cottage. Never had she dreamt of ending up in Treweham Hall as Lady Cavendish-Blake.

'What's going on in that mind of yours?' Tobias came and put his arm round her shoulders.

She laughed. 'Just how your life can take such a sudden change of direction.' There was a moment's pause.

'Let's hope Marcus can cope with the direction his is about to take.'

She hugged her husband, knowing how defensive Tobias was about all his family. 'He will,' she reassured him.

67

'Do I look nice, Daddy?' Emily stood before Daniel proudly wearing her new school uniform.

'Emily, you look fantastic.' He smiled with a tear in his eye. At times such as this, it hit him what Jenna had been robbed of. Then a dark voice taunted him. If Jenna was still here, would he be the one looking at their daughter in her school uniform? Or would Emily be starting at a city school in Liverpool, not a small village school in Treweham?

It was no good going over and over such thoughts in his mind. This is where they were now, and they each had to deal with it in their own way. Emily appeared to be doing fine on the whole. Now and then, night-time especially, he could hear her cry, but thankfully this was happening less and less now. She didn't seem quite as clingy either.

Daniel honestly believed that moving to a new location and new home had been the right decision. It had given them both something to focus on and represented a fresh beginning, a new start. His parents had been impressed with what he'd done with Keeper's Cottage and they loved the area. Now it was Emily's first day at school and his parents were staying again. They wanted to be there to welcome

Emily home in the afternoon and hear all about her big day.

'Right, ready to go, Sweet Pea?'

'Yes!'

Together they went, hand in hand, down the footpath and onto the main road leading to the school. All the time Emily chatted away, no sign of any nerves, Daniel noticed with relief. As they approached the quaint, small school nestled amongst the trees, he realised if anything, it was his chest that was tightening at the thought of letting go of her tiny hand to say goodbye.

Knowing smiles were exchanged amongst parents all having similar thoughts as their children skipped along beside them. Only one little girl was reluctant to leave her mummy's side.

'Daddy, what's the matter with her?' asked Emily, seeing how she was clinging to her mum's legs.

'I think maybe she needs a friend to go in with.'

Immediately Emily went over. 'Come on, let's go in together. What's your name?'

The girl stood still for a moment and stared. After a gentle coaxing from her mum she replied, 'Ella.'

Emily held her hand out. 'Let's go, Ella.'

Daniel stood back with pride. That's my girl, he thought. 'Bye, Emily!' he called.

Emily looked over her shoulder. 'Bye, Daddy!' she chirped back, whilst practically frogmarching Ella into school, making the rest of the parents laugh.

Not wanting to go straight back he called at The Templar on the way home. Well, he had a vested interest in it now, he reminded himself happily.

'Well, if it isn't the new co-owner,' said Dermot as he entered the bar.

'Hi, Dermot.' Daniel smiled. 'Is Christie about?'

'No. She's gone to see her solicitor. Lots to sort out I believe.'

True to his word, Stephen had acted swiftly and all had signed the necessary paperwork sealing the transaction.

'Yes and all for the best,' he replied.

'I'll say.' Dermot held his hand out to shake Daniel's. 'Congratulations, good man yaself.'

'Thanks. I'm just so glad Stephen accepted the offer.'

Dermot gave a shake of his head. 'Got more than he deserved if you ask me. Still, it's good to know The Templar's in safe hands now.'

'It certainly is, Dermot.'

68

'Come on, Finula!' shouted Marcus as he slammed down the boot of the Range Rover. As usual it was jam-packed with everything that Finula had managed to ram in. Although, to be fair to his wife, they would be staying at Treweham Hall for the foreseeable future. He still felt daunted by what lay ahead for him and Finula, whom he thought hadn't fully grasped the situation. Whereas he was rather pensive, she seemed to be excited about living in the Hall. It bothered him that Finula didn't appear to be prepared for the onslaught, or maybe he was being a tad dramatic?

Then he cast his mind back to Tobias and the way he had been hounded practically all his life. For Marcus, caution was his watchword, always had been. It was the way he operated, unlike his carefree wife. But then, wasn't that what had attracted him to her in the first place? His mouth twitched whilst watching her fluster and faff about, double-checking she'd locked the door, patting her pocket to make sure her phone was there, looking inside her bag, then checking the door again. Finally, she clambered into the passenger's seat beside him.

'Phew!' she puffed. 'I think that's everything done.' She quickly glanced behind her to the back seat. 'Did you see me pack my cookery books?'

'Yes,' he lied, half laughing.

'What's so funny?'

'You are.'

'Why?' she asked surprised.

'Stop fussing.' He leant over and kissed her. 'Time to go.'

Finula grinned, she couldn't wait to get back to Treweham; not that she didn't like Shropshire – far from it – but she still regarded Treweham as home, and it was where her dad was. Plus, having Treweham Hall as a base meant living alongside her best friend and cutie-pie godson. She turned sideways and took in Marcus' profile. That frown had come back. Recognising it as a sign of stress, she gently patted his lap. They exchanged a knowing smile and set off.

Within a couple of hours they were sweeping onto the gravel driveway of Treweham Hall. Finula's heart gave a leap of joy as she saw Megan standing at the entrance, ready to greet them.

'Leave your stuff. I'll get Henry to sort it,' she called.

'How the other half live,' muttered Marcus to himself. He grabbed his laptop, not wanting to leave that behind.

'Megan!' gushed Finula, hugging her.

'Tobias is in a meeting, but he'll join us later,' Megan told them.

'Hi, Megan.' Marcus kissed her cheek.

'I'll show you your rooms – they're amazing.' She smiled.

'Oh, I can't wait to see them.' Finula was at fever pitch. Marcus couldn't help but be infected by her excitement. He had to concede that being in this huge fortress of a place left him feeling far more assured than at home in his humble cottage.

The documentary was due to be aired that night. Tobias had arranged for a large screen to be erected in the Hall library for all the family to watch together. Marcus was uneasy knowing that Beatrice, Tobias and Sebastian's mam would be there too. It didn't bode well having your husband's first illegitimate son announced on TV for all to witness. Still, it was the truth, and it couldn't be hidden forever, no matter how convenient Beatrice would find it.

For him, it was a small price to pay, considering all the hardship his mam had had to endure. A part of him was comforted, knowing she was finally getting some recognition, even though she wasn't there to acknowledge it.

A cocktail of emotions ran through him as Megan led them to their rooms. It still hadn't truly sunk in that this was his actual ancestral home.

'OMG!' Finula's face lit up as they entered their drawing room. 'It's fabulous!'

'I know,' Megan agreed and looked to Marcus for his reaction. He couldn't speak. Then after a moment's pause he answered.

'Thanks.' It seemed somewhat of an understatement, but was heartfelt nonetheless.

'Right, I'm going to leave you to settle in. Your stuff will be brought up shortly.' Megan left, sensing Marcus' apprehension. She recalled how Treweham Hall had intimidated her when first stepping inside its majestic walls. Typical of Finula though to come in guns blazing. She chuckled to herself at the thought.

A Green and Pleasant Land? was due to start at 9pm. It had been Marcus' idea to put a question mark after the title, because the documentary was tackling burning issues about poverty and the homeless in comparison to the rich flourishing in country estates. At the time he was commissioned to produce the documentary, he'd been more than happy to expose the affluent, but back then his parentage hadn't been in question. Now, the hint of hypocrisy left a bitter taste. It didn't sit comfortably with him. Although he had Cavendish-Blake blood running through his veins, he hadn't been born and bred into the aristocratic lifestyle. He was ill-equipped, untrained.

If only he could steal just a small sample of his wife's enthusiasm, he thought bleakly, watching her gasp in awe at all the rooms. He had two hours to get his act together and compose himself. Two hours before he was sat in front of that large screen with all of them scrutinising his work. Two hours before the world would learn who he really was. Swallowing, he decided to take refuge and sink into that enormous bath.

'Finula, I'm going to have a long, hot soak,' he said, taking off his jacket.

'Want me to join you?' She raised her eyebrow and gave him a sexy grin.

'Darlin', I need some space.' Then seeing her face fall, he quickly added, 'Sorry, Finula, I'm just...' He stopped and stared out of the window.

'You're what?' asked Finula gently.

'I'm scared.' He gulped.

'Of what? The documentary? Don't be, I know it'll be brilliant – everyone's going to be amazed by it.'

'Of the outcome and the impact it's going to have on us.'

Finula looked into his troubled eyes. He really was a tortured soul at times and not always with good reason. Yes, she accepted there would be media attention, that was obvious, but it would calm down. She'd seen it happen with Tobias and Megan, especially at the time of their wedding. She walked over to him and put her arms round his waist.

'Now listen to me, together we'll weather the storm. We're amongst family and friends who care about us. The press won't be here forever. You'll soon be yesterday's news. Believe me, I've seen it happen before with Tobias.' Then as though the thought had just occurred to her she added, 'What do you think your mum would make of the documentary?'

He paused, then answered. 'I think she'd be proud… and glad I've been recognised.'

'Exactly. I'm sure she'd be pleased that you've found your brothers too.'

'Yes, yes she would.' He smiled warmly into her eyes. Where the hell would he be without her?

That evening the whole family gathered together to watch the documentary. The air was heavy with anticipation, excitement and suspense. All had good seating positions with a full view of the big screen, except the Dowager. Beatrice had chosen to sit discreetly at the back of the room. Tobias, Megan, Marcus, Finula, Sebastian and Jamie all sat together enjoying drinks and canapés before the start.

Marcus was feeling much more relaxed after Finula's wise words, a long, soothing bath and a couple of Jameson whiskeys. Every now and then he'd catch Finula's eye and he'd get a reassuring smile. Then the grandfather clock chimed, it was time for the documentary to start. The title *Green and Pleasant Land* shone onto the screen accompanied by sweet, choral music, only to turn into a more sinister tune, as the question mark gradually appeared after the title, indicating that perhaps the land wasn't so green and pleasant after all. It set the tone perfectly, signifying that the story about to be told wasn't going to be just about the quintessential, quaint English countryside, but would expose the great injustice too – of poor housing, poverty and how the vulnerable were forced to cope.

The village of Treweham was spellbound. All the villagers who had taken part in the documentary sat glued to their screens. At The Templar, all the locals gathered round the large TV with avid interest.

True to form, the documentary provoked many emotions, which all Marcus' work was notorious for. He had the absolute skill to evoke sympathy and despair at families being evicted; anger at all the idiotic bureaucracy and envy mingled with awe at the vast, impressive country estates of the aristocracy. It highlighted the inequality and discrimination of the class system and the great chasm between the classes. When the culmination of the interview came, the whole audience across the country was riveted. There they were, the two Cavendish-Blake brothers, familiar faces to the nation, plus one. The opening lines from Jamie, who had interviewed them, spelled it out completely.

'Thank you, gentlemen, for agreeing to be interviewed. Marcus, it must be especially challenging for you?'

'In a way, yes. Then again, I'm glad it's all out in the open now,' Marcus had calmly replied, giving direct eye contact to the camera.

'How did you feel when learning of your true parentage?'

'I was always led to believe that my father had been killed in an accident. To be told the truth by my dying mam was astonishing.'

'Tobias and Sebastian, how does it feel to have Marcus suddenly in your lives?' Jamie had continued.

'He's our brother and the family accepts this,' Tobias had answered resolutely. 'I'm sure if our father had known of Marcus' existence, then we would have been brought up with him.'

'Diaries, written by Father, prove he knew nothing about Marcus, which is a tragedy,' continued Sebastian.

'But they do document a relationship with my mam,' Marcus had explained.

'And the DNA tests confirmed we all share the same father,' Tobias had stated.

And so the interview continued; three brothers united in one family. They spoke agreeably together, giving clear, concise answers, gelling seamlessly, with the picture of their father hanging above, looking down on them.

The documentary ended with the same choral music it had started with, gradually fading with the subtitles rising up from the screen. There in bold letters was Marcus Devlin's name as producer. A short silence followed. Then Tobias raised his glass.

'Well done, Marcus.' All agreed and saluted him. The door closed quietly as Beatrice tactfully vacated the room.

69

As expected, the following morning in Treweham was chaos. Tabloids went wild with, *"The Cavendish-Blakes' hidden secret"*; *"Devlin's a toff!"* headlines to the more sedate articles stating: *"the rather embarrassing announcement from one of England's finest aristocratic lineage."* Marcus threw the newspapers on the table. So, he was a "rather embarrassing announcement" was he? The bastards. Then, on hearing his name, his head turned towards the TV.

'The village of Treweham is once again in the public eye,' said the news reporter. Marcus blinked. Was that The Templar in the background? It was! The bloody reporter was stood outside The Templar. 'Here, home to the Cavendish-Blake family, the village is alive with news from Treweham Hall. The documentary *Green and Pleasant Land?* last night gave the explosive revelation that the documentary's own producer, Marcus Devlin, is in fact the firstborn son of the late Lord Richard Cavendish-Blake, sending shock waves through the nation.'

Marcus rolled his eyes at the sensationalism being whipped up by the presenter.

'Marcus spoke candidly about the secret his own mother had kept from him.'

Marcus' jaw clenched at the mention of his mam. Then, to his horror, a picture of her holding him as a baby suddenly appeared on the screen. Where the feck did they get hold of that? His eyes widened as more snapshots of his childhood home in Ireland spilled onto the screen. That pretty whitewashed cottage with the hills in the background was there, for all and sundry to see; another of him as a toddler running through the wild flower meadows – again with his beloved mam, then more of him growing up, school photographs, his teenage years at university, him receiving awards, to the one that absolutely enraged him – a wedding picture of him and Finula. *Who the hell had given them that?*

His hands curled into fists. He was livid. Then the reporter was back with her chirpy spiel. 'So, to get a picture of how Marcus is coping with the shock of his parentage, we have local vet, Nick Fletcher, to give us some inside knowledge.' *Who the feck's Nick Fletcher?* raged Marcus. He'd never set eyes on the guy. Then, he vaguely remembered a couple of his TV crew had interviewed him for the documentary and had shot some footage of his veterinary surgery. So, that must make him a close friend, he thought incredulously, almost choking on the complete brazenness of the pillock.

'Nick, tell us about Marcus and how he must be feeling right now.'

'Well obviously Marcus has a lot of adjusting to do, but I'm sure he'll get a lot of support from his wife, Finula.'

Marcus' eyes narrowed.

'So you know his wife then?' asked the reporter.

'Yes.' Nick gave a slight laugh, faking embarrassment. 'I was actually her boyfriend, before she met Marcus.'

Marcus' mind flashed back again. He did seem to recall Finula mentioning how he had two-timed her with Sebastian. Neither of them had known at the time that Nick was bisexual and he had very deceitfully dated them both, causing heartache to both parties once found out. The *shite*. Marcus was incensed.

'I'm also a close friend of Sebastian Cavendish-Blake,' gloated Nick with a wide smile.

Marcus wanted to punch the TV screen; instead he switched it off with disgust. He stood up and looked out of the window. The cast-iron gates of Treweham Hall were locked securely, but beyond them he could just make out the rows of journalists, photographers and news reporters lining up. He closed his eyes, wanting to block it all out. Just then Finula entered the room. On seeing Marcus' face, she instantly knew what had happened. That and seeing the discarded newspapers on the table.

'They're all out there,' he stated flatly, pointing to the window, 'like vultures.'

'I know,' she replied quietly.

'Nick Fletcher's just been on TV, by the way, saying how close he is to you and Sebastian.'

Finula's head shot up. 'What?' she spat. She quickly turned the TV back on, just to get the tail end of the interview.

'Thanks, Nick, for sharing this with us.'

'My pleasure.' He beamed smugly.

'The cheeky bastard!' Finula bellowed.

'I thought so,' remarked Marcus calmly. For the first time ever, his wife was showing real emotion over the whole episode.

'They're outside The Templar.' She squinted at the screen. 'Don't say they've tried to get hold of my dad.'

She immediately reached for her phone inside her bag as Marcus said evenly, 'I wouldn't bother trying to ring him.' He tipped his head towards the TV. There, on national television, was Dermot standing outside the pub.

'Now listen here,' he told the reporter with force, 'my son-in-law is a fine man and an asset to the Cavendish-Blake family and my Finula is lucky to have him as a husband. That's all I've got to say on the matter – now clear off.' And with that he strode back into The Templar leaving the interviewer somewhat staggered.

'Good for you, Dad!' shouted Finula and fell onto the sofa in hysterics. Marcus too couldn't stop laughing. Together they howled, unable to stop.

Sebastian wasn't laughing. He had seen the interview with Nick Fletcher and he wanted to slap the sly dog's face. How dare he appear on TV and say those things? Didn't he realise the effect it would have on all concerned? Of course he did, but he simply didn't care. That had been Nick Fletcher all over: selfish. Would their love affair be plastered all over the papers next? How much was Nick getting? Or did he do it purely for the limelight? He could feel an anxious sensation settle in the pit of his stomach. Stress, something he could well do without, especially with his condition.

Jamie turned off the TV. 'Don't watch any more. He's so not worth it.'

Sebastian turned to face him. 'You're absolutely right. He

isn't.' Deciding there and then not to let Nick get to him, he made a concerted effort to block him out.

Tobias, on the other hand, had quietly taken in the morning's events. Besides scanning all the newspapers, he too had seen Nick Fletcher pontificating on TV. How he would love to bury that bastard. Once before he had come to blows with him when he had tried, in a drunken stupor, to kiss Megan. Tobias had punched the living daylights out of him – obviously Nick still hadn't learnt his lesson, judging by the way he was still dabbling with his family. The newspapers he could handle: nothing there that he hadn't been expecting. It was now a case of riding the media wave, until it all died down again. He looked towards the entrance of the Hall where half of Fleet Street seemed to be camped out and shook his head. Didn't they ever give up?

He rang the estate office.

'Good morning, Lord Cavendish-Blake,' answered the estate manager.

'Good morning, Percy. I want maximum security,' he said sternly.

'Yes, Sir, it has been arranged, as of last evening.'

'Excellent. Nobody is to leave this Hall without being escorted. Do I make myself clear?'

'Yes, Sir, absolutely.' Tobias put the phone down and fixed his eyes on the TV screen.

'Baby Edward is the son and heir to Lord Tobias Cavendish-Blake, but will the sudden announcement change things?' asked yet another reporter appearing outside Treweham Hall this time. Tobias gritted his teeth. He wanted to shoot the fucking lot of them. Just then Megan entered the room carrying his son. Immediately his mood changed at seeing them.

'Oh don't watch any more – please, Tobias,' said Megan wearily.

'I won't.' He flicked it off with the remote control and opened his arms to hold Edward. 'Come here, you,' he said kissing his chubby cheeks. Edward gurgled in delight. This is what mattered, he told himself, family – not what the scavengers outside alleged.

70

As predicted, Treweham recovered from yet another press invasion. Within a fortnight, as the autumn nights drew further in and the mornings brought a nip in the air, gradually a calmness descended upon the village.

The Templar wasn't quite as manic as it had been, much to the relief of Dermot and Christie. Even more of a relief to them was the knowledge that Stephen had now received his money and was officially no longer joint owner of The Templar. This in turn had speeded up the divorce process and Christie was eagerly awaiting the decree absolute to be declared imminently. Knowing that she would no longer be Stephen's wife and he had no hold over her, or her business, was more than enough to put a spring in Christie's step.

Dermot had seemed a whole lot cheerier too. Not least at being dubbed "a legend" by the village due to his response to the pesky reporters on TV, but because he was at last now able to leave The Templar. Instead of getting emotional whilst packing his belongings, he found himself rather comforted. His retirement was well overdue and by God, he'd earned it. After serving the good people of Treweham for over thirty years, it was well and truly time to call last orders.

Tonight would be his last night. Christie and the staff had seen to it that instead of pulling pints behind the bar, he would be sat on the opposite side drinking them. All of the regulars would want to say goodbye and buy him a fond farewell drink. Even though he'd still be living in his cosy, little cottage in Treweham, he'd no longer be their landlord. Dermot was a popular member of the community. Being a pub landlord had often meant being a good listener, as customers had poured out their hearts to him. He was discreet and knew how to keep a secret. He also knew when to intervene, especially when sensing trouble.

'So, how does it feel to be leaving at last?' Christie smiled warmly at Dermot. She'd so miss this gentle, kind man. If it hadn't been for him, her life at The Templar would never have run as smoothly as it had, especially under the circumstances. He had been an absolute rock to her and she'd never forget that. Suddenly her eyes started to fill.

'Now come on, Christie,' he softly reproached. 'I'm only down the road. You don't get rid of me that easily.'

'Seriously though, thanks, Dermot.' She swallowed, barely getting the words out.

'It's my pleasure. I couldn't be leaving the pub in better hands. I take it Daniel will be here tonight?'

'Of course – he wouldn't miss your leaving do.'

'Should think not, as the joint owner.' He gave her a wink, making her laugh. 'I said it'd all work out in the end, didn't I?' He eyed her thoughtfully. She'd come a long way since that morning landing up at The Templar alone and in tears.

'Yes, you did.' They looked at each other. No more words were necessary.

They were interrupted by Daniel as he came into the bar

with Emily. Turning, Dermot grinned at seeing what was following them. A chocolate-brown Labrador puppy.

'Look what we've got!' Emily burst out.

'Oh, what a sweetie!' Christie knelt down to stroke its velvety-soft face. 'What's he called?'

'We haven't named him yet,' said Daniel. 'There you go, Dermot—' he handed him a bottle of Baileys Irish Cream '—all the best.'

'Ah, good man, thanks, very much.'

'Can we call him Dermot?' asked Emily, making them laugh.

'No, we can't call the puppy Dermot,' said Daniel smiling.

'How about Bailey, after my favourite drink?' suggested Dermot, holding up the bottle.

'That's a nice name,' said Christie.

Emily looked up to Daniel for confirmation. 'Shall we?'

'Yes, Bailey sounds good.'

'Come on, Bailey.' Emily took his lead. 'Let's play outside.' She led the puppy through the French doors onto the lawn.

'She's a good kid,' remarked Dermot. 'Settled in at school OK?'

'Yes, thanks, she loves it.' Daniel paused, then added, 'Emily loves it here, in Treweham. I think she feels more settled.' Hardly surprising considering how Emily had been shipped from pillar to post previously. Still nobody came out and actually said that; but all thought it. 'So, all set then?' Daniel changed the subject.

'Sure am.' Dermot nodded. 'You ready to run this pub?'

'I'm more of a sleeping partner really.' Daniel grinned.

'I bet you bloody are.' Dermot smirked, as Christie burst into giggles.

71

Christie stretched slowly with satisfaction and gazed out of the window. Last night's starry sky had been so spectacular she hadn't wanted to shut it out. The blind in the small sash window remained open, allowing the view of the lush, green hills to shine brightly in the distance. She sank back in the goose-down pillows and contemplated. Since sending Dermot off with a rip-snorting hell of a leaving bash, she had confidently taken the helm. Knowing she always had Daniel's input if needed gave her that extra reassurance of assertively running The Templar. Also, having had Dermot's support had given her a boost.

Christie had been fully accepted and approved by the locals, which meant an awful lot to her. They'd also welcomed the news of Daniel having a stake in the pub. Together they were now regarded as fully-fledged villagers. A huge honour indeed, Dermot had told them. It was strange having him call in now as a customer, but still comforting.

They were all due to meet up that night. Daniel had decided to throw a house-warming party, to celebrate the completion of Keeper's Cottage. The garden had been landscaped and a fence now surrounded his land from the footpath. The outbuilding had been converted into a work studio as planned, with skylight windows blasting out daylight, making it an ideal space for him to sit and draw plans, while Bailey sat contently by his feet. Daniel would always make sure he had finished working by 3pm, in order to pick Emily up from school.

Often, when she had been bathed and tucked up in bed, he would squeeze another hour or two into his work schedule. His parents were in the process of moving nearby. Wanting to be hands-on grandparents to Emily and a support to their son, they had sold their house and bought a bungalow in the next village to Treweham. Daniel was so glad of the helping hands and was pleased they were close by.

He was making good progress on the project he had been commissioned to do. Being happy and content made all the difference to his creativity he realised – that and a good work-life balance. This had in turn made him consider Christie's lifestyle. After seeing the way she dedicated almost every hour God sent to The Templar, Daniel was beginning to grow concerned. Not only as her partner, but also as joint owner of the pub, he wanted to shoulder more responsibility. Obviously he couldn't be there at her side running The Templar when he had Emily and his own career, but an idea was beginning to take root, which he wanted to suggest to Christie.

The more he considered it, the more appealing it became. Perhaps tonight at his house-warming party he would run it past her, he thought, as he leisurely made his way back home from dropping Emily off at school. He had a lot to do today. He'd planned to do two hours' work in the studio, then tidy up and prepare for the party. His parents were due to arrive later that afternoon, plus the caterers would be delivering the buffet. He wanted to stock up on booze too. The three bottles of wine in his rack wouldn't last two minutes amongst the guests.

Daniel was looking forward to meeting all his neighbours properly after deciding to invite those who lived nearby but whom hadn't spoken a great deal to, apart from small talk in the pub. Now, as his roots were firmly grounded in Treweham, he wanted to be on good terms with as many people as possible.

As early evening came a mildness filled the dusky air. Tobias and Megan trampled through the fallen, rusty-brown leaves in the damp wood. The smell of wood smoke wafted through the trees and an owl hooted in the distance.

'There's something romantic about wandering through the woods in dusk, isn't there?' remarked Megan as she held Tobias' hand.

'Do you remember our first encounter in Quercus Woods, Megan?' Tobias laughed, the sexy flashback giving him a stir.

Megan giggled. 'Do I ever.' She squeezed his hand and he lowered his face to kiss her. Marcus and Finula followed at a distance behind them with Sebastian and Jamie. Laughter could be heard as they all fumbled their way through the semi-darkness to Keeper's Cottage.

Sebastian was in exceptionally good form, having been offered a major role in a BBC drama, which a casting director had headhunted him for.

'So, the show's not over yet,' he'd remarked wryly to a beaming Jamie, who knew more than anyone how much it meant to him.

By the time they arrived the party was in full swing. Daniel opened the patio doors on seeing them emerge from the trees.

'Hi!' he called, waving them over. They joined the crowd, already in good cheer. Dylan and Flora had been amongst the first guests to arrive. Flora, now several months pregnant, was showing, but also fighting fatigue. Dylan, as protective as ever, was keen to get there early, to come home early. The last thing he wanted was Flora exhausted. The way he fussed over her was endearing to others who witnessed it, but exasperating for Flora.

'I'm fine, Dylan,' she hissed as he provided a chair for her to sit on.

'I know, but just rest your legs,' he insisted as Flora rolled her eyes, making Gary and Tracy Belcher, who were stood talking to them, stifle laughter.

'So, how's our Phoenix?' asked Gary, throwing back his pint.

Immediately Flora's face softened. 'Oh, he's fine, Gary. Feel free to come and visit him anytime.'

'We will.' Tracy smiled. 'I'm looking forward to his next race.'

'Doubt you'll be riding him though, eh, Flora?' roared Gary, whilst thumping Dylan on his back.

Dermot arrived next. Finula rushed over and hugged him.

'How's my girl?' He loved having his daughter in Treweham again.

'I'm good, thanks.'

'And how's Marcus?' he asked, ever mindful of his son-in-law's unwanted media attention.

'He's good too. Things are settling down now. We'll be heading back to Shropshire.'

'Oh, I see.' Dermot couldn't help the disappointment in his voice.

'But after Christmas,' she quickly added.

'After Christmas?' he replied in surprise. 'So, you'll be here until then?'

'Yep.' She beamed. 'You'll have to put up with us until then.'

'I'll manage.' He smiled back.

Christie was the last to arrive. Reluctant to leave a busy bar, the staff eventually persuaded her to go. Daniel immediately saw her walking up the footpath. He opened the front door and met her halfway.

'Hello, you.' He kissed her lingeringly.

'Hi,' she replied after a long, sensuous kiss.

'Christie, come with me.' He caught her hand and walked her to the back of the cottage. A full moon shone on the secluded garden. Music and laughter could be heard from the house inside. Daniel gently sat her down on the bench by his studio. 'Christie, I want you to move in with me—'

'But—'

'No, please hear me out. I want us to be a family together, not you working flat out at The Templar.'

'I can't give up The Templar,' she replied, almost incredulously.

'No, and I don't want you to. But let's employ a live-in assistant manager. You still have overall say on the running of the place, but you'd be here, with me and Emily.'

Christie was speechless. A lump formed in her throat.

Then, that hollow, gutted feeling overwhelmed her. Taking a deep breath she looked directly at him.

'Daniel, I can't...'

He raised his head sharply.

'You know I... may not be able to have children.'

His shoulders relaxed. 'Christie, you and Emily are all I need.' He took both her hands in his and stared at her. 'I love you, Christie.'

Her heart leapt. Then it all fell into place, so naturally, so clearly, like night follows day; *he* was all she needed. Simple as.

Looking into those gorgeous, pale blue eyes she gave a quivering smile back. 'And I love you, Daniel.'

Acknowledgements

Having worked many years for the Court Service, I have drawn on my experiences for this book and would like to thank my colleague, Mark Adamson, Deputy Justice's Clerk, for his sharp legal mind and advise on family law.

It's time to say a fond farewell to the Cotswolds, as this is the last novel in the Treweham Hall series. It was a pleasure researching property in this area for Daniel's storyline and hopefully one day would love a bolthole of my very own in a village exactly like Treweham.

Big thanks as always to the Aria Publishing Team, especially Rhea Kurien, my lovely editor for her wise words and support.

I'd also like to say a huge thank you for all the kind words given by the reviewers and readers so far in my writing journey – it really does make it all worthwhile.

Love Sasha x

About the Author

SASHA MORGAN lives in a village by the coast in Lancashire with her husband and has one grown up son. She writes mainly contemporary fiction with a touch of 'spice', which she attributes to all the Jilly Cooper novels she read as a teenager! Besides writing, she loves drinking wine, country walks and curling up with a good book.

Hello from Aria

We hope you enjoyed this book! If you did let us know, we'd love to hear from you.

We are Aria, a dynamic digital-first fiction imprint from award-winning independent publishers Head of Zeus. At heart, we're committed to publishing fantastic commercial fiction – from romance and sagas to crime, thrillers and historical fiction. Visit us online and discover a community of like-minded fiction fans!

We're also on the look out for tomorrow's superstar authors. So, if you're a budding writer looking for a publisher, we'd love to hear from you.
You can submit your book online at ariafiction.com/we-want-read-your-book

You can find us at:
Email: aria@headofzeus.com
Website: www.ariafiction.com
Submissions: www.ariafiction.com/we-want-read-your-book

- @ariafiction
- @Aria_Fiction
- @ariafiction

Printed and bound by CPI Group (UK) Ltd, Croydon, CR0 4YY
20/03/2026
02075568-0003